The
Keeper
of the
Irish Secret

BOOKS BY SUSANNE O'LEARY

The Road Trip

A Holiday to Remember

SANDY COVE SERIES

Secrets of Willow House

Sisters of Willow House

Dreams of Willow House

Daughters of Wild Rose Bay

Memories of Wild Rose Bay

Miracles in Wild Rose Bay

STARLIGHT COTTAGES SERIES

The Lost Girls of Ireland

The Lost Secret of Ireland

The Lost Promise of Ireland

The Lost House of Ireland

The Lost Letters of Ireland

The Lost Mother of Ireland

Susanne O'Leary

The
Keeper
of the
Irish Secret

bookouture

Published by Bookouture in 2024

An imprint of Storyfire Ltd.
Carmelite House
50 Victoria Embankment
London EC4Y 0DZ

www.bookouture.com

ISBN: 978-1-83525-086-0
eBook ISBN: 978-1-83525-085-3

1

On a wet and windy January afternoon on the Dingle Peninsula, Sylvia Fleury was sitting at her desk in the study of the old manor house writing the guest list for the Magnolia tea party at the beginning of March. It was an old tradition that went back more than a hundred years, but then it had been known as the Magnolia Ball, because the large magnolia tree beside the house was usually in bloom by that time. It was the most popular event of early spring, held on the first Saturday in March, with friends and family happy to dress up and dance the night away after the cold and wet winter. Dingle town, on the south shore of the Dingle Peninsula, was the perfect place for such a party, as spring was in the air all around South Kerry by then.

As time went by and the family money dwindled, the Magnolia Ball became a tea party instead – less grand, but perhaps more relaxed, and definitively less expensive to hold.

Sylvia had loved this event ever since she had arrived at Magnolia Manor as a young bride, nearly sixty years ago, so in love with her new husband and excited at the prospect of living in the legendary house that held so much history – and family secrets. 'If the walls could speak, we'd hear a thing or two we might not want to know,' her father-in-law Cornelius Fleury had said with a wink. What those secrets were had only been hinted at, and she had forgotten about them as time – and life – went on.

But now, as she sat there looking out the window, she thought of the shocking family secret, which concerned Cornelius, that had so recently been revealed. It could threaten her very existence in this house, and also compromise the legacy she hoped to leave to her three granddaughters.

Her gaze drifted to the two photos in silver frames on her desk. One was of her husband, Liam, and son, Fred, so tragically killed in a sailing accident over twenty-five years ago. Both smiling with their arms around each other, so handsome and sweet. And then the photo of her granddaughters, Fred's three girls – Lily, Rose and Violet – now grown up, but in that photo still little girls on the cusp of life. Lily, the eldest, with her dark hair and brown eyes, so like her father and Sylvia too – Rose the image of her blonde, blue-eyed mother – and then the baby, Violet, a mixture of both with dark eyes, red hair and that mischievous smile. 'A lovely bouquet,' their grandfather had called them, as their names went so well with the Fleury family name.

The girls had overcome the loss of their father and grandfather and grown up to be independent and strong. Sylvia was so proud of them, and had been happy to feel she would leave them the house and land to manage for future generations. But now, with this news that had come in a letter from France just before Christmas, she knew this might not be possible.

Sylvia shivered and went back to her guest list. Better not think about it right now. Live for the day, her grandmother had always said, and at this moment it seemed like the best policy.

She'd focus on the party, which might be the last one she hosted. And if it was, it had to be the best one ever. The Fleurys of Magnolia Manor had to go out in style.

Surrounded by lush subtropical gardens, the house was situated on a headland just off Dingle town on the southern side of the Dingle Peninsula in County Kerry. The white stucco building had been built as a summer residence in the early 1800s by a Fleury who had made a pile of money importing spices from the far east. Very grand for a summer house, Sylvia had thought when she'd first seen it, as the house had four large reception rooms, one of which had been used as a ballroom in the glory days. There were ten bedrooms, a huge kitchen with butlers' pantries, servants' quarters and all kinds of other rooms and nooks and crannies that made it impossible to keep track of anything. Then there was the conservatory, which used to be crammed with tropical plants and even a large cage with exotic birds.

Oh those were wonderful times, Sylvia thought, as memories of the balls flitted through her mind. The women in beautiful gowns, the men in white tie and tails. And the music... 'The Blue Danube' played by a live orchestra, the candlelit ballroom, the smell of perfume and cigar smoke, the laughter and flirting and clinking of champagne glasses – all the fun they had without a care in the world. How things had changed as the money dwindled away.

These days, Sylvia lived in only three rooms: the little study off the library, her bedroom and the former butlers' sitting room that she used as a living room. Everything else was closed up or in need of repair, like the once extraordinary conservatory, and the greenhouse in the now overgrown garden, both sadly derelict. Formal occasions, such as the Magnolia party, were held in the dining room and library, cleaned and aired for the occasion by Nora, the housekeeper, without whom Sylvia couldn't manage anything at all these days, including cooking a meal for herself.

Darling Nora. She was much more than a housekeeper, she was a dear friend and someone who had been with the family since her teens, as her mother had been the manor's house-keeper before her. Nora lived in a cottage nearby with her husband, Martin, who helped out from time to time if anything vital needed to be fixed or there was some heavy work to be done.

Sylvia turned at a knock on the door, and Nora entered carrying a tray with a cup of coffee and a digestive biscuit with strawberry jam.

'It must be eleven o'clock,' Sylvia said as Nora placed the little tray on the desk beside the list and the invitation cards.

'It is,' Nora agreed. 'I knew you'd be wanting a break from writing the invitations. How far have you got?'

Sylvia sighed and picked up the cup. 'I haven't even started. Everyone on the list is my age or older. I'm wondering if I should call these people up and find out if they're still alive before I write the invitations.'

Nora giggled. 'Not sure that would be appreciated.'

'Probably not. Sit down.' Sylvia pointed at a chair beside the desk. 'I need a chat.'

'I will, in a minute, I'll just get the fire going again.' Nora went to the fireplace and put a log on the smouldering embers. 'It's quite chilly today.'

Sylvia rubbed her cold hands together. 'Yes, it is. Thank you, Nora.' She looked at the list. 'I'll just write out the invita-tions and send them off. If they're dead they won't show up and then I'll strike them off the list. Oh,' she sighed. 'This is the problem with growing old. All one's contemporaries pass away and then there's nobody left of your own age. Makes me feel lonely at times. All alone in this huge mausoleum.'

'The huge family home you love,' Nora reminded her.

'One I've not been able to look after properly,' she said, worried. 'What will they think of it? Of me?'

'You still have the girls. Lily, Rose and Violet. Maybe you should invite them? They'd liven up the party no end.'

Sylvia frowned at the mention of her three granddaughters. Should she invite them this year? It might result in them coming and asking all kinds of questions she didn't want to answer. But still... Nora might be right. The girls would distract everyone. They'd inject some life and youth to the party. Maybe she could even include some suitable young men on the list?

'Maybe,' she said out loud, still considering the suggestion. 'I'll think about it.'

If the girls came to the party, they'd start going through the house and then they might find out what she had been trying to keep from them. That she'd been struggling. And the long-forgotten secret that had suddenly appeared – after years of denial and cover-ups – could be revealed as well. *It might be risky*, she thought. She knew they would have to be told eventually. But not yet.

'I think they'd love to come,' Nora remarked. She jumped to her feet as a cacophony of barking could be heard. 'Someone is coming up the drive. Could be the postman. I'll go and see. Let me know if you need anything else.'

'Thanks,' Sylvia said absentmindedly while she went back to her task. Then she got up as well and looked through the window. Judging by the excited barking of the dogs, someone a lot more popular than the postman had just arrived.

She peered through the window that had a side view of the entrance door and saw a silver car she didn't recognise. Then the driver's side door opened and a woman got out. A young woman with dark hair tied back in a ponytail, dressed in a black puffa jacket, jeans and boots. Sylvia gave a start of surprise. It was Lily.

She watched as Lily bent down to greet each of the excited

dogs in turn and then looked up at the house. Even from this distance, Sylvia could see the sadness in her granddaughter's eyes. Poor Lily. She was still upset.

But what was she doing here?

2

Lily laughed as the dogs barked and yelped and jumped up at her in their excitement, and she momentarily forgot her problems. She loved dogs, and four of them running at her barking furiously didn't faze her at all. She sank to her knees on the wet gravel and let them lick her while she hugged them all in turn: Vicky the lurcher, Amy the black-and-white border collie, Bunty the ancient Jack Russel and finally, the star of the show, an Irish setter aptly named Princess.

'Hello, darlings,' she shouted, trying to turn her face away from the doggy kisses. 'I haven't seen you for ages. I'm so happy to see you again.' She felt a dart of guilt as she tried to remember the last time she had visited her grandmother. It must have been more than a year – or even two. She had intended to come but things had been so stressful at home. Work had been very busy, to the point that she had decided to hand in her notice. She had no idea what she was going to do next – but what the last year had taught her was that she could start again if she *had* to. And what better place to do it than Dingle. A place she loved.

Magnolia Manor had been a little like a fairy-tale castle to

Lily and her sisters when they were children. The big rambling house with its overgrown subtropical garden was a wonderful place to spend the holidays. They'd played hide-and-seek in the vast rooms and long corridors, hiding in cupboards and wardrobes. They'd shrieked with fear at the creaking of floors and long shadows, as the imagined ghosts of past generations of Fleurys seemed to glide around in dark rooms, where draughts from the old windows made the curtains flutter.

Lily smiled at the memories of being deliciously excited and terrified at the same time. In those days, when both their grandfather and father had still been alive, it had been a wonderful family place, where Christmas was magical and everything was an adventure.

But then a double tragedy had struck. Her father and her grandfather had died in a boating accident just off the Blasket Islands. A massive tsunami-like wave had capsized their sailing boat and they'd both drowned. Lily had been twelve years old at the time, Rose ten and Violet only four. Both their father and grandfather gone at the same time.

Lily had been heartbroken, but she had her mother, Patricia, to keep her strong: holding her and her sisters at night, sharing memories of their father with them, and being the light to guide them, the strongest force imaginable, doing the work of both mother and father. Stony-faced with grief, she'd brought the girls back to Dublin where she tried her best to cope with suddenly being a single mother of three children. She had been amazing. And now that the girls were grown up, she had married again and moved to Donegal with her lovely new husband, but she was always there for them if they needed her.

Lily remembered that Sylvia had been devastated too – having lost both her husband and only child – and that she had been all alone in the aftermath. She'd locked herself in her room after the funeral and stayed there without eating or drinking for several days. When she'd emerged, ashen-faced, she'd declared that they had to go on living and the children had to be taken care of. Sylvia had helped Patricia financially for several years, making sure the girls were safe and well and got the best education, which she paid for. Her support was a great help; all three girls did well at school and went on to university and various colleges. But it couldn't get rid of the heartbreak. Twenty-five years had passed since that tragedy, but the memory was still vivid in Lily's heart.

Lily got up as the dogs calmed down and ran off into the garden. She could see a curtain twitching in a window, and knew she was being watched. She looked up at the house, noticing ivy growing out of control over some of the windows. There were few lights on and curtains shut in many of the rooms. The last time she'd seen Magnolia Manor it had looked old and tired– but this was something else. It was even worse than when she'd last seen it. Her grandmother had a keen eye for detail and exceptional standards, she tried her best with the gardens and the rooms, but it looked like she'd been struggling to maintain every aspect of the grand abode.

She touched the gnarled trunk of the old magnolia tree beside the entrance for good luck, as she always did. Then she went up the steps and stood at the ornate front door, which opened just as she was about to ring the bell.

Nora peered out. 'Hello, Lily,' she said and opened the door wider. 'Long time no see.'

'That's for sure,' Lily said and put her arms around Nora. 'Far too long. But you haven't changed a bit.' It was true. Nora was still the tall, wiry woman, now in her sixties, with the short mid-brown hair and kind grey eyes behind horn-rimmed glasses that Lily remembered from long ago.

'Neither have you,' Nora said, smiling. 'The same pretty face and your grandmother's dark hair and eyes. And that dimple when you smile,' she added, pinching Lily's cheek.

'Not much to smile about now,' Lily said glumly.

Nora nodded. 'I heard about the divorce. I'm so sorry. It must be hard.'

Lily sighed and shrugged. 'That's what happens when you marry for all the wrong reasons. Well, you know the story. Should never have happened. But I'm moving on and that's why I'm here.'

'Oh?' Nora moved towards the open door. 'Come in and tell me. Your granny will be so happy to see you.'

'She'll be cross with me for not coming to see her for so long,' Lily said as she followed Nora into the vast hall, their footsteps ringing out on the marble floor. She looked up at the walls adorned with antlers from deer killed generations ago, the huge fireplace that used to blaze with logs, now empty, the pale winter light through the tall windows making the room feel colder still.

'She's in the study,' Nora said. 'Go in and say hello. There's a fire there so you'll be warm.'

'Okay.' Lily was about to take off her jacket but changed her mind. 'I'll keep this on for the moment.'

'Good idea,' Nora agreed and led the way through the main corridor, opening the door to the study. 'I'll bring you a cup of coffee and biscuits.'

'Digestives with strawberry jam?' Lily asked with a smile.

'Of course.'

'Great. I love the old traditions.'

Lily stepped into the study and stood inside the doorway for a moment, looking at her grandmother at the desk. She was dressed in a tartan skirt, navy cardigan and gold ballerina slippers. Her greying dark hair was held back from her forehead with a velvet hairband. She seemed so preoccupied by her task she hadn't noticed Lily step in. The room was warmed by the smouldering embers in the fireplace and an electric radiator near the desk. Everything looked the same as always: the faded oriental rug on the parquet floor, the bookcase crammed with books and photos, the mahogany desk by the window and the deep red velvet curtains. It even smelled exactly the same: a mixture of woodsmoke, old books and rose petals from the bowl of potpourri on the little table by the sofa, a smell Lily always associated with Magnolia Manor.

Sylvia turned from her writing. 'Lily,' she said and got up. 'What are you doing here?'

'Hello, Granny.' Lily went to Sylvia's side and kissed her grandmother on her slightly wrinkled but silky-soft cheek, breathing in the familiar Chanel No.5 perfume she always wore. 'So lovely to see you.'

'Is it?' Sylvia asked, stepping back to look at Lily. 'You haven't been here for such a long time. I thought you had forgotten about me. Or maybe you thought I was dead?'

Lily laughed. 'No, I knew you had to be alive. You're a tough old cookie.' Then she met Sylvia's gaze and was, as always, taken aback by how alike they were, as Sylvia smiled playfully at her. The same thick dark hair, which in Sylvia's case was sprinkled with grey, the same velvet brown eyes, regular features and square jaw. It had always seemed amazing to Lily that she looked like her grandmother, rather than either of her parents. 'You look good,' she said, despite thinking that Sylvia looked unusually pale and thin. There was also a hint in those dark eyes that told Lily her grandmother was deeply worried about something.

'Good for eighty-two you mean?' Sylvia asked.

'Good for any age,' Lily argued. 'How are you?' she asked earnestly.

Sylvia made a dismissive gesture. 'Stop blathering. Let's go and sit and you'll tell me why you're here. I don't believe for a second that you came just to visit me.'

'Well, partly,' Lily said as she sank down on the sofa. 'But I do have another reason to be here. It's about a job.'

Sylvia put another log on the fire before she sat down. 'A

job?' she asked. 'But I thought you were working for this big legal firm in Dublin?'

Lily swallowed nervously before she replied. 'I'm not working there any more...' She waited for the scathing reply she knew would come. Sylvia didn't like quitters. It was giving up, she had always told the girls, and 'a Fleury never gives up'.

But Sylvia didn't seem to take the news of Lily's quitting with much interest.

'I see,' was all she said.

And then the door opened to admit Nora with Lily's cup of coffee and biscuits, and that part of the conversation ended. Nora was followed by Princess, who pranced to Sylvia's side and sat down prettily, looking adoringly at her mistress.

Lily laughed. 'She's such a diva.'

Sylvia patted the dog on the head. 'She's a sweetheart.'

'Where are the others?' Lily asked Nora.

'In the boot room,' Nora replied, putting the cup on the coffee table. 'They were all so muddy, I had to lock them in there. But Princess doesn't like mud, so she was allowed in here.'

'Good girl,' Sylvia said approvingly, patting Princess on the head.

Princess wagged her tail and lay down on the carpet in front of the fire, closing her eyes.

'She knows on which side her bread is buttered,' Nora said with a laugh. 'I'll go and clean up the others and then I'll do the ironing. Are you staying for lunch, Lily?'

'No, thanks.' Lily shot a look at Sylvia. 'I have an appointment in town just before twelve, so I'll grab a sandwich there afterwards.'

'But you'll be back to stay the night?' Nora asked.

'Stay?' Sylvia said, sounding alarmed. She looked at Lily with what appeared to be a hint of panic. 'You've come to stay? In the house?'

'Well, I...' Lily hadn't planned to mention the subject of her accommodation so soon. She had wanted to come to it slowly so Sylvia would get used to the idea. 'No, not in the house,' she said. 'I'll stay in a B&B in town for a few nights. And then, if I get this job, I thought you might let me take the gatehouse. I'll pay rent of course,' she added quickly. 'I know the last tenants moved out, so I thought maybe you're looking for another one?'

'I'm not.' Sylvia glanced at Nora. 'The gatehouse? Is that even fit for anyone to live in? The last tenants moved out five years ago. I'd say it's a bit of a wreck by now. What do you think, Nora?'

Lily was shocked – the gatehouse in disrepair too?

'Lily and I could go and look at it together,' Nora suggested. 'It'll be cold, as it has no central heating, but apart from that, it's perfectly habitable.'

Sylvia let out a snort. 'Habitable, yes, for anyone who isn't used to a comfortable apartment in Dublin. It would be madness for you to stay there, Lily.'

'I'm sure it'll be fine,' Lily argued. 'I can take a bit of discomfort, you know.'

She was surprised that Sylvia wasn't being more welcoming. It wasn't as if she wanted to stay with her in the big house. She knew her grandmother was independent – she had her ways of doing things, and Lily didn't want to get in the way of that; that's why she'd booked the B&B. Though, now she was here and could see that Sylvia was struggling, she wished she'd been checking in on her more often. She felt bad that her grandmother wasn't managing the house very well. Lily felt she had got here just in time.

'Well, I suppose you'll survive,' Sylvia remarked, folding her hands in her lap. 'After all, this house isn't much better. My bedroom is warm but any of the others would be freezing cold. It can only be a temporary arrangement for you to live there. You should look for somewhere more modern if you plan to settle down here in Dingle.' Her eyes were warm as she looked at Lily. 'That old house could be too much for you to cope with after the upset you've been through. I only want you to be comfortable.'

'Maybe,' Lily replied, wondering why Sylvia seemed so reluctant for her to live in the gatehouse. 'But it'll be fine for now.'

'True.' Nora stood at the door ready to leave the room. 'Give me a shout if you want to take a look at the gatehouse, Lily.'

'I will,' Lily promised. 'I have your mobile number.'

'Grand.' Nora nodded and left.

Sylvia turned her gaze on Lily. 'So where is this job in Dingle?'

Lily squirmed. 'Well... Actually, I wasn't going to tell you right now. I mean, I don't know if I'll get it, so...' She didn't want to jinx the outcome by telling her grandmother what she was doing. She was nervous enough about the interview without Sylvia making negative comments. She was sure to disapprove even if the job was with a high-profile firm, which it definitively was not.

But Lily didn't care. She needed to decompress after all that had happened. This job was what she wanted and it seemed to suit her perfectly. She had longed to go to Kerry all through the hard times of the divorce proceedings. The rugged mountains, the spectacular views of the Atlantic Ocean, the clean air all seemed like the perfect remedy for a broken heart and a stressed-out brain. The idea of staying at the gatehouse had seemed ideal. This way she would be close to Sylvia but still keep her independence. If the gatehouse wasn't too cold and damp. It probably was, she realised, and it would need a lot of work to get it comfortable. But she'd tackle that problem later. It had been a tough year, and there was too much riding on her plan. She desperately needed this change and to create a home for herself after all the pain of the breakup and quitting her job.

And then there was the idea she and her sisters had dreamt up. Their plan for the house.

Lily checked her watch and got up. 'I'd better get going. I'll see you later, Granny.' She bent down and planted a kiss on Sylvia's cheek.

Sylvia nodded. 'Very well, dear. I'd better get back to my invitations.'

'The Magnolia party?' Lily asked.

'Yes. I just this minute had the idea of holding it in the ball-room this year and inviting a lot more people than usual. I might as well warn you that includes you and your sisters. We need young people, Nora tells me. And there'll be some suitable young men for you all as well. A perfect opportunity to find a better match.'

'Oh please,' Lily pleaded, 'no match making, Granny. Rose might come, but Vi is still in LA, so you can forget about her. But please don't invite what you call *suitable* men.'

Being set up was the last thing Lily wanted. She had been so hurt by everything that had happened with Simon. When they had met, and he had proposed so quickly after their first few dates, she had thought all her dreams had come true. He had swept her off her feet and she had thought she was the luckiest woman alive. But the cracks had appeared very quickly when the reality of the imagined big house had dawned on him. She was no heiress to a fortune or a grand mansion, but simply a member of an old family.

'I really don't want to meet anyone right now,' she said. 'I'm not ready.'

Sylvia waved her hand. 'We'll see about that.'

'Yes. But I have to go now, so we can discuss it later.'

Sylvia nodded. 'Off you go. You don't want to be late for your interview. It gives a very bad impression.'

'Bye for now,' Lily said. 'I'll keep you posted.'

Sylvia smiled. 'Good. Break a leg.'

Lily stopped on her way to the door. 'What?'

'Isn't that what they say for good luck nowadays?'

Lily laughed. 'If you're an actor about to go on stage, yes. But I suppose it fits here, as I'm about to perform in some way, so thanks. See you later, Granny.' She left the room without waiting for a reply, still smiling.

Lily had always loved her granny. So strong and brave in all weathers, standing up to anyone who tried to put her down. When she was younger, she had been known to 'take no prisoners' and always spoke up against unfair treatment of anyone, especially her granddaughters. She still had that feisty look in her eyes, even if there was something worrying her. She appeared strict and forbidding at times, but Lily knew Sylvia's hard shell hid a heart of gold. Her granny had always been her rock and a haven to come to when life was rough.

But right now, Lily had other things on her mind. The job interview. She felt butterflies in her stomach as she drove down the long avenue to the front entrance, where she stopped briefly and looked at the gatehouse. It was a nice-looking building with a blue front door and leaded windows. She knew it was early Victorian, having replaced the previous building that had stood there when the manor house was being built. With a sitting room, a large kitchen-diner downstairs and three bedrooms upstairs, it was bigger than most gatehouses. It would suit Lily perfectly. *If* she got the job. Everything depended on that. *But you will get it*, she told herself as she turned onto the main road to Dingle town. *Of course you will.*

Then there was her other mission, the one she had been assigned to get started by her sisters. It would be a much bigger challenge than the job interview. It was, in fact, the main reason she was thinking of leaving Dublin and settling in the south west. It would involve a long campaign, lots of arguments and maybe even a family crisis. Despite all the problems that would arise, Lily knew it was the only way. *One step at a time,* she thought. *It will take a long time and a lot of patience. But I know it will be worth the struggle.*

3

Despite her nervousness about the interview, Lily found herself enjoying the short drive to Dingle town. When she crossed the little bridge, she felt a dart of nostalgia as she remembered the Sunday drives into town with her grandfather, when she and her sisters were very little. It had been such a treat to sit on the leather seats of the old Ford and then have a meal of fish and chips in his preferred restaurant on the quays, watching the fishing boats come into the harbour and unloading all the catch that was to be sold to shops and restaurants. Then he would take them to the ice cream parlour further up the street and buy them each a cone of whipped ice cream topped with a Cadbury's flake. Sundays with Granddad had been such fun for them all.

Now, as she drove slowly along the harbour, Lily saw that nothing much had changed. Dingle town was still the same, its waterfront lined with quirky shops, cute pubs and restaurants. She passed the fish warehouse and Oceanworld, the aquarium, where you could see all kinds of marine life, including sharks and other amazing sea creatures, in huge tanks. It was a popular place for families and also a very interesting place to visit for adults who loved the ocean. Lily promised herself to take Sylvia for a visit soon.

She was nearing her destination and needed to find a place to park and a moment to gather her thoughts before the interview. As it was a quiet Monday in January, she had no problem finding a space right outside the solicitor's office where she would be working should she get the job. It was situated on Green Street, which wound its way up the hill, like most streets in this charming little town.

Lily sat in the car for a moment while she looked at the brass plaque on the wall of the tall Victorian house. It said: *W. Quinn solicitors.* She didn't know who W. Quinn was, only that they were the person she had sent her CV to when she had seen the advertisement about the position as legal secretary and assistant. *What does W stand for?* she wondered. *William? Wanda? Is it a man or a woman? Well, there's only one way to find out.*

Lily glanced in the rear-view mirror, smoothed her hair, touched up her lipstick and then got out of the car and rang the bell beside the brass plaque. There was a buzzing sound and she pushed the door open, stepping inside an entrance hall with a console table and a tall mirror, an ornate staircase leading to the upper floors. A sign said there was an architect's office, a chiropodist and a dentist upstairs. The ground floor seemed to only house the solicitor's and an accountant. The solicitor's door to the left was open and she peered in to see an empty reception area with a desk on which stood a computer. Then another door opened and out walked a tall man with a shock of pale blonde hair and piercing blue eyes.

'How can I help you?' he asked, looking as if she was disturbing him.

'Are you... Mr Quinn, the solicitor?' she asked, amazed at his height. He had to be at least six foot four.

'I am indeed,' he replied in a strong Kerry accent. 'And you are...?'

'Lily Fleury. I'm here for the job.'

'The job?' He looked confused. Then he brightened. 'Oh, of course. The secretary job.'

'Legal secretary,' she corrected.

'Oh yeah, that one.' He stepped aside and opened the door wider. 'Please come in and we'll chat. I'm afraid I haven't had time to look at your application yet. Thought I'd talk to you in person instead of reading your CV in detail. A much better way to assess someone you might be working with.'

'Oh.' Lily crossed the reception area and followed him into a room that was flooded with light from a tall window that looked onto the street. A large desk littered with piles of papers and binders and a computer screen stood by the window.

Mr Quinn went behind the desk and gestured towards a chair in front of it before he sat down in a leather office chair. 'So,' he said, turning to the screen. 'Your CV... Oh yes, here it is.' He looked at her and frowned. 'Hmm. Lily Fleury... Quite a famous name around here. Are you related to the Magnolia Manor family?'

Lily nodded. 'Yes.' She didn't elaborate despite knowing he'd find out how she was related to the Fleurys very quickly.

'I see.' He paused while he read through the email and lifted an eyebrow. 'You worked at Malone and O'Mahony in Dublin as a legal secretary for twelve years?'

Lily nodded again. 'That's right. I got the job nearly straight away after college,' she said, wondering why she was telling him this. He might feel she was too qualified for him. She really wanted this job, even though it wouldn't be as exciting as her old one. Or as exhausting.

'Very well-known firm.' He looked at her with a touch of suspicion. 'So why are you here looking for a job with me? Not the best career move, I would have thought. You weren't let go, were you?'

'As in fired?' Lily asked with rising irritation. Was she really going to work for this awkward man with very little manners? He was staring at her as if she was a witness in court. 'No, I wasn't. I quit on my own accord.'

'You quit? Why?' he asked. 'Was it about pay? Or did you have a problem with your boss?'

'No, the money was good and my boss was quite nice, if a little unfocused,' she said, remembering the chaos she had to deal with every morning and the briefs she had to read out to him on the phone just before a court case, while he was busy with other things.

'Why did you quit, then?' Quinn insisted, directing his ice-blue stare at Lily. 'I mean, if the pay was good and your boss was okay, what was the problem?'

'I... well I didn't feel fulfilled,' Lily tried, becoming increasingly nervous under his gaze. 'And I also had some issues in my private life that were quite stressful. I need a change of scene.'

'So you came to Dingle to chill out and rest?'

'Something like that,' Lily agreed, beginning to feel frustrated. Why was he questioning her like this? It wasn't a good start to a possible working relationship.

'There won't be much chilling in this office,' he said with a hint of a smile as he gestured across the mess on the desk. 'As you can see, I'm a one-man band and my office is a mess. Quite a step down from your previous position.'

Lily shrugged. 'I don't mind. I want to spend some time with my family here in Dingle and I need a job.'

'So you'd be prepared to work for less money than in Dublin?'

'That depends on how much less.'

'How does two thousand a month sound to you?'

'Eh...' Lily hesitated. It sounded terrible compared to her

Dublin salary. But here life would be a lot less expensive, of course. 'Five days a week, no overtime?' she said.

He nodded. 'Yes, with occasional exceptions, but that would be very rare. And the usual annual leave and all bank holidays off, of course.'

Lily took a deep breath while she considered the offer. 'Okay. That's fine. And I have very good references,' she said and opened her handbag.

'I'm sure you do. No need to show them to me.' Quinn turned off his computer and suddenly smiled at her, showing a row of perfect teeth. He looked at once more friendly. 'You know what?'

Lily blinked, amazed at the change in his demeanour, and looks. When he smiled he was quite good looking. 'No, what?'

'You're hired. When can you start?'

She was delighted but a little shocked. 'I'd need to look over the contract first,' she said. *But phew, I got the job*, she thought. *He seems quite nice even if he's a little strange. But I won't accept just yet. Better not to look too eager.*

'Yeah, but I'd need to know soon.' He gestured at the piles of papers. 'All this needs to be sorted and filed. I haven't had a secretary for over a week. The last one left to go to Galway to marry a farmer up there, thank goodness.'

'Thank goodness?' Lily echoed. 'You were happy she left?'

'Yes. Nice girl but totally useless. Spent most of her time making long chains out of paperclips while she listened to her Spotify playlist and looked at wedding dresses online. Awful music too. Drove me nuts, to be honest, but I didn't have the heart to fire her. That's why there's such a mess here. And the coffee machine is broken too.'

He suddenly looked so stressed she had to laugh.

'I see what you mean,' she said. 'Don't worry, I don't do those things at work. But before I start, we have to draw up a contract.'

He looked contrite. 'Of course. Hey, it's nearly lunch time. Could we go down the street and grab a sandwich and work it all out? And then we'll come back here and you could type up the contract and we'll sign it and then we're in business.'

She couldn't help feeling a dart of sympathy for him despite his odd behaviour. 'It's a bit unusual, but, well, this is Kerry, so yeah why not? And I'm starving,' she confessed.

He got up from the desk. 'Great.' He held out his hand. 'Welcome to the Quinn firm. My first name is Wolfgang; may I call you Lily?'

'Of course,' she said. 'That's quite all right, Mr... eh, Wolfgang. Not exactly a Kerry name,' she added, intrigued. With his tall frame, blonde hair and chiselled features, she had guessed he was of either Scandinavian, German or Dutch ancestry, despite his local accent.

'My mother was German,' he explained, confirming her guess. 'She named me after my grandfather in Munich. But my dad's from Killorglin, so I'm half native.' He held the door open and she went out into the reception area. 'Your domain,' he said, gesturing at the desk. 'I will get you a better computer and anything else you might need.' He pointed at a door in the far wall. 'There is a little utility room there where your predecessor used to make coffee or tea and so on. Just a small scullery really.'

'I'm not going to make coffee,' Lily said primly. 'That will not be part of my job.' She fixed him with a steely look to make sure he realised that she was going to be taken seriously. That was one of the reasons she had quit her job in Dublin. All the men, including the male legal secretaries, had assumed she would make coffee just because she was a woman. And there were other things too. Things that hadn't been expressed openly, but there was a general feeling that women were somehow inferior. So last century, Lily had thought, but hadn't dared to say.

The last straw had been when she had been sent out for

sandwiches on a wet and windy Monday. She had put up with it
for years because she didn't want to cause a row, but now she had
suddenly felt she had enough of men ordering her around. Men
like her ex-husband who thought they could snap their fingers at
women and get served. She had marched into the office of the
senior partner and given him her notice. He hadn't protested or
asked her why she was leaving, just shrugged and said, 'Fine.'
That, combined with the divorce settlement that had not been in
her favour, made her desperately want a change of scene. It had
shocked her that they could treat her like this, even though they
knew how devastated she had been after Simon had left her.

All this was going through her mind as she stared at the man
who might be her new boss. 'I'm a legal secretary, not a wait-
ress,' she said to emphasise her point, looking at him sternly.

'Of course,' he agreed amiably, looking a little surprised by
her tone. 'We used to take turns. I'm the one who broke the
machine, actually. That will be replaced, of course, and I'll
make you as many cups of coffee as you like, so you'll have time
to get some kind of order of the filing and all the rest. And
please tell me now if you don't want the job, just so I can look
for someone else.'

'Well, I...' Lily stopped in the middle of the floor and looked
around. The reception area was quite nice, with a window that
had a view down the steep hill all the way to the harbour where
the blue water of the ocean glinted. A thick green carpet
covered the floor and the small desk was made of some kind of
inlaid wood. The light from the window brightened the whole
room and she knew it could be made quite inviting with plants
and a few nice prints on the wall, so that anyone who had to
wait to go in to see Wolfgang felt comfortable. *Oh*, she thought,
suddenly feeling how much she wanted to work here, *this is a
lot nicer than my cubbyhole of an office in Dublin. A window
looking down to the sea, and the town I love on the doorstep.*

'This could be really nice, with just a few touches that wouldn't be too expensive,' she suggested.

'I'll give you carte blanche to do what you like,' Wolfgang said, looking relieved.

'Great.' Lily shot him a reassuring smile. 'I do want the job, and I accept your offer.'

He beamed that wide smile at her again. 'Wonderful. What a relief. You had me quite worried there when you looked so serious. Let's go and iron out the details, so.' He held the door open for her and they went through the hall and out into the sunlit street. 'By the way,' he added, 'my friends call me Wolfie. I know it's a weird name that some people laugh at, but my mother loved her dad so I never felt I could hurt her feelings and change it. And now that she's dead, I feel that even more strongly.'

'I understand completely,' Lily said, feeling a surge of empathy for him. 'And I like Wolfie. It's cute,' she said without thinking.

He blushed and cleared his throat. 'Eh, okay. Here's the café anyway. Let's have a sandwich and discuss everything.'

They went inside the charming little café with light blue wainscoting on the walls, small round tables scattered across the creaking wooden floor and a view of the harbour through the bay window. The room smelled strongly of freshly brewed coffee and woodsmoke from logs that crackled in the fireplace on the far side.

Wolfgang pulled out a chair for Lily, who sat down, impressed with this unusual chivalry. Simon had not been this considerate, especially when their marriage was heading for the rocks.

'What would you like?' he asked. 'Lunch is on me to celebrate your new job.'

'Oh thank you,' Lily replied, scanning the blackboard over

the counter. 'I see they have wild Atlantic prawn sandwiches, so I'd love one of those.'

'Good choice,' he agreed. 'I'll join you in that one. And water, coffee and perhaps a cinnamon bun to finish?'

'Coffee, yes, but not the bun,' Lily replied, remembering her diet. She felt she had put on far too much weight over Christmas, as a result of comfort eating after the divorce. During that time, food was her only friend and she didn't care what she looked like, feeling that nobody would want her anyway, so why bother?

'Okay.' Wolfgang went to the counter to order while Lily waited, relieved he had made no remark about her refusing the bun like some men in her acquaintance would have done. Besides, she wanted to keep their relationship strictly professional, even if it was nice to work with a man she found very nice looking. He was a bit awkward and she guessed he could be grumpy, but those were minor matters.

He arrived back at the table with the sandwiches and two glasses of water on a tray. Lily reached for the sandwich and took a huge bite, the taste of prawns in homemade mayonnaise laced with dill hitting her tastebuds.

'Oh, that's delicious,' she said when she had swallowed. 'Nothing like wild Atlantic prawns.'

'Very nice,' he agreed, devouring his sandwich in a few bites. Then he strode to the counter to fetch the coffee and his bun that he devoured with equal speed.

'You were hungry,' Lily remarked as she sedately sipped her coffee and tried not to laugh. She couldn't imagine him in court or negotiating a contract with a client, but maybe he was different when he was working. 'So you mainly deal with conveyancing, is that correct?' she asked. 'What other kinds of cases do you normally handle?'

Wolfie swallowed his mouthful. 'Wills and stuff like that.

Some litigations from time to time and divorce settlements. No criminal cases at all.'

Lily nodded. 'I see. So then my work is mostly typing up contracts and wills and things like that?'

'Yes, but also, with your experience, I would expect to consult you about legal details and correct procedures, as you worked with a firm that handled such a variety of cases. Would that be okay?'

'Of course. I'll help with anything I can,' she replied, beginning to look forward to the job. She hadn't known if the role would involve legal work. She knew she could handle all of that too and was delighted at the prospect.

'Right, then,' he said and got up so suddenly he nearly knocked his chair over. 'Let's go back to the office and draw up that contract. And then maybe you could take a look at the accounts and also see if we can get some kind of order with the files.'

'Hold on just a minute,' Lily protested. 'I didn't say I could start straight away. I only just arrived and I haven't unloaded my car or been to the B&B or...' She paused. 'I need to get organised and settle in.' *And I want to look at the gatehouse and try to start working on Granny so she'll agree to our plans*, she thought. 'Today is Friday,' she continued. 'So why don't I start working at your office on Monday?'

His face fell. 'Oh. Right, okay. Well, how about we just do the contract then?'

'Great.' Lily nodded and gulped down the last of her coffee. Then she changed her mind, feeling everything was happening too fast. 'Eh, maybe you could send over a draft contract when you've drawn it up? It would just be a standard contract. I'm feeling a little overwhelmed with all this and moving house as well.'

'Oh,' he said, looking sheepish. 'Of course. I was so

desperate to get some order in the office and then you arrived like a gift from heaven with your fantastic experience, I felt I needed to grab you before you went somewhere else. Metaphorically speaking, of course,' he added, looking even more awkward.

Lily had to laugh. He was so beguiling standing there trying to explain why he was so anxious to get her help. 'I understand, of course. And don't worry, I'm not looking for any other job or going anywhere at all. I'll be staying at the Oceanview B&B, so maybe you can drop in the contract there once it's ready?'

He nodded, looking relieved. 'Of course. Sorry about rushing you like that. I'll leave you to finish your coffee.'

'Great. Thank you.' Lily smiled at him. 'And thanks for lunch. See you on Monday.'

'Okay. I'll go back to the office now to see if I can sort some of the paperwork,' he said, clearly not looking forward to it.

'Leave it until Monday,' Lily suggested, suspecting he'd just mess it up further. 'I'll go through it all then and set up a new system. No need to worry about it today.'

Wolfie let out a sigh of relief. 'You really are a gift from heaven.'

Lily laughed. 'I wouldn't go that far. You might change your mind when you get to know me better.'

'I'm sure I won't.' He started to walk away. 'Bye for now, Lily. See you Monday. Have a nice weekend.'

'You too.'

Lily watched him walk out, thinking she would have her work cut out for her on Monday. The whole filing system would probably have to be changed. It could turn out to be a more stressful job than she had imagined. But she had accepted the offer and the salary, so now she had to cope with it all. And it seemed Wolfie desperately needed her help. It would be a challenge, but she had always loved putting things in order, even if this was a lot more organising than she had bargained for.

Well, she could always quit if it proved to be too difficult.

She just needed to stay on for a bit and put the other plan in action. The plan Rose had dreamt up – to restore Magnolia Manor to its former glory, and to live there themselves. Then they would realise the rest of the plan – to use some of the formal rooms for weddings and celebrations and turn the green-house into a little garden centre and café that Lily would run. It had seemed such a good idea at the time, but now that Lily was here and had seen what a state the house was in, and that pained look in her grandmother's eyes... Was it going to be more difficult than they had thought?

But oh, the house had to be rescued before it was too late. It meant so much to her now she had lost everything, all her hopes and dreams of a family and a career crumbled to nothing after her breakup with the man she had thought loved her as much as she loved him. She needed to restart her life and build it on a more solid foundation. The new job was a start. Then she would work on her plans for the house. Magnolia Manor was so much a part of her, and had been the safe place she knew she could always return to, it just had to be saved.

But she had been surprised that Sylvia had sent out such negative vibes at the suggestion of Lily living in the gatehouse. Perhaps convincing Granny would be more of an uphill battle than she thought.

4

Later that day, Lily stood in the small garden of the gatehouse with Nora, looking at the front door. It had originally been painted a beautiful light blue, but now the paint had flaked off, exposing the wood.

Lily rattled the keys in her hand. 'I suppose it will be horribly damp and mouldy in there. I thought it was in a better state. Do you know how much work it needs, Nora?'

'I have no idea,' Nora said. 'I haven't been in there for years. We just locked it up when the last tenant left five years ago and forgot about it. Martin and I were so busy with the garden and the bit of the main house that Sylvia lives in that we just forgot about this place. In any case, I think there were plans to simply pull it down.'

'Pull it down?' Lily exclaimed as she kept looking at the house that, with its slate roof, dormer windows upstairs and French door leading out to a tiny patio, looked like something from a Victorian painting. 'But it's such a nice little house. And the roof looks okay too.'

'It's not a bad house,' Nora agreed, starting up the front steps. 'But it's not very comfortable. No central heating for a start. Come on, Lily,' she urged. 'Open the door so you can take a look for yourself. And then you might change your mind and ask your granny for a room in the main house.'

'I don't think she wants me there for some reason,' Lily said as she followed Nora. 'Anyway, one step at a time.' She put the large key in the lock and tried to turn it. 'It seems to be stuck,' she muttered, giving it another twist. The lock finally turned and Lily pushed at the door that slowly opened with a loud creak. 'The wood must have warped or something,' she said and peered into a hall with light green wainscoting and a mahogany hallstand. She went inside and stood there for a moment, breathing in the air that was slightly musty but not as damp as she had feared. 'No smell of mould,' she said. 'In fact I can smell a little whiff of woodsmoke and a hint of lavender. Quite pleasant, really.'

'You're right.' Nora came in, pulling the door shut behind her. 'It's surprisingly fresh.'

They continued into a corridor, past a staircase that rose to the upper floor and walked into a bright kitchen that opened into a living room. There was woodburning stove at the far end of the kitchen and the living room had a fireplace. Wide oak planks covered the floors and the windows overlooked the eastern end of the famous Magnolia Manor gardens.

Lily peered through the dirty pane. 'Lovely view, even if it's all so overgrown. But that makes it look like a jungle. It's nice and kind of mysterious. I'd half expect Tarzan swinging from a vine out there.'

Nora laughed and opened a cupboard. 'Let's see if there is anything useful here. I see some crockery. Old fashioned but it'll do.' She closed the door and looked at Lily. 'You didn't tell me about your job interview. How did it go?'

Lily turned from the window. 'Great. I got the job. You're looking at the new legal secretary of W. Quinn solicitors. Hmm, why is that in plural?' she asked as if to herself. 'There's only one solicitor.'

'Wolfgang's father works there too,' Nora replied. 'Or did until recently. He might have retired. Wolfie is a nice lad, though. He helped me with my mother's estate when she died a few years ago. Went out of his way to sort everything.'

'Does Granny use him?' Lily asked. 'Never thought of that. Could make things awkward.'

'No, she has a solicitor in Tralee,' Nora replied as she opened drawers and looked into the larder. 'There's cutlery and a few saucepans and a cast-iron frying pan.'

'Good,' Lily said absentmindedly, turning back to the window. 'I can see the path we used to walk down to the jetty. Oh, how I loved the summers here and the feeling of constantly being on an adventure.'

'You girls ran wild all over the place,' Nora said with a fond smile.

'We did.' Lily paused and studied the overgrown garden, remembering Violet trailing behind her and Rose, shouting at them to wait for her. She was dying to tell someone about her plan, and if she couldn't tell Granny yet, perhaps she could tell Nora. 'This house could be made into something amazing. An adventure trail for kids, or a park. And there could be a garden centre by the glasshouses. An outdoor café in the summer and boat trips and...' She stopped and sighed. 'We have this plan you see. Rose and Violet and I. We want to restore Magnolia and live here with Granny. And then use the formal rooms like the ballroom and drawing room for a wedding venue and such. And I would run it all, including the garden centre.'

'Is that why you're here?' Nora asked and Lily nodded. 'You mean you'd give up your job as legal secretary?' Nora asked.

'I would,' Lily replied. 'It has always been my dream to have a little garden centre. You know how I love plants and growing things. The whole thing would be a huge undertaking, but wouldn't it be fantastic?'

Nora closed the cupboard door. 'Yes, it would indeed. But I wonder what Sylvia will think.'

'We're not going to tell her yet.'

Nora nodded. 'Good idea. I won't breathe a word to her either for now. I like your plan, though. The house has to be saved somehow before it falls down. And that lad who does the garden with Martin said very much the same thing.'

'What lad?' Lily asked. 'Granny never mentioned anyone else apart from Martin.'

'Oh he only comes here from time to time. He runs a gardening and house maintenance service.'

'Really? What's his name?' Lily asked, intrigued.

'Dominic Doyle,' Nora replied.

'Oh? Never heard that name before. Is he from around here?'

'No, he's from Kenmare,' Nora explained. 'He came here a few years ago and set up business doing all sorts of jobs like landscaping, tending gardens for people who have holiday homes and building patios and decks. Sylvia used to hire him in the spring to help clear up around the house after the winter, but she hasn't been as on top of all of that lately.'

Lily looked at Nora thoughtfully. 'So this Dominic would do all kinds of work, then? If we – Granny, I mean – wanted to develop the gardens or repair the glasshouses?'

Nora nodded. 'He'd be your man. He can hire in people to help out too. But Sylvia wouldn't want to do anything like that, I'm sure.'

'I suppose not,' Lily said, deciding to leave the subject alone for now. But a grain of an idea was beginning to grow and she couldn't wait to talk to her sister Rose about it. 'Let's have a look upstairs,' she said and walked out of the kitchen. 'I hope the bedrooms aren't too bad. And there is a bathroom, isn't there?'

'There is,' Nora said as she followed Lily up the creaking staircase. 'It was put in sometime in the seventies so it could be a bit outdated.'

'As long as it works,' Lily replied as she arrived at the landing.

The two double bedrooms were in good condition with iron beds, but no mattresses, and flowery wallpaper that was a little old fashioned but quite nice, Lily decided.

'I have to get a mattress and some bedclothes,' she muttered.

'I'm sure you can find sheets and blankets in the manor,' Nora suggested.

'Yeah. I'll have a root around in the linen cupboard,' Lily agreed.

The bathroom units were a riot of green, which made her laugh. 'Avocado was all the rage fifty years ago, as far as I can tell,' she said. 'But hey, there's a bath, a shower and a toilet, so who am I to complain?'

'The water is heated by the back boiler of the stove,' Nora announced. 'You might want to put in something more modern.'

'Eventually, yes. The tiles on the floor are gorgeous.'

'That's from the Victorian bathroom that was here before,' Nora remarked. 'Pity that was ripped out.'

'A real shame,' Lily agreed. 'But look at this sweet fireplace. I can light a fire before I get into the bath.'

'I'd put in one of those bathroom heaters,' Nora suggested. 'In fact, I'd put electric heaters in all the bedrooms.'

'You're right. And I will,' Lily agreed as she opened the door to the smallest bedroom. She knew the two of them were getting carried away dreaming up ideas to improve the gatehouse. Sylvia hadn't agreed to anything yet, and truthfully Lily felt worried to ask her now she'd seen how tired she looked. *One step at a time*, she thought. 'I bet this one is empty,' she said but stopped on the threshold of the third bedroom and stared at an object in the far corner of the room. 'What!' she exclaimed and pointed. 'What is *he* doing here?'

'Who?' Nora asked as she joined Lily in the doorway.

'Him,' Lily said. 'My great-grandfather, Cornelius Fleury. That's his portrait that used to hang over the fireplace in the library. I always loved it, but what on earth is it doing here?'

'I have no idea,' Nora said as they both stared at the oval oil painting propped against the far wall. It was of a man in morning suit standing against the backdrop of the huge fireplace in the library. A handsome man with wavy brown hair and moustache and large hazel eyes that gazed at them with a mischievous look as if he was about to wink at them.

Lily walked into the room that was empty except for a narrow bed, the painting and a leather trunk. She tried to remember what Sylvia had said about their great-grandfather, her father-in-law.

'Granny said he was very charming and kind to her when she first arrived here.'

Nora nodded. 'Yes, he was, she told me. Charming man, according to everyone who knew him. He died sometime in the early nineteen seventies, I think.'

'That's right.' Lily stared at the face in the portrait. 'He was ninety years old then. But why is he here? And what's in that trunk?' It was big with a brass lock and the leather darkened by damp and time. It sat there like something dark, mysterious and oddly threatening.

'Only one way to find out,' Nora said. 'Open it and take a look.'

Lily shivered. 'No, I can't. There could be a body in there or something.'

Nora laughed and went to the trunk. 'I bet there isn't.' She touched the leather. 'Could be locked of course.' She tried to lift the lid. 'It's not,' she said, taking a step back. 'But it's very heavy.'

'Go on. Open it,' Lily urged, wrapping her arms around herself, feeling suddenly cold. 'Just take a peek inside and then close it. Just to make sure there's nothing scary in it.'

Nora looked slightly apprehensive as she slowly heaved the lid open and peered into the trunk. 'Stacks of letters and photos are all I can see. And then some small boxes and a riding crop.'

'All of Cornelius's things?' Lily walked closer, looked into the trunk and touched a packet of letters. 'Weren't these in the library too? In that big cupboard?'

Nora nodded and let go of the lid, which closed with a bang that made them both jump. 'Yes, they were until quite recently.'

'But why are they here now?' Lily asked, staring at Nora. 'And who put them here? I can't imagine Granny carting it all over here by herself.'

Nora looked thoughtful. 'I don't know, but I have been worried about your granny,' she said and Lily inched closer. She and Nora had always had a special bond.

'Why?' Lily asked.

'She received a letter about two weeks before Christmas and she hasn't been the same since. She was white as a sheet after reading it and got into her car and drove off, speeding up the main road. I was so worried about her and expected to hear from the Guards any moment that she had been in an accident. I nearly called them but Martin told me to calm down. Sylvia was a sensible woman, he said, and she wouldn't do anything stupid.'

'Normally, no,' Lily agreed and sat down on the window seat. 'But anyone can be distracted by something that upset them. She didn't say anything about what was in the letter?'

'No. It had a foreign stamp, that's all I know,' Nora said, still standing by the trunk. 'And it seemed to be from some kind of legal firm as far as I could tell from the sender.'

'Legal?' Lily asked. 'Can you remember what was written on it?'

Nora shook her head. 'No.'

'Then what happened?'

'She was gone most of the day and then came back exhausted but calmer. Then it was Christmas and she went to stay with her sister Joan on the family farm on the other side of Dingle, and Martin and I went off to spend the holidays in Cork with our daughter. We came back just after New Year's and Sylvia didn't want to talk about it.'

Lily looked down at the trunk and the portrait. 'When did these things get moved into here?'

'I have no idea.' Nora kept staring at the portrait. 'I never noticed anything being moved out of the house.'

'So she could have done it while you were away?'

'Of course she could. And now, when I think about it, Dominic said he had done some kind of job for her just after New Year's.'

'He could have been who helped her, I suppose.' Lily looked at Nora for an answer.

Nora nodded, touching the trunk. 'He could. He has a little utility truck he goes around in between jobs.'

'Not too much to handle for a strong man.'

'Easy for Dominic. He's as strong as an ox.'

'And a young man,' Lily assumed.

'Not that young. Late thirties, I think,' Nora said with a fond smile. 'Lives in an old house on a bit of land above Ventry beach. He's on the beach in the early morning with his strange-looking dog following him.'

'Really? I love dogs. I'd love to say hello.'

'You can go over to Ventry in the early hours.'

'I might,' Lily said and got up. 'But now we have to make a plan. Do you think Granny might give me some furniture?'

'I'm sure she would,' Nora replied as they walked out of the room. 'There's a lot of furniture in rooms that are never used.

But...' Nora stopped on the landing. 'You might have to be very diplomatic.'

'As in sneaky?' Lily asked with a conspiratorial grin.

'If you like.' Nora frowned. 'She seems a little worried about you going around the house. She said something about closing off all the rooms except the library to everyone.'

'Including me and my sisters?' Lily suggested, taken aback by the serious look in Nora's kind eyes.

'*Especially* you,' Nora said.

5

Later that night after dinner in a lovely little fish restaurant, Lily prepared for bed in Oceanview B&B. It was a nice place with five bedrooms in a house overlooking the harbour. The 'ocean view' was just a glimpse of the sea through the bathroom window, but that was just a minor detail as the room was so comfortable, with a big bed piled with cushions and a soft wool carpet. The hostess, a chatty woman who introduced herself as Megan Slattery, had been full of questions, which Lily tried to reply to as blandly as she could. She didn't want to reveal too much. The Fleury family had always attracted a lot of attention, but with everything that Lily had been through, and her need for peace and quiet, she didn't want to tell her life story quite yet. She doubted her divorce was something her ancestry would have been proud of, and she felt like she needed to get back on her feet before reacquainting herself with the community. Lily simply told Mrs Slattery she had suddenly decided to visit, and that her room at Magnolia Manor wasn't ready yet, which put an end to the questions.

As she was the only guest the house was quiet, and Lily looked forward to crawling in under the duvet and going to sleep lulled by the distant murmur of the sea. In her pyjamas, she leaned out of the window and looked up at the starlit sky, a balmy breeze playing with her hair. Spring was in the air already here in the south west, which surprised visitors who had never been to this part of Kerry. She felt a sudden dart of happiness at having escaped from her sorrows and hectic life. She would finally have a home again, and a bed to call her own – not just Rose's couch. It would be quite busy here too, with many obstacles and problems, but she felt that it would be easier to cope in such lovely surroundings.

She had tried not to think about the divorce but, in idle moments like this, she couldn't stop the memories from tumbling into her mind. The marriage had been a huge mistake right from the start. She knew she shouldn't have let herself be carried away by Simon. But when they'd met and he had looked at her across the room at that party, she'd fallen head over heels for him. He had such a handsome face and his deep voice had compelled her. When he started whispering sweet nothings into her ear during those first dates, when he had taken her to romantic restaurants, she knew she was in love. He had seemed so interested in her and her family, fascinated by the old house in Kerry. She had taken this to mean he understood her completely and wanted to be part of her life with all it entailed.

Her mother had been so excited to organise the wedding; and Sean, her new husband, was so keen to walk Lily down the aisle. She had gone along with the fairy-tale image, the ring, the dress, the flowers and walking down the aisle to marry a man that every girl in Dublin had been in love with – or so it seemed. Simon had been what she had thought was the dream come true of love and marriage and, eventually, a family.

But it had all started to crumble shortly after that fairy-tale wedding.

Lily had first thought it all changed when Simon had seen the decrepit state of Magnolia Manor. Rather than a perfect mansion, Magnolia Manor was old and unloved, the family's money slowly running out. Looking back, she realised that perhaps even at the start, he had fallen in love with her name and not her.

Lily was glad he'd shown his cards. The day they had visited Sylvia, he didn't see the magic of the gardens, the view over Dingle Bay in the mellow sunshine, the old house with its towers, bay windows and tangle of roses over the south wall. He'd given away his true intentions. But they were already married by then.

She'd tried to forget the cracks she'd seen in his perfect façade, and believe that he loved her. She tried her best to be the kind of wife she thought Simon wanted, but it was no use. Despite the occasional fun events like dinners with friends or watching a movie they both liked, nothing seemed to please him. And she couldn't forget the look in his eyes when he discovered she was no heiress, or the slow realisation that he didn't really love her. Then the day came when he told Lily he wanted to leave, that the marriage had been a mistake and that he was sorry but...

Although Lily had felt in her bones that it would happen eventually, the blow was still brutal. She felt as if she had been struck by a physical force, even if he had never lifted a hand to hurt her. Devastated, she moved out of the apartment that she had loved and went to stay with Rose until she found a place to rent near her office.

The divorce proceedings had been so painful. Her solicitor had told her to claim half the apartment, as there had been no prenup, and she had agreed, but then halfway through the court case she had given up and said she'd let him have it. They'd chosen it together, but most of the money had come from him, and she just wanted it all to end as soon as possible. She was left with nothing, except an empty feeling and a pain in her heart, and she had buried herself in work, taking on whatever she was asked to do and then some, until she felt she could take no more and quit.

Then Rose had started talking about Magnolia Manor and all its potential for development and Lily agreed to start 'working on Granny' to get things started. And now, here she was in Dingle, looking out into the starry night, feeling that she could at last relax and breathe. It was over. Time to move on.

Lily took the elastic out of her hair and shook it out, letting it bounce around her face. It made her feel free and careless and ready to face whatever challenges would come her way. She was in the place she had always thought of as home and that was a wonderful feeling, despite her worry about Granny's strange behaviour, the portrait she had found in the gatehouse and that mysterious letter that had sent Sylvia racing out of town in such a hurry.

Despite her feelings of peace, Lily could tell something was going on, and she was determined to find out what it was before she could even think about her quest.

6

Lily woke up to the delicious smell of fried bacon. Normally, she would only have a smoothie or yogurt for breakfast as she raced out of the door, but now with that smell in her nostrils she knew she wouldn't be able to resist a full Irish. Twenty minutes later, she was sitting in the breakfast room of the B&B looking at a plate loaded with bacon, black pudding, sausages, a fried egg, mushrooms and a grilled tomato.

'I wasn't going to do this,' she said as Mrs Slattery arrived with a basket of homemade soda bread. 'But I can't resist this. It's too delicious to miss.'

Mrs Slattery smiled and put the basket on the table. 'I didn't mean to tempt you, but you looked as if you needed a bit of cheering up.'

'Well, yes, I do,' Lily admitted. 'But things are improving, so I'm feeling quite cheerful about everything.'

'That's grand. So everything is all right with your grand-mother?' Mrs Slattery asked as she hovered at the table.

'Oh yes. She's in good form,' Lily replied, sensing Mrs Slattery was in the mood for a gossip.

'And the house is still standing I've seen. So the Magnolia party will go ahead as usual?'

'Of course,' Lily said, dying to dig into her breakfast. 'Why wouldn't it?'

'Oh you never know,' Mrs Slattery said as if she hoped some disaster had befallen the family. 'Things might happen to prevent it. Or someone could get sick, or there could be a bad storm or—'

'Oh I don't think anything will stop us doing the party as usual,' Lily interrupted. 'My sisters and I will all be there to help out. And the house is still solid.'

'That's good to hear. So,' she continued. 'Your sisters will be here soon too?'

'No, not really,' Lily replied, looking longingly at her plate. 'Maybe for the party, of course. But that's a long way away.'

'I suppose,' Mrs Slattery mused. 'I remember you girls around town with your grandfather when I was working in the ice cream parlour. Lovely man.'

'Yes, he was.' Lily paused and smiled at Mrs Slattery. 'I can't wait to get stuck into this.' She cut off a piece of sausage and popped it into her mouth, looking defiantly at Mrs Slattery as she chewed, hoping it would stop the chatter.

'Enjoy,' Mrs Slattery said before she moved off. 'Let me know if you need anything else.'

Lily waved her fork in the air and then dug in, promising herself to skip lunch that day. It was all delicious and, when she had cleaned the plate, she complimented Mrs Slattery on her excellent cooking skills when she came back with more tea.

Mrs Slattery thanked her and said it was lovely to see someone enjoying their food instead of counting calories. 'But most of my guests seem to like my version of the full Irish,' she added.

'I'm not surprised.'

'So,' Mrs Slattery started after a brief pause, looking as if she was in the mood for another chat. 'You're going to work for Wolfie Quinn?'

Lily wiped her mouth with her napkin, trying not to look too shocked. But of course, this was a small town and everyone knew what was happening. Someone must have seen her go into the office and guessed why she was there.

'That's right. Starting on Monday. Do you know him?'

'I know who he is of course, like I know most people around here,' Mrs Slattery replied. 'He seems to be a good enough solicitor. But he and his dad keep themselves to themselves, if you know what I mean. Could be because they handle people's affairs, so they want to be discreet. But your grandmother could tell you more, I'm sure. She used to go into that office quite a lot for a while.'

'Did she?' Lily stared at Mrs Slattery. 'I had no idea. Nora said...' She stopped. 'Well, that's something I should talk to her about.'

'Or your grandmother,' Mrs Slattery suggested with a knowing look.

'Maybe.' Suddenly uncomfortable, Lily got up from the table. 'I have to go. I'll see you later.'

Mrs Slattery looked disappointed. 'Okay,' she said as she loaded her tray with the breakfast dishes. 'You're staying another few days, is that right?'

'Eh, yes, maybe. Not sure,' Lily replied as she hovered in the door. 'Depends on how soon I can get the gatehouse liveable. I'll let you know.'

Mrs Slattery nodded. 'That's fine. No rush at all.'

Lily walked out into the bright sunshine, her mind full of what Mrs Slattery had said. Her grandmother had obviously consulted Wolfie about something. But why had Nora said he wasn't Sylvia's solicitor? Something strange was going on, that was becoming increasingly clear. But what? Lily shook her head as she got into her car that was parked outside the B&B. Only one way to find out. She would go straight to her grandmother and ask what on earth was going on.

When Lily drove through the gates of Magnolia Manor, she noticed a battered pickup truck beside the steps of the gate-house and an odd-looking dog sitting by the open front door. Intrigued, she pulled up behind the truck and got out. The dog was large, woolly and white except for a big black patch over one eye. He got up and wagged his tail, cocking his head and looking at Lily with lovely doggy eyes. Enchanted, she crouched down and scratched him behind his ear.

'Aren't you the loveliest dog,' she said while he licked her face. 'Who do you belong to then? And what on earth is going on?' she added as she heard loud noises coming from the living room.

Frowning, she got up, walked inside and caught sight of two men carrying a sofa that they placed in front of the fireplace, on top of a blue and red rug beside two easy chairs. Lily stopped and stared at them.

'What's going on here?' she exclaimed.

One of the men, who was tall with black hair and a five o'clock shadow on his square chin, turned around.

'Oh, hi,' he said. 'You must be Lily Fleury.' He smiled as he studied her for a moment. 'You're the spit of your granny.'

'Yes, I'm Lily Fleury. Who are you?' she enquired, slightly self-conscious as she returned his gaze.

He held out his hand. 'Dominic Doyle. And this is Con,' he said, gesturing at his companion, a gangly youth with fair hair and a face full of freckles.

Hi,' Lily said absentmindedly as she shook Dominic's hand. 'Hello, Con. What are you doing here?'

'We've delivered some furniture from the manor,' Dominic

said. 'A request from your grandmother. There's a lot more than the sofa and chairs.'

'Like what?' Lily stared at the sofa, astonished that Sylvia would have been so generous after having been so negative about Lily living in the gatehouse. She knew the rug, sofa and chairs had come from the small drawing room.

'A kitchen table, a nearly new mattress, a bedside lamp and two boxes with bedclothes,' Dominic replied. 'We've nearly finished bringing everything in.'

'There's a few more lamps and stuff in the truck,' Con cut in. 'Then we're done.'

'And then Con can go to the Saturday hurling match,' Dominic remarked with a grin, which made him look a lot more cheerful.

Lily noticed that his eyes were dark green, like jade, and also that he was good looking in a wild Kerry way. 'That's very kind of Granny,' she said and started to back out of the room. 'I'll call into her to say thanks.'

'She won't be there,' Dominic warned. 'I saw her drive out of the gate and up road towards Ventry a few minutes ago. In any case, she told me to let you know that she wanted you to be comfortable while you live here, even though it's only for a short while.'

'Oh. Then I'll just give her a call on her mobile and go and see her later. But what did she mean by that strange message?'

Dominic shrugged. 'No idea. I'm just the messenger. And hey, maybe you could go upstairs and check that we put the mattress on the right bed? The one in the front bedroom, we thought. And there are a few boxes and stuff you might want to look at. Just to make sure all is in order and up to Dublin standards, ya know?'

His teasing tone made Lily bristle. 'I had no idea these things were being delivered,' she said stiffly. 'My grandmother seems to be up to all kinds of things she never shared with me or my sisters.'

'Ah well, if you were around a bit more, you might have been better informed,' Dominic remarked.

Lily knew what he meant, despite the bland look on his face. Sylvia was obviously closer to this man than Lily had thought and might have complained about her granddaughters' long absences.

'Well, that is...'

'None of my business?' he filled in.

'Something like that. I'll go and check what you put upstairs,' Lily said and marched out of the room, her face burning.

He'd made her feel flustered and confused for some reason, possibly because she felt guilty about not having been in touch with her grandmother. There was something insolent in the way he looked at her, as if he knew everything about her – most of it bad. What had Sylvia told him about Lily and her sisters? That they were spoilt brats? Lily didn't want to think about it.

She raced up the stairs and into the front bedroom, where a nearly brand new mattress sat on the bed and two half-open boxes full of pillows, blankets and sheets had been put on the floor. On closer inspection, Lily saw that the sheets were the very special monogrammed linen ones reserved for guests and that the pillows were new. The blankets were the thick wool Foxford blankets they had slept under as children; she remembered cuddling in under them as a small child, feeling warm and protected and safe. How lovely of Granny to do this. Lily pulled her phone out of her handbag and dialled Sylvia's number. She answered after several rings.

'Hello, I'm driving. Please call back later.'

'Granny, it's me—' Lily started, but Sylvia had hung up. Lily sighed and rang Nora, who answered straight away.

'Hello, Lily, what's the matter?'

'I just... I wanted to talk to Granny to say thanks for all the stuff she had sent over to the gatehouse but she's driving, so...'

'I know. She's on her way to bridge with her friends near Ventry,' Nora said. 'They play every Saturday morning. She'll be back later this afternoon when she's been to lunch with the ladies who do the flower arranging at the church, and then she is having tea with the board members of the nursing home, and then she's meeting the seniors' walking group to plan their outing to the lakes of Killarney.' Nora drew breath. 'She's very busy.'

'That's putting it mildly,' Lily said with a laugh. She felt a little less worried about Granny now. She was glad she'd been keeping up with her usual social engagements. But it made her wonder why she'd stopped maintaining the manor. 'What's she doing tomorrow, bungee jumping off Mount Brandon?'

'No, that's on Tuesdays,' Nora quipped.

Lily giggled. Nora was always such fun. 'So I suppose today is not the day to talk to her?'

'Not really. Try tomorrow after mass. In fact, just call in and catch her when she's reading the Sunday papers in the study. Usually a good time to have a chat with her.'

'Great. I'll do that. Thanks, Nora.' Lily hung up and walked downstairs again, feeling much calmer. Whatever this Dominic said next would have no effect on her. He could try to annoy her as much as he wanted, she would not react. He might be Granny's confidant, but he would not be allowed to stick his nose into Lily's business. She'd just ignore him.

There was no sign of Dominic or his helper in the living room and, when Lily looked out the front door, she saw they were getting into the truck, the dog already sitting in the bed at the back, panting. She went outside to say goodbye.

'You're off, then?' she said.

'Yup.' Dominic paused before he got in. 'The stuff all okay?' he asked.

Lily shrugged. 'No idea what you mean, I didn't order anything so I can't comment.'

Dominic nodded. 'I see. Well, your granny gave me a list that I left on the kitchen table. Take a look at that to get an idea of what we brought. If you need anything else give me a shout.'

The dog suddenly barked.

'Shut up, Larry,' Dominic told him and got into the truck. 'See ya around, Princess,' he shouted through the open window before he took off in a shower of gravel, driving through the gates at breakneck speed.

Nearly dizzy after his whirlwind departure, Lily sank down on the step and stared at the truck as it disappeared up the road to Dingle town. She realised she had forgotten to ask him about the portrait and the trunk with old letters and photos, but he would probably have been evasive about it anyway.

Then she started to laugh, shook her head and got up again. 'What an odd man,' she muttered. 'And full of himself, too.'

She went inside to check the list of the items that had been delivered. It looked as if the house had been nearly fully furnished and made comfortable – or at least habitable. All she needed to do now was to clean it from top to bottom and get a fire started in both the fireplace and the woodburning stove. There would be no electricity until she could set up an account, but she saw that there were two brass candlesticks and a paraffin oil lamp on the kitchen counter, so Granny must have thought she'd be able to manage with that until the electricity was switched on. And she would, she decided, feeling she'd rather be uncomfortable, cold and in darkness than put up with more questions from Mrs Slattery at the Oceanview B&B. It was Saturday and Granny was away and Lily had no other plans. She'd get stuck in and get herself as comfortable as possible. No better way to start her new life.

7

When dusk was falling, Lily looked around the kitchen of the gatehouse feeling she had achieved the nearly impossible. Everything was clean and tidy, the countertops shining after a good polish, the flagstones on the floor had been swept and washed and a few logs burning in the stove spread a welcome warmth through the little house. Lily sat down on a kitchen chair to rest her aching back and looked through the now-clean window at the garden bathed in a mellow light from the setting sun. The camellia bush down the path was already in bloom and some of the shrubs were beginning to shoot green leaves. She had always agreed with the saying that 'Kerry has no seasons, only weather,' as it was mostly mild even if windy and wet at this time of year. It was the abundant rain and mild temperatures that made it a gardener's delight.

In the early days of the manor, it must have been such a joy to plant this garden. Even two hundred years later, it was mostly overgrown but still such a haven of peace and tranquillity. It had also been a place of adventure for her as a child, playing hide-and-seek and ghosts and pirates and other games with her sisters and local children when they were here on holiday. The memories tumbled through Lily's mind as she sat there, making her smile. Then, as darkness fell, she lit the paraffin oil lamp and went into the living room to light the fire. Just as the flames started to flicker around the kindling and logs, her phone rang. It was Rose.

'Hi,' she said, sounding cross. 'Why haven't you called me? I thought we agreed you'd be in touch when you had talked to Granny.'

'I haven't managed to talk to her yet,' Lily confessed as she sat down on the sofa.

'What? But you've been there since yesterday!' Rose exclaimed.

Lily could hear what sounded like crockery being knocked together in the background. 'What's all that noise?' she asked.

'I'm cooking dinner for Gavin. Special night. We've been together two years today.'

'Congratulations,' Lily said, even though she had never quite approved of Rose being in a relationship with her boss.

'Thanks, that's very sweet of you.' Rose paused. 'I'm going to give him a home-cooked meal for the first time ever.'

'A home-cooked meal?' Lily said incredulously. Rose was beautiful and smart but not what anyone would call domestic. 'You've never even boiled an egg.'

'Yeah, well I'm trying to learn. I'm doing a grilled steak and potato gratin that I bought ready made but he won't notice. Never mind that. He's not home yet so I have plenty of time. So what about our plan? I thought you'd at least have had a little chat with Granny by now.'

'I was going to, but things got in the way,' Lily tried to explain. 'I had the job interview yesterday. Got the job, by the way, and then I had a look at the gatehouse, which wasn't exactly in great nick. I've spent the whole day cleaning it. And Granny seems odd... She doesn't seem to want me to stay for too long. And the house is even more crumbling and unloved than ever before. I have a feeling she's really been struggling to look after it...'

'Poor Granny,' Rose remarked. 'She wants to be independent and show us she can manage on her own all the time. I wish she had told us she needed help.'

'She doesn't want to be a burden on us, I think,' Lily said with desperation in her voice. 'And now she is hiding something. She keeps disappearing. And then there's the business of the portrait and the box full of letters and photos...' Lily went on to tell Rose what she had found in the small bedroom in the gatehouse.

Rose gasped. 'What? Great-grandpa Cornelius's portrait and old trunk were thrown out of the manor? Did she kick him out of the house? Granny must have discovered something awful in his past. He was supposed to be a bit of a rascal, according to family history. But I never thought much of it. Have you had a look at the stuff in the trunk?'

'No,' Lily protested. 'I haven't had a chance.'

Rose sighed. 'I know, you only arrived yesterday and you've been busy cleaning and getting a job. But had I been there I'd have at least had a peek.'

'Of course you would.' Lily knew Rose would have gone through most of the trunk by now. She wouldn't have put a job and where to live on the top of her list of priorities. But that was Rose. Lily was different. 'I like order,' she said.

Rose sighed. 'Don't I know it. You used to catalogue your underwear and socks when we were kids.'

'I did not,' Lily protested.

'You would have if you could,' Rose teased. 'But I have to go. Gavin will be home soon and I have to do my hair and set the table and put the gratin in the oven. Call me tomorrow and let me know what you've found out and how far you got with Granny.'

'Okay. But I have to make sure the battery on my phone doesn't run out. There's no electricity here at the moment.'

'I see. We'll talk soon. Bye for now. Don't kill yourself cleaning.'

She hung up before Lily had a chance to say goodbye.

Lily sighed as she put her phone back in her bag. Rose was her usual self, such a mixture of brains and beauty and a burning ambition to make it big in the world of real estate. Rose and Gavin would make a fabulous corporate couple; they might marry one day and even have their wedding in the gardens of Magnolia Manor... That would bring them all together once they had realised their dreams of doing up the manor and returning it to its former glory. But that was all pie in the sky at the moment. No time to dream right now.

As darkness fell over the lush gardens and the stars began to sparkle in the midnight blue sky, Lily realised that spending the night in the gatehouse would not be very comfortable. She had to get the electricity turned on and buy heaters for the bedrooms. It was all very well to love camping, but the house was chilly despite the fires and she knew it would take at least a week for the stone walls to warm up. She had to give up the notion of staying here and go back to the Oceanview B&B and Mrs Slattery for at least a couple of days. Not ideal but the best option right now. Carrying the paraffin oil lamp, she went upstairs to get her overnight bag that she had left on the bed. On her way back down, she stopped as a thought struck her. Why not have a look at the trunk in the small bedroom? She could take away some of the letters to look at tonight. It might throw some light on whatever it was that had made Granny 'evict' Cornelius's portrait and trunk from the manor, as Rose had put it.

Holding the lamp high, Lily opened the door to the small bedroom, the hinges squeaking loudly. There was an eerie feeling in the room as the lamp cast shadows all around. Lily hesitated in the doorway and then shook herself and went in. The floorboards creaked as she walked to the trunk and she glanced at Cornelius's face in the portrait. He seemed to follow her with his gaze, which felt scary, but she told herself not to be silly. She opened the trunk, but she couldn't see the contents clearly, and she grabbed what looked like a leatherbound diary or journal with the initials CF in gold lettering on the front. It had to mean Cornelius Fleury. Maybe what was in this diary would throw some light on what Cornelius had been up to and why his things had been put in the gatehouse. She'd bring it back to the B&B and look at it more closely.

It was a start, and Lily had a strange feeling that if she could find some kind of clue in the diary, it might help convince Sylvia and make it possible to put their plans for the house into action. *The past meeting the future, that's what we could create,* she thought as she went down the stairs clutching the leather-bound book.

8

All was quiet in the B&B when Lily arrived and she went upstairs to her bedroom grateful that she hadn't checked out. It was comfortable and warm, a sharp contrast to the current feel of the gatehouse. She would stay until at least Monday when she might be able to get the electricity turned on. And she'd go and buy an electric heater for the front bedroom on her lunch hour. All this seemed like a good plan and, feeling satisfied, Lily sat down on the bed and opened Cornelius's old diary. It smelled of damp, rose petals and smoke. She ran her fingers over the soft leather and then opened it slowly and reverently, believing the contents to be like a message from the past. A message from someone she had never known, born over a hundred years ago, but who had lived in the manor all his life, and presumably loved it as much as she did.

But when Lily opened the book, she discovered that instead of the diary of her great-grandfather, it was a kind of notebook full of exquisite drawings of flowers and birds, and the person it had belonged to was a woman. Caroline Fleury, it said on the flyleaf. This was the sketchbook of Cornelius's wife, Caroline, Lily's great-grandmother, renowned for her beauty and gentle, kind soul. Her portrait hung in the library and Lily had often stared at it, meeting the gaze from the lovely hooded blue eyes and admiring the lavender silk gown she was dressed in. Lily's heart sank. It was a nice discovery, but not what she had hoped to find.

Still, as Lily turned the pages, she marvelled at the fine drawings and the skill and talent of the artist. There were little notes at the bottom of each sketch, with details of where each plant had been found. The birds were mostly small – finches and thrushes – but there were also sea birds and birds of prey, their feathers drawn in beautiful detail with depth and colours that were true to life even after so many years. Lily kept turning the pages until she came to the end, where the last few pages held no pictures but were covered in writing that was hard to decipher. The script was quite faint, as the ink had faded, but some of it was legible. A date on the last page said *19 April 1922* and then:

He's gone to Paris again, staying at the same hotel. He's there to meet a cousin and to buy a painting for the drawing room. I know he's telling the truth, but I do worry sometimes that he's gone back to his old ways, smoking and drinking too much... and then the other activity, betting on horses and playing cards for money. He's often elated when he comes back but the last time he looked very poorly, pale and tired with a haunted look in his lovely eyes. Then he cheered up after a few days and when that letter arrived from Etienne Bernard he seemed calmer afterwards. But now I'm worried about what he's doing over there, so far away from the family and this house that we both love.

I don't like Etienne Bernard. He seems false to me with his hand kissing and beautiful clothes. Good looking, yes, and so polite it makes me want to scream. I'm always happy when his visits end. And now Cornelius is over there with him. I hope

*and pray that all will be well. Drawing and painting help keep
my mind off my worries. Thank goodness for this garden and
the shoreline where I can sit and draw beautiful birds and
follow their flight across the deep blue water of the ocean. It
soothes my soul and seems to heal my heart.*

Lily stared at the words, reading them several times. Poor
Caroline seemed so worried and sad. Had Cornelius led some
kind of double life? This was not the great-grandfather she had
heard so much about. He had been a legend in the family as a
kind, jovial man who everyone loved. They had seen photos of
him tending the gardens, working on the farm, having picnics
on the beach with his wife and son, Lily's grandfather, the
picture of domestic bliss. Caroline had looked so happy in those
photos, gazing at her husband with such love in her eyes. Lily
and her sisters had enjoyed looking through the family albums
as children, giggling at the clothes, the long skirts that got
shorter and shorter, the bucket hats, the funny-looking shoes. It
had all seemed so idyllic and sweet. But here, Lily suddenly met
a woman who was distressed and worried and far from happy.
What had been going on behind the lovely façade?

Lily put the album on the bedside table, feeling confused.
She would have to ask Granny what she knew and also what
had prompted the sudden aversion to Cornelius's portrait. She
knew it would be hard to get anything out of Sylvia that she
didn't want to share, but she would have to try all the same.

But that was for another day. Lily was getting hungry. It
was past seven and time for dinner. She decided to try the pub
down the street from the B&B. As it was Saturday night, they
were sure to have some kind of music evening. She suddenly
felt in the mood for some good Irish food and music to cheer her
up. She knew she would meet people she knew – *or at least
people who know people I know*, she thought with amusement.
She might even meet someone whose granny might have heard

some old family gossip. You never knew what might turn up during an idle conversation...

The pub was of the traditional variety: the flagstones on the floor strewn with sawdust, the wainscoting on the walls hung with framed photos of the town and harbour in bygone days, the bar counter made of rough timber, and rows of bottles on shelves behind it. Sods of turf blazed in the fireplace, spreading a welcome warmth; the smell of lamb stew mingled with the turf smoke and just a whiff of garlic and herbs. Lily knew she was in for a treat. Apart from a few people sitting at the bar, the pub was empty and Lily looked around for a suitable table.

'Hiya,' a waiter with black curly hair and prominent teeth, dressed in a worn fisherman's sweater, greeted her as she hesitated at a table near the fireplace. 'You're here to eat or just for a drink?'

'A bit of both,' Lily said, smiling back at him.

'Great. You can sit anywhere. There's only two things on the menu – stew or sausages and chips. You can have either chips or boiled spuds with the stew.'

'I'll have the stew with boiled spuds, please. And a glass of Guinness.'

'Better make it a pint,' he suggested. 'We'll be packed in about half an hour and then you'll have a job getting another drink. The Fiddler's Elbow are playing tonight, and they're fierce popular.'

'Okay. Thanks.' Lily sat down at the table. 'I used to think it wasn't ladylike to order a pint.'

'Ah sure things have changed,' the waiter said, grinning. 'Ladies are thin on the ground these days. A dying breed, dontcha know? Or maybe they just decided to be equal? If you can't beat 'em, join 'em kind of thing,' he added with a wink.

Lily smiled. 'And isn't it a relief for us all?'

'A blessed relief,' he agreed. 'I'll be back with your pint in a tick. And the stew will be here before you know it.'

He walked away, leaving Lily grinning, having enjoyed the conversation enormously. It was such a treat to be back in Kerry, in a pub that was so welcoming, with a waiter who had this easy way of talking.

A man and a woman sat down at the table beside Lily's. 'Hi there,' the woman said. 'Are you here for the music?'

'And the food,' Lily replied. 'I heard both are good.'

'Top notch,' the man said.

They fell into an easy conversation, talking about the weather, the town and how it was so lively even in the middle of winter. The couple were from Cork and were spending the weekend in Dingle, planning to do the Mount Brandon walk the following day. The pub became increasingly crowded as the band arrived and started to tune their instruments: a banjo, a fiddle, a tin whistle and a bodhrán – the small handheld drum. When they started to play it was no longer possible to talk. Lily was soon spellbound by the lovely rhythmic sounds, the beauty of the tunes that seemed to be imprinted in her heart and soul from early childhood. The music had such depth of feeling and conjured up images of the landscape, the history of the people who had lived and worked here for hundreds of years, their sadness at the loss of loved ones who had emigrated or died. Lily was nearly in a trance, only coming to her senses when the music suddenly stopped. She noticed the plate of fragrant stew that had been put in front of her and started to eat it, enjoying every bite, washed down with bittersweet Guinness.

'What an evening, eh?' the man at the neighbouring table said as he finished his dinner. 'The music is fantastic and the food is amazing. This food is nearly as good as my mammy's.' He took a swig of his pint and looked expectantly at the band. 'They're taking a break and then their singer will be on. I've heard his voice is fabulous.'

'And he's not bad looking either,' the woman cut in, winking at Lily.

'Sounds like a real treat, so,' Lily remarked.

She didn't have to wait long. The lights dimmed and the musicians struck up a lilting ballad. Then a man carrying a guitar stepped into the light, sat down on a stool and started to sing, his voice low at first, and then stronger as he strummed his guitar and sang the first bars of 'The Mountains of Mourne'. Deep and melodious with a touch of hoarseness, his voice was truly magical. Lily listened intently. He was bent over the guitar and lost in the music, his eyes closed so it was difficult to see his features clearly. It wasn't until he looked up to smile as a thank you for the applause that Lily saw who he was. Dominic Doyle, the rude man she had met that morning. She stared at him, shocked at the discovery. How weird that he had such a talent and such a sweet voice.

Dominic hadn't spotted Lily in the audience and she shrank back into the shadows while he started to sing 'You Raise Me Up' followed by 'Fields of Gold', two of her favourite songs, both of which were sung so beautifully it brought tears to her eyes. He went on to sing some Irish songs, ending with a lively rendition of 'Brown Eyed Girl' to rousing applause, cheering and whistling. Dominic declined the shouts of 'encore!' with a wave and disappeared behind the bar while the band played a final song.

'Ooh,' the woman beside Lily sighed, her hands to her heart. 'I will dream of him all night. That voice, that face, those green eyes...'

Lily nodded, lost for words, knowing her sleep would be equally affected. The fact that she had found him cheeky to the point of rudeness when they met earlier didn't seem to matter right now. The voice and those eyes glimmering in the dim light had touched her in a very strange way.

But it was late and she was tired. It was time to leave. She realised that it wouldn't be possible to meet anyone with whom she could have a conversation about the past in this crowded pub. Suddenly exhausted, she got up, looking for her credit card in her handbag to pay at the till on the way out while she said goodbye to the nice couple beside her.

'Enjoy the walk tomorrow,' she said.

They thanked her and said they knew they would and she waved at them as she pushed through the crowd to the till at the entrance.

'Your bill has already been settled,' the waiter said, his voice loud in the din of the pub. 'Dominic Doyle said it was on him. A friend of yours?'

'Eh, not... not exactly,' Lily replied, feeling confused. Why had Dominic paid for her meal? It was a kind gesture that she didn't understand. 'He works for my grandmother,' she explained.

The young man nodded. 'Oh yeah, Mrs Fleury. So you're a Fleury, then?'

Lily nodded. 'Yes. Do you know my grandmother?'

'Don't everybody?' he asked with a grin. 'Sylvia Fleury is a legend around here. Very nice lady too. You must be very fond of her.'

'Yes, I am,' Lily replied. 'I'm so lucky to have a grandmother like her.'

'You're steeped. But I have a feeling we're connected in some way. My granny knew your great-granny, I remember now.'

'My great-grandmother, Caroline?' Lily asked, feeling her heart beat faster. 'Could I ask you some questions about her?'

'That's the lady I meant.' He smiled and shook his head as the pub became even noisier. 'But it's not possible to talk here,' he shouted. 'Come back during the week when it's less packed. Not next week though. I'll be away. I'll give you a shout when

I'm back if you give me your number. Then I can tell you about it.' He handed her a napkin. 'Do you have a pen?'

'I do.' Lily fished one out of her handbag, quickly scribbled her number on the napkin and handed it back. 'There.'

He nodded. 'Great. My name is Brian. I'll call you when I'm back.'

'Thanks, Brian,' Lily said, waving as she left the pub.

The street was blissfully quiet, the clamour from the pub barely audible. Lily breathed in the fresh, cool air, grateful to be outside the hot, stuffy bar. The stars twinkled in the dark sky and the smell of turf smoke mingled with the salty tang from the harbour as she made her way back to the Oceanview B&B. She wondered what the waiter would tell her when they met up. What was that he had said? His granny had known her great-grandmother. Maybe she'd find a trail she could follow.

9

The phone rang early the following morning. Lily grunted and peered at the caller ID. Rose. But it was seven o'clock. Why was she up at this hour? 'Hi, Rose,' she said. 'You're up early. Everything all right?'

'Fine,' Rose replied. 'It's just that Gavin went on a business trip to New York and had to leave early, so I'm all alone for a bit. Thought I'd come and see you. I'll take some time off and come down to Kerry. We can do up the gatehouse together and work on Granny. Why don't I come down tomorrow?'

'I don't know...' Lily hesitated. Things were so up in the air, with the gatehouse not ready and a new job and... 'I haven't even moved into the gatehouse. I'm still at this B&B and I'm starting at the solicitor's office tomorrow and...'

'I won't be in your way,' Rose promised. 'It's been hectic here and I feel like a break.'

'Well...' Lily paused. 'Could you hold off for a bit until I have the gatehouse ready? Better to be comfortable if you need a holiday.'

'I suppose you're right,' Rose replied. 'I've been doing so well lately and got a huge commission selling a house in Killiney that went for nearly a million. Gavin was so pleased with me. He won't mind if I take some extra leave. Could be good for us to be apart for a while too. Wouldn't it be fun for you and me to be together like the old times?'

'I'd love to see you,' Lily said. 'I'll give you a shout when things are a bit more organised.'

'Okay. I get that you're a bit stressed right now. I'll come when things settle down for you,' Rose promised.

'Great. And when you do come, you can have a go at Granny. She dotes on you so you might have a better chance to get her to listen.'

'I'll do my best. See you soon, Lily-lou. I miss you.'

'I miss you too, Rosie-roo.' Lily felt herself soften at the pet name her grandfather had made up for her. Rose had been 'Rosie-roo' and Violet 'Violetta'. He had loved them dearly and spoilt them rotten. After the tragic accident, when both Sylvia and their mother had been paralysed with grief, Lily had taken care of her sisters and still did to some extent. In any case, they always turned to her when they needed help or a shoulder to cry on. 'Just give me a little time to get the house organised. Don't expect miracles though.'

'I won't,' Rose promised, sounding more cheerful. 'See you soon, sweetie.'

'Bye for now.' Lily hung up, feeling relieved. She did miss her sister but felt she couldn't cope with looking after Rose on top of everything else, even if it would be nice to have her around.

Lily lay there for a while, staring into the darkness, trying to go back to sleep. But she gave up after an hour, flung the bedclothes back and got out of bed. She padded across the carpet to the bathroom and peered out through the little window from where she could see the ocean. The sun was rising behind the hill, giving the whole bay a golden hue. Tiny ripples on the water told her there was only a slight breeze.

Good running weather. Lily went to her suitcase and rummaged around for her leggings, T-shirt and light jacket. The shoes were at the bottom and she managed to pull them out without having to unpack the whole case. Then, when she was ready, she tiptoed down the stairs and managed to get out without being confronted by Mrs Slattery, who seemed to be in the kitchen making breakfast.

Once outside, Lily breathed in the cool, clean air and looked down the street, trying to decide where to go. The back road to Ventry wouldn't be too busy this early on a Sunday morning, and it was a lovely road lined with green fields sloping down to the sea. The beach in Ventry was also nice; she had often gone there for a swim in the summer. It would take her about half an hour to get to the beach and she could get a coffee at the little shop before heading back. She nodded. Good choice.

She set off down the quiet street and onto the main road, past the little houses all painted in bright colours and then over the bridge before she turned right onto the back road. She ran at an easy pace, not trying to keep a set time, simply enjoying the run, the beautiful surroundings and the wind in her hair. She hadn't kept up her running schedule so she wasn't as fit as she used to be, but she decided there and then to take it up again. There was nothing like a run in the early morning to get that feeling of wellbeing.

Lily had to slow to a walk several times before she reached Ventry, the little hamlet with the holiday cottages that lined the road sloping down to the curved beach. She passed a quirky house she had often admired, situated behind a high wall and just above the beach. She could see a tiny but lush garden on a ledge perched high above the sand and the slate roof with the chimney sticking up. A dog barked as she passed and she wondered who lived there now. Years ago, the house had been occupied by an artist who was renowned for his beautiful seascapes. But he had died a long time ago and the house had been abandoned for a number of years. Now it seemed to have been restored and was occupied again, which was nice as it was such a beautiful little house in a stunning location.

Lily felt a dart of envy as she made her way down the overgrown concrete path to the beach. Wouldn't it be the perfect place to live? She had always imagined herself living there, with a dog and a cat and maybe a husband and a baby or two... She laughed at herself and those dreams she had when she was very young. She had thought it would be easy to be grown up and in charge of her life. But now, at the age of thirty-seven, she knew better and longed to be a young girl again with all those hopes and dreams yet to be realised, her whole life ahead of her.

Lily jumped from the path onto the sand and sat down, looking out across the little bay, enjoying the peace and the sound of the waves and the distant cry of seagulls. She leaned her elbows on her knees and gazed out all the way to the horizon where the blue sky met the darker blue water.

She jumped as something wet hit her ear and turned to discover a shaggy white dog beside her, licking her, wagging his tail. She recognised him immediately. It was Dominic's dog.

Lily laughed and scratched him behind his ear. 'Hi, Larry, where did you come from?' She looked back across the beach and saw the outline of a man walking towards her. As he drew closer, she saw it was Dominic dressed in jeans and a dark green hoodie.

He stopped in front of her. 'Hi there, Lily. You're out and about early. Did you run all the way here?'

'Not quite,' she confessed. 'I ran and walked and then ran again. I'm trying to get my fitness back.'

He crouched beside her. 'It can be hard to get back to it. But you made it here, whatever your pace. Well done. You do look a bit hot and tired though.'

'I know,' she started, realising she must be very sweaty. She wiped her face with the sleeve of her jacket. 'I forgot to take a bottle of water with me too.'

'I'll get you a bottle from the shop,' Dominic offered. 'I was on my way to get the Sunday papers when Larry did a runner. He must have known you were here. He seems to like you.'

'Or he just likes sweaty people,' Lily joked as Larry sniffed at her face.

'Could be.' Dominic got up. 'I'll go and get you the water. Won't be long. Larry, you stay and keep the lady company.' He ran down the beach and up the slope, returning within minutes with a bottle of water and two paper mugs. 'I brought you coffee as well. Thought you might like some to give you energy for the run back.'

'Thanks, that's perfect.' Lily took the bottle, unscrewed the cap and drank deeply before she smiled at him. 'That was heaven. Just what I needed.'

He offered her one of the mugs. 'Coffee? I figured you were a latte girl.'

Lily took the mug. 'I usually go for an Americano. But a latte is fine too. Thank you.'

'Okay. I'll remember that.' He smiled, drank from the other cup and then sat down on the sand beside her. 'I'm Americano too, and espresso from time to time.'

'I see.' Lily suddenly felt awkward. 'Eh, thank you for paying for my meal last night,' she said after a moment's silence. 'There really was no need. And now I owe you for coffee too.'

He waved his hand. 'There's no need. You're welcome. Thought I should do something to apologise for being a bit rude when we met. I didn't mean to upset you or anything.'

She raised an eyebrow. 'You just wanted to tease me then?' she asked.

He grinned. 'Yeah. You were standing there so prim and proper, looking at me as if I was something the cat dragged in. So I decided to annoy you.'

'You succeeded brilliantly,' Lily retorted. 'I bet you were one of those boys who pulled the girls' hair in junior infants.'

'I'm afraid you're right,' he said with mock contrition. 'I was an awful little brat. But I reformed.'

'Now you just annoy people and then pay for their dinners? Must be an expensive little hobby.'

'Hmm, well. Touché. You win. Can we stop the needling now?'

Lily had to laugh, feeling satisfied she had won their argument – or whatever it was. 'Okay. As you've declared me the winner.' She held out her hand. 'Truce?'

He grabbed it in a strong grip. 'Until the next time.' He held her hand for a moment, during which their eyes met and she felt a jolt of something happening between them.

'I'll be ready.' Lily sipped her coffee, looking at him over the rim of the mug. He was good looking in a careless way, with the strong jaw and straight nose. His luminous green eyes met hers again for a second before they both looked away. 'Strange to be here,' she said, looking out over the water. 'We used to swim in this bay when we were kids. When my dad was still alive,' she added wistfully. 'He died when I was twelve and I still miss him so much, even after all these years.'

'And the memories come alive when you're in a place you used to go to with him?' he asked softly.

'Yes. I don't think I'll ever get over losing him.'

'Must be hard to grow up without a father,' Dominic said with empathy in his voice. 'I suppose you'll always feel the loss.'

'I think you're right.'

'Yeah.' They sat there in silence, both deep in thought as Lily felt comforted by his understanding.

'I was wondering,' she said after a while, 'about the portrait and that trunk in the small bedroom. Was it you who moved it all?'

Dominic nodded and put the paper mug on the sand.

'Yes, it was. That was just before Christmas. Sylvia phoned me and asked me to come and move it all. She needed help to take the painting down from its place in the drawing room. It's very heavy. Then she asked me to put it where you found it.'

'Did she say why she wanted to move it?'

'No. Just that she wanted it out of the way. I thought she was clearing the room to use it for something else. She did seem very stressed about something. I didn't ask what was going on. Didn't think it was any of my business.'

'She wouldn't have told you anyway. I wonder what's troubling her,' Lily muttered as if to herself. 'It has something to do with Cornelius, but what?'

'Cornelius?' Dominic asked. 'Is that the dude in the portrait?'

Lily let out a laugh. 'Yes, that's the dude. My great-grandfather. Her father-in-law.'

'Oh.' Dominic was silent for a moment. 'I guess it is a bit weird that she wanted all his stuff moved out of the main house.'

'Isn't it? But you don't know why?'

'No.'

Lily looked at Dominic for a while. 'You and Granny are quite close I gather?'

'In a way. She was a great help when I first came here. Made sure everyone knew about me and my business and got me some good contracts for renovations and landscaping. And I did a bit of work for her as well.'

'So you run your business from your house?' Lily looked up the hill. 'Where is it?'

'I have a shed and workshop up there.' Dominic pointed behind a group of houses. 'But I live in that house on the edge of the beach. Got it for a song as it was very run down.'

'You mean that house behind the wall?' Lily asked pointing at the house she had just passed. 'I always loved it. I wanted to live there when I was younger. I'm so glad it has an owner again.'

'It's such a nice spot too,' Dominic remarked. 'Very quiet with stunning views. It makes me feel so at one with the ocean.'

'I can imagine.' Lily felt a dart of envy. 'A heavenly spot.'

'On a good day,' he said with a laugh. 'You won't want to be there during a storm. But then I move up to the shed until the wind drops as the waves might hit the house. It never has though, but you never know. I have an old donkey I adopted in the field beside it. I like animals. They never argue.'

'They are the best companions. I might get a dog myself when I'm a bit more settled. Or I could take over one of Granny's dogs – Princess and I have always had a very special bond.'

'And you and your grandmother?' he asked gently.

'We're very close. You wouldn't think so the way she often corrects me and my sisters. She is strict but has a heart of pure gold,' Lily said, smiling fondly.

'Oh she can slap me down too,' Dominic said with a grin. 'But I know she's an old softie deep down. I'd do anything for her.'

'Me too,' Lily agreed, touched by the warmth in his voice. 'And I want to help her get Magnolia restored. There is so much to do there. I don't really know where to start. But I think the gardens might be cleared up first. And the greenhouse. I'd love to...' She stopped.

'To do what?'

She wondered if she should say anything. But for some reason, despite it all, she thought she could trust him. 'To have a little garden centre there. I have always loved plants and growing things,' she said.

'I know what you mean,' he said, looking at her with interest. 'I'm very much into gardening too. I grow all my own vegetables and I have a lean-to greenhouse behind my shed. I grow all sorts of weird things there. I love seeing the seedlings grow into plants.'

'That's amazing,' Lily said, feeling as if she had found a kindred spirit. 'Maybe you could help me get the greenhouses repaired?'

'I'd like that very much. And I could do some work on the house too once you get the restoration started. I know the place inside out by now.'

'That would be fantastic.'

'We could draw up a plan,' he suggested. 'It'll be quite a long project though.'

'Yes, and the first step would be to convince Granny.' Lily got up and brushed the sand off her bottom. 'I'm afraid I haven't told her about this idea yet.' She looked up at the bright sky. 'I have to go. I'm going to see if I can catch her. She'll be home from mass and reading the papers in the study. A good moment to get her to listen.'

Dominic gathered the mugs and scrambled to his feet. 'I'd better be off too. Here, Larry,' he called to the dog that had wandered off down the beach. Then he looked at Lily thoughtfully. 'The café here has freshly made pastries,' he said. 'Your granny loves them. Especially their Danish.'

'Oh?' Lily hesitated for a moment, wondering how he knew. Sylvia had always been a bit of a mystery to Lily: a beautiful, kind and generous grandmother, but also a little reticent. She certainly didn't know which pastries she liked.

Sylvia was quite reserved and didn't often show her feelings. Lily had always gauged her grandmother's moods by looking into her eyes or listening to her tone of voice. She had learned to read the vibes of irritation, sadness or worry by changes in body language or facial expressions. But Granny never spoke openly about her feelings – like most people of that generation. They had been brought up to get on with it and not complain or explain. But Sylvia was obviously sharing more of her innermost feelings with Dominic than her granddaughters. Lily felt a dart of irritation at his insight into her grandmother's life, but then she realised he was just trying to be helpful. His empathy was obvious and Sylvia probably needed someone to lean on at times. Her granddaughters hadn't been around much to shoulder that burden, she thought guiltily.

'Good tip,' she said. 'I'll get her some of those for later.'

'Might put her in a good mood,' he suggested, waggling his dark eyebrows. 'In case you need her to talk about... whatever.'

Lily smiled. 'Yeah, that would help.'

'And I won't tell her. About the plan,' he added, smiling at her.

'Thank you,' Lily replied. 'And thanks for the water and the coffee as well,' she said, moving away. 'Oh, and I meant to tell you how much I enjoyed your singing last night. You have a beautiful voice.'

'Thank you,' he said, looking suddenly shy. 'The band is great too. Fantastic musicians.'

'They are,' Lily agreed. 'I loved listening to them. Bye for now.'

'See you around,' he replied.

Lily walked swiftly up the beach and then broke into a run when she reached the concrete path, trying her best to keep a good pace in case Dominic was still watching. She didn't quite know why she wanted to impress him. She wasn't looking for someone to flirt with after all she'd been through. She pushed those thoughts away and slowed her pace as she reached the café, where she bought two Danish pastries before she walked back down the road, thinking about what she was going to say to her grandmother. It would take a little clever planning to ask questions in a casual way that wouldn't annoy or upset, but she really wanted to find out why she had moved Cornelius's things. And start laying the groundwork for her and her sisters' ideas. Now that she had Dominic's promise of help with the renovations, she felt she had a solid backup and someone outside the family to assist with their plan. The warm glow of his sympathy and understanding lasted all the way back to Magnolia Manor.

Lily found Sylvia by the fire in the study engrossed in the Sunday papers, a cup of coffee on the little table beside her. She looked suddenly frail to Lily, as if all the world's troubles were weighing heavily on her shoulders. What was she struggling with? Lily wondered. Something truly serious must be on her mind. Lily wished Granny would share it with her so she could help in some way. But she knew asking questions would be no use. Better to wait for the right moment.

Sylvia put down her newspaper as Lily entered and smiled, her eyes suddenly brightening. 'Hello, Lily. How nice to see you. You're looking a little flushed.'

'I've been out running.' Lily kissed her grandmother's cheek. 'Lovely to see you too. I brought some buns from the little café in Ventry. I haven't had breakfast yet.'

'Thank you, darling, that's very kind,' Sylvia said, smiling at Lily. 'Go and make yourself some coffee in the kitchen and put those on a plate and we'll have them together.'

'I will.' Lily stopped in the doorway. 'I got the job, by the way. I'm starting at the solicitor's office tomorrow.'

'Yes, I was happy to hear that from Nora. Well done.'

'Thank you. I'll be back in a sec.'

Lily went to the kitchen to make herself some coffee. The smell of herbs and spices and fried bacon still lingered as the sun shone in through the tall windows that overlooked the courtyard. She was surprised to see a brand new Nespresso machine on the counter beside the old woodburning stove. She also noticed the old electric cooker had been replaced with an induction hob and wall-mounted oven. So Granny had done a little modernising. Probably for Nora, who did most of the cooking. But the rest of the large kitchen was the same as ever, with the wooden worktops, the huge pine table marked by innumerable baking sessions and all kind of food preparations through several centuries. Lily liked to imagine the cooks and housekeepers ruling the roost along with an army of household staff back in the day.

Lily had always loved this warm, welcoming kitchen where she had spent many happy hours during her childhood, helping Nora with baking and cooking. She looked around, thinking about the potential in the old house. If only she had a free hand to do what she had dreamt of for a long time. But Sylvia might not agree. It was a huge undertaking that would demand a lot of work and money. Better to wait until they had a concrete plan and some kind of financial help. A project on paper to present to Sylvia that was all ready to go...

When Lily returned to the study with her coffee and the pastries on a plate, Sylvia folded the newspaper and put it away.

'Sit down on the sofa and tell me. Have you moved into the gatehouse?'

Lily sat down, putting her cup and the plate with the pastries on the coffee table. 'Not yet. I'm staying at a B&B in Dingle until I can get the electricity sorted. But I meant to thank you for the things you sent over. That'll be a great help with settling in.'

'Settling in *temporarily*,' Sylvia corrected with a stern look. 'I hope you understand that.'

'So you said. But why?' Lily asked. 'I thought you might like having me close.'

Sylvia looked away. 'Oh,' she said airily, 'that isn't the issue. I think you should be more independent and get a house that's modern and comfortable. The gatehouse is sweet but there are a lot of problems with it. The roof, the cracks in the walls, the plumbing all need to be looked at and repaired. I'm sure you don't want to have to deal with all of that.'

'I wouldn't mind taking care of that. It's such a nice little house,' Lily argued. 'I can tackle each problem as it comes up.'

'You might be sorry you took it on,' Sylvia said darkly. 'In any case, I'm not happy with you living there permanently and that's that,' she ended as if the subject was closed.

'I understand,' Lily said, knowing she shouldn't pursue the issue right now. Sylvia's mouth was set in a tight line and that was a signal to move on to other things.

'That's settled then. And how are you going to cope when Rose comes?' Sylvia asked, taking a bite of her Danish.

'What?' Lily stared at her grandmother, wondering for a second if she was psychic. 'How did you know she was coming?'

'She just called me. Told me she is coming in two weeks to see me. She misses me, she says.' Sylvia nibbled on her Danish again. 'I've missed her too.'

'I know you have,' Lily said. 'The two of you have always been close.'

'Yes,' Sylvia said, looking a little guilty. 'Not that I don't love you and Violet too.'

'Of course,' Lily agreed. 'I know that. We're all quite like you, really.'

'Volatile, your grandfather used to say,' Sylvia remarked with a fond smile.

'And full of devilment,' Lily filled in, smiling at her grandmother. 'He always said if we weren't up to mischief, we were planning it. And so were you.'

'I'm a little long in the tooth for devilment,' Sylvia said, taking another bite of her pastry. 'These are very good. How clever of you to guess that the café in Ventry makes my favourite Danish.'

'Actually,' Lily confessed, 'it was Dominic's idea. I bumped into him on the beach and he told me you love them.'

'He's a nice lad,' Sylvia said. 'Very kind and helpful.'

'So he seems.' Lily was quiet for a while, wondering how she would bring up the subject of the painting and the trunk. Then she decided not to beat about the bush and just ask. 'Granny,' she started carefully. 'Why did you have Great-grandpa Cornelius's portrait moved to the gatehouse? And that trunk with all his stuff?'

Sylvia's hand holding the last of the pastry froze. 'I knew you were going to ask me that. Silly of me to have it put there.'

'Yes. But why did you?' Lily insisted.

Sylvia looked at Lily for a long time without replying. Then she put the Danish back on the plate as if she had suddenly lost her appetite. Her face pale, she looked away and then back at Lily. 'I don't want to talk about him. Not now, not ever.'

'But...' Lily protested.

'I don't want to say anything about it right now,' Sylvia said firmly. 'It will all come out one day,' she started to mumble. 'But right now there's nothing much we can do, so there's no point discussing it.'

Lily felt a dart of fear. 'What are you talking about? Are you sick, Granny?'

'Of course not,' Sylvia exclaimed. 'I'm as fit as a fiddle. This is not about me. It's about us – the family.' She took a deep breath. 'I've recently discovered we might be in for some difficult times. But nothing might happen, so there is no need to worry anyone,' she added quickly. 'We'll cross that bridge when and if we have to. Right now, everything is fine. We're all well and my granddaughters are coming back home. Can't we just enjoy the present without worrying about the future?'

Lily decided to stay calm for now and not show her alarm at what Sylvia had just said, even though she wondered what on earth 'difficult times' meant.

'Yes, we can enjoy the present, Granny,' she said. 'But maybe it's better to know what's ahead?' she tried. 'Then we can be better prepared. "Forewarned is forearmed," Granddad used to say.'

'Carpe diem, *I* say,' Sylvia declared with feeling. 'Let's enjoy the moment, the day, and not fret too much about the dark clouds on the horizon.'

'What dark clouds?' Lily asked even though she knew she wouldn't get a straight answer. 'Granny, I can see you're very worried about something. What difficulties could be ahead for the family? Wouldn't you feel better if you told me?'

'I don't want to talk about it,' Sylvia snapped. 'The subject is closed. Tell me about your new job and what we should do to organise the gatehouse now that Rose is coming.'

Lily gave up. She thought of Dominic and the plans he was drawing up. She felt sad that she might have to tell him she couldn't do up the house any more. She couldn't deny that she was looking forward to stealing some moments of his time. Perhaps she should just continue with it anyway. What Sylvia had said echoed through her mind. It would all come out one day, she had said. But what would come out? And how could it affect them all?

10

The next few days were busy but satisfying. Lily moved into the gatehouse, pleased to check out of the B&B. Despite the comfy bed, she was so fed up with Mrs Slattery and her constant chatter and questions. Also, she had not been pleased when Lily had not turned up for breakfast that Sunday morning. Lily had tried to explain that she had been to see her grandmother, but Mrs Slattery was still miffed.

'You could have told me last night that you wouldn't be here for breakfast. Then I wouldn't have cooked a whole full Irish for you that I had to throw away.'

'Oh, no!' Lily exclaimed. 'Did you have to?'

'No,' Mrs Slattery admitted. 'I had it all ready to cook, but when you didn't appear, I put it back in the fridge. Maybe you'd like it tomorrow?'

'No thanks.' Lily smiled apologetically. 'I won't be here. I'm checking out today.'

'I see,' Mrs Slattery said, her eyes suddenly cold. 'Well, that's most unfortunate. I thought you'd stay for at least a week.'

'I said I wasn't sure,' Lily retorted.

'Well I thought you had nowhere to go, so I took it you needed to stay here for the week,' Mrs Slattery shot back.

'Yes, but now the gatehouse is fine to stay in even if a little chilly. I like being close to the house and my granny, you see.'

'I'll get your bill, so,' Mrs Slattery snapped.

Lily went upstairs to pack her things, then paid the bill and thanked Mrs Slattery for 'a very nice stay', before she carried her suitcase down the stairs and put it in the car. She drove off with a huge sense of relief, despite the prospect of spending the next few days in a cold house with no electricity. But she'd manage, and Rose was coming soon and all would be well. For a while.

Her conversation with Dominic on the beach was still fresh in Lily's mind and it gave her a good feeling to know she had his support. His promise of help with the clearing up of the gardens and repairs of the greenhouse was also something to look forward to. Their shared love of plants and growing things had been a nice surprise; she looked forward to meeting him again to make plans for how they could work together.

Everything fell into place by Thursday afternoon. Nora had managed to get the electricity turned on. Her nephew worked at the ESB office in Tralee and they agreed to connect the gatehouse on the promise of Lily signing the contract and paying the connection fee straight away. After a few evenings in the house lit only by candles and a paraffin oil lamp, Lily was prepared to do anything to get connected, so she happily paid the deposit and arranged for the direct debit. That done, she got stuck into her new job at Wolfgang Quinn's office, where she started to tackle the files and documents, which she discovered would be quite a difficult task. Everything was in a muddle and even Wolfie's list of clients was all mixed up.

'In what kind of order are the clients organised?' Lily asked him after an exasperating few days trying to make some kind of sense of it all. 'The names are not in alphabetical order.'

'Order?' Wolfgang asked, looking confused. 'I have no idea. Maybe by their first names? Or by what kind of thing we do for them?'

'First names?' Lily shook her head. 'Your filing system is impossible to understand. I've never seen anything so messy.'

'I know.' Wolfgang looked a little sheepish. 'I left it all to that girl. Shouldn't have, I suppose. But at the time, I was busy with a huge litigation case, so I was out of the office a lot. I suspect she was too busy organising her wedding to bother with the filing system.' He gestured at the piles of papers on his desk. 'I was hoping you could start by getting this stuff off my desk and sorted.'

'Okay.' Lily pushed all the documents together into a pile and then gathered them up in her arms. 'I'll do these and set up a new system. It'll take a while though, so don't expect me to do anything else for a day or two.'

'Of course I won't,' Wolfgang promised. 'I'll leave you alone while you do that. I'll even answer the phone and make coffee.'

Lily smiled. 'You're amazing, Wolfgang.'

'No, I'm not,' he protested. 'You are. Most people would run out of the office screaming. But you're taking it on like a... a...'

'Like a Fleury,' Lily filled in. 'We don't give up, you see.'

'Admirable,' Wolfgang said, looking impressed.

Lily smiled and went back to her office, piling the documents onto her desk. Then she started the humungous task of getting things in order, which she secretly enjoyed. This was something she was good at and actually loved doing.

She removed her jacket, rolled up her sleeves and started work while the phone rang in the main office and Wolfgang dealt with the many calls. Quite a weird situation, but as Lily worked, she quickly realised she would be very happy here and that Wolfgang was one of the nicest men she had ever met, even if he had his head in the clouds most times. The thing about him, though, was that he had a very sharp legal brain, which

Lily discovered during her reorganising of the documents and papers of past and current cases.

By the end of the week, she had managed to sort out most of the paperwork and had neatly arranged it in the filing cabinet according to a system she had used at her old office. Then she started on the computer files, which was another headache. But by the following week, that too was more than halfway done and Wolfgang was so impressed he gave Lily a raise, promoted her to office manager and took her out to lunch at the best restaurant in Dingle. 'Just to make sure you don't leave for another firm,' he said. Lily promised she would stay as long as he kept being so nice, but she knew by then she wouldn't leave simply because she had never felt as happy in any job, or as appreciated.

Rose arrived on a blustery afternoon two weeks later in her little red car. Dressed in jeans, a light blue hoodie and trainers, she looked a little pale but very pretty, her blonde hair cut very short and her blue eyes calm and determined.

'I took two weeks off, but I brought my laptop and stuff so I can do some work from here,' she explained. 'Gavin is still away and I couldn't bear to stay in the flat all alone. I'll be free to go on outings and things with you, isn't that brilliant?'

'You might be on holiday, but I'm not,' Lily remarked, staring at Rose as she unloaded her luggage in front of the gate-house. 'I have my new job, then this house needs some doing up and then there's Granny and all that stuff with her.'

Rose pulled a bright yellow suitcase from the boot. 'I can help you with the house and with Granny. Keep her company and get her in a good mood. That should smooth the way for our plan, don't you think? I also want to suss out this area for the firm. They're thinking of opening a branch here. I'll do a little market research for that. Kerry is getting very popular with people who want to do up old houses or just build new ones. I mean,' she said, making a sweeping gesture across the gardens, the hills and the ocean glittering through the trees, 'this place is unique. Wild and romantic and absolutely stunning.'

'That's true,' Lily agreed. 'But do we really want a lot of people building new houses all over the place?'

'Well, it won't be that many, I'm sure,' Rose soothed. 'Don't worry. We won't turn Dingle into some kind of playground for the nouveau riche. They'll still want to go to Marbella.'

'The weather is better there,' Lily said, grabbing Rose's suitcase. 'Let's get all this stuff in before it starts to rain, then we'll light the fire and have dinner. I'm afraid it's just a frozen pizza tonight. I haven't had the time to shop for anything fancy.'

'That's okay. I brought wine and a chocolate cake from that French shop in Killarney.'

'Lovely,' Lily said with a laugh. Rose always knew how to turn an everyday dinner into a party. 'Have you called in to Granny to say hello?'

'Yup,' Rose replied. 'And she invited us both to dinner tomorrow night. She couldn't tonight because of bingo in the church hall.'

'She is always doing something,' Lily remarked. 'But good for her. Always up for the craic.'

Later, as they ate pizza and drank wine in front of the fire in the living room, Lily told Rose what their grandmother had said a couple of weeks ago about dark clouds on the horizon. 'She said that whatever it is might affect us all,' Lily ended.

Rose stopped eating and stared at Lily. 'That sounds scary. What on earth did she mean? Is there some kind of threat out there to our family? Or has it to do with the house? Or her health?'

'She says there's nothing wrong with her health,' Lily replied. 'I think it has something to do with Cornelius. Some kind of old scandal that has been discovered.'

'Is that why Granny threw him out of the house, do you think?' Rose asked.

'Could be.' Lily took a swig of wine. 'There was a hint of that in the little book of drawings I found that belonged to Great-granny Caroline. According to what she wrote, she was seriously worried about something Cornelius was doing in Paris. I think this must be what Granny discovered before she threw whatever he had left out of the house, along with his portrait.'

'Maybe she's being blackmailed?' Rose suggested. 'Someone could be threatening to reveal this dirty secret and we'll all have to pay for it.'

'Or he had a child out of wedlock and now this person's great-grandchild wants a part of our inheritance,' Lily pondered.

Rose shook her head and tucked her legs under her, reaching for her glass of wine on the coffee table. 'Nah, that couldn't happen. Illegitimate children can't usually claim inheritance. You should know that, with all that legal stuff you studied.'

'I do know,' Lily argued. 'Illegitimate children have the same rights as children of a marriage.'

'Okay,' Rose said. 'But I doubt it's the case. Why now after all these years? It has to be something else.'

'Yes, but what?' Lily asked. 'It's beginning to really bug me. And if whatever Granny is worried about doesn't happen, we'll never find out what it was.'

'So why make it into a big problem before you have to?' Rose drained her glass and got up. 'How about that cake then? I'm in the mood for some chocolate.'

'Okay,' Lily said without enthusiasm.

Rose stopped on her way to the kitchen. 'I know you're worried. So why don't we go through the trunk and see if we can find some kind of clue to it all?'

'Right now?' Lily asked, startled.

'After a bit of cake. It's too delicious to ignore. Then we'll have the energy to tackle the trunk.'

'It's a bit late, but okay,' Lily said with a resigned sigh. Rose always acted on impulse; Lily knew she had to agree to get her sister's help and support, before her enthusiasm waned.

When Rose came back with two large slices of chocolate cake, they quickly devoured them and hurried upstairs to the back bedroom, switching on lights as they went.

'Thank goodness we have power,' Lily remarked as she opened the door. 'We couldn't do this in the dark.'

'I hope there's a lightbulb in the lamp in the ceiling,' Rose said, groping for the switch just inside the door. The room was suddenly bathed in light and Rose gave a little shriek as she caught sight of the portrait. 'Holy moly, you gave me a fright, Great-grandpa!'

'I know. He keeps staring at me.'

'I love that naughty look in his eyes though,' Rose said with a giggle. 'I think he was a bit of a rascal.'

'I bet he was,' Lily said grimly. 'Doing something that might make us all miserable.'

Rose pulled the bedspread off the bed. 'I'm going to cover him up. I don't want him to watch us going through his stuff.'

Lily giggled, the wine and chocolate cake having improved her mood. Rose was turning it into an adventure, the way she always had when they were children. 'You mad thing,' she said as Rose delved into the trunk.

'I know, but I can't resist old trunks like this.' Rose sneezed as she blew dust off a cardboard box. She opened it and looked inside. 'A whole lot of cravats.' She pulled out a blue one with a pattern of red dots. 'Pure silk and really lovely. I'm going to nick a few of these to use as scarves. Here,' she said and tossed one with a paisley pattern in pink and purple. 'You have this one. Tie it around your ponytail.'

'It's gorgeous,' Lily agreed. 'But it doesn't give us any clues.'

'True.' Rose dug deeper into the trunk. 'I'm not sure there'll be anything here. Caroline's notebook with the drawings was probably the only thing. There's a riding crop and a cane with a silver handle. And a red velvet waistcoat, a leather wallet with visiting cards. Oh, here at the bottom, there are two round cardboard things with numbers on them in gold...' She held them up for Lily to see.

'I think they're chips from a casino,' Lily said after she had examined them. 'Nowadays they're made of plastic, but they must have been made of cardboard in those days. I have a feeling Cornelius was a secret gambler. I also think only Caroline knew this and didn't tell anyone. Maybe he went to Paris or Deauville to the casino there.'

'Could be.' Rose dived back in. 'Nothing much left except some bits of paper that I can't read and a...' Rose stopped and looked at an envelope. 'A letter to Cornelius from someone in Paris.'

'Open it,' Lily urged, feeling excited. 'That could be our clue.'

'Oh no,' Rose groaned. 'It's empty. The letter or whatever it was isn't there. There's a name and address on the back of it though.'

'Let me see.' Lily snatched the envelope. She turned it over and read the name and address on the back. 'Etienne Bernard, 21 rue de la Pompe, Paris XVI,' she read out loud. 'Oh, I recognise that name... Where did I see it?' Lily thought for a moment and then it came to her. 'He was the man Caroline mentioned in her notebook. The one she didn't like who kissed her hand and was so polite it made her want to scream.'

Rose giggled. 'Really? I like Caroline even better now. I wish I had met her.'

'She died over fifty years ago. But yes, she seems amazing. And she had to cope with Cornelius and his wild ways.'

Rose got up and brushed the dust from her hands. 'Okay that's it. All we got was an envelope with a name on it. That doesn't tell us anything.'

'Not really,' Lily said, feeling disappointed.

'We'll have to go straight to the source,' Rose declared as she closed the trunk.

'What source?' Lily said, confused.

'Granny, of course.' Rose sighed and shook her head. 'You haven't got very far with her, have you?'

'No, she shut me down,' Lily protested. She started to walk out of the room. 'Come on, time for bed.'

'Yes, Mammy.' Rose stopped in the door. 'How is she, by the way? Our mum, I mean. Have you been in touch with her lately?'

'Yes. I spoke to her just before I left Dublin,' Lily replied. 'She says they'll come down at Easter.' Their mother and Sean lived on a farm in Donegal and were not often in Dublin. The girls and their mother had a good, if slightly distant relationship, which made Lily a little sad. But their mother had seemed relieved when all her daughters had moved on in their chosen careers and she had left for the north with Sean, as if starting a whole new life.

'That'll be nice.' Rose yawned. 'I'm really tired now. It's a long drive from Dublin.'

'I made the bed for you in the other bedroom,' Lily said, switching off the light in the small bedroom and closing the door behind her. 'I managed to get you a brand new mattress and Granny gave us her best linen sheets.'

'Lovely,' Rose said and yawned again. 'I brought my duvet and pillows so I'll just pop those on the bed and get into my pjs. Can I have the bathroom first?'

'You can,' Lily said. 'I'll go down and tidy up. We have no dishwasher so it'll take a little while.'

'Okay. But I'll do the dishes tomorrow,' Rose promised.

'When we'll be at Granny's for dinner where there is a dishwasher.'

'I know,' Rose said with a smirk. 'I'll load it and switch it on. Night, night, Lily-lou.'

'Night, Rosie-roo,' Lily said and kissed her sister on the cheek. 'I'm so glad you came.'

'Me too,' Rose agreed with a fond smile.

Later, as Lily got ready for bed, she discovered the scrunched-up envelope in the pocket of her jeans. She must have tucked it in there while they were putting the things back in the old trunk. She looked at the name on the back of it. Etienne Bernard. Who was he? And what was his connection with Cornelius and the Fleurys?

11

'I've been in touch with Vi,' Rose said when they were walking up the avenue to Magnolia Manor the next evening.

'Is she still in LA?' Lily linked arms with Rose. It was dark but the light from the full moon illuminated the gardens so brightly it was nearly like walking in daylight. A soft breeze played with their hair, bringing with it a salty tang of seaweed from the bay.

'Not any more. She's on her way to London to audition for a part in a movie that's going to be shot here, in Ireland. Some mediaeval thing in an Irish castle. Tipperary, I think.'

'Oh. I had no idea,' Lily said, slightly miffed she hadn't been informed.

'Her agent told her only yesterday so she hopped on a plane and now she's on her way. If she gets the part, she'll be able to come here for weekends.'

'That would be great.' Lily felt a flutter of joy at the thought of the three of them together for a while. It didn't happen often but when it did they had such fun together. 'Granny will be so pleased.'

'I know,' Rose agreed as the dark shape of the manor rose in front of them. 'No light in any window. Gosh, this place looks spooky in the moonlight.'

'Spooky and lonely,' Lily remarked. 'I don't know how Granny lives here all alone.'

'I know why,' Rose said. 'She loves this place and would never leave even if it was falling down. It's where she was so happy with Granddad, and where our own dad was born. She could never give it up.'

'I think you're right. The Fleurys have always lived here so she couldn't move out of it. She doesn't mind a bit of discomfort either. And, even in this state, it's still a beautiful house.' Lily pulled Rose to the side of the building. 'Come on, she'll be in the kitchen cooking.'

As they arrived at the back door, there was a cacophony of barking. Rose laughed and opened the door, neatly stepping aside as all the dogs rushed out into the dark, barking furiously. Then they both leapt inside and pulled the door shut behind them. This was an old trick they always played on the dogs to avoid being jumped all over. They usually calmed down after a while and whined to be let in, then the door was opened again for more civilised greetings.

They found Sylvia at the stove, dressed in black slacks and a dark green sweater, putting plates in to warm. The table was set for three with the old crockery – decorated with a design of wild flowers – that they always used for casual evenings.

Sylvia turned around with a warm smile when they entered. 'Hello, lovely girls. Supper is ready. Sit down at the table and I'll serve you.'

'You shouldn't serve us,' Rose protested. 'We should look after you.'

'Nonsense,' Sylvia said with a snort. 'I'm not that old yet. Why can't I look after my girls the way I always do?'

'You can,' Rose said, going over to hug her grandmother before she sat down. 'Serve away, Granny. It smells delicious.'

'My chicken and herb casserole,' Sylvia said proudly. 'The only dish I do well. Lily, go and let the dogs in. I think they've calmed down.'

Lily did as she was told; the dogs trotted in and greeted the girls by wagging their tails and sniffing at them while they were being patted and cooed at. Then Sylvia shooed them out into the utility room and served the supper.

They chatted while they ate and Rose told Sylvia about Violet and how she might be able to come for a visit, which seemed to make her very happy. At least for a moment. But Lily noticed an undertone of sadness as Sylvia told them how wonderful it was that the sisters would be together at Magnolia Manor, even if it was only for a while. Her smile looked forced and didn't reach her eyes, and she talked nervously and didn't eat much, another sign that something was amiss.

Rose didn't seem to notice her grandmother's distress but went on about the house and how it should 'be brought to life again'.

Sylvia sighed and pushed her plate away. 'Please, Rose, stop going on about it. I know you'll want to change things around here when the house is yours, but I don't want to talk about it right now.'

'Why not?' Lily cut in. 'Granny, you can't let the house fall down around you. It has to be repaired. Or if you want to move to a house of your own, maybe you could let us take over? We could find somewhere for you nearby. A nice little bungalow with proper heating and a little garden and—'

Sylvia stared at Lily, her face white. 'I can't,' she said in a near whisper.

'Why not?' Lily asked, shocked at how upset Sylvia was. 'What's the matter, Granny?'

Sylvia's shoulders slumped. 'I might as well tell you. It'll all come out soon anyway.'

'What?' Lily asked, her heart contracting.

Sylvia looked at both her granddaughters, then said hoarsely, 'I couldn't sell this house even if I wanted to.'

'Why not?' Rose asked.

'Because it isn't mine to sell,' Sylvia said and burst into tears.

Lily and Rose looked at each other in shock and then at Sylvia, who was still crying inconsolably into her napkin. Princess came out of the utility room, padded to Sylvia's side and put a paw on her knee. They all sat there in silence until Lily finally spoke.

'Can you tell us what's going on, Granny?' she asked softly.

Sylvia drew in a ragged breath and groped for her handkerchief in the pocket of her slacks. 'I will. Just give me a moment.'

'Go into the study with Lily and sit by the fire,' Rose suggested. 'I'll make you a cup of tea and tidy up here.'

Sylvia nodded. 'Thank you, darling Rose.'

She slowly got to her feet and Lily put her arm around her. With Princess trotting behind them, they made their way to the study. The fire was nearly out so Lily put a log on it and used the bellows to fan it until flames started to flicker. The smell of woodsmoke and the soft lamplight made the room cosy; Sylvia seemed to calm down a little as she sat on the sofa. Princess sat on the floor, leaning against her mistress as if trying to protect her from some kind of danger.

Lily wrapped a cashmere shawl around her grandmother's shoulders and gave her a quick hug, breathing in the jasmine scent Sylvia always wore. It reminded Lily of her childhood, when her grandmother had been their rock. But now the tables were turned and Lily knew she would have to support her, which felt frightening and comforting at the same time. She sat beside Sylvia as Rose came in with a cup of tea.

Sylvia took the cup in both hands and sipped the tea before she looked up at Lily and Rose with sad eyes. 'Sit down, Rose,' she said. 'And I'll tell you everything.'

Rose sat on the chair beside the sofa and looked fondly at Sylvia. 'Take your time, Granny. No rush.'

Holding her cup, Sylvia took another few sips before she spoke. 'It's about Cornelius,' she started. 'You must have guessed all this has something to do with him.'

'Yes,' Lily said. 'But we figured that whatever he did was a long time ago. Why are you so upset about it?'

'A long time ago, yes.' Sylvia put the cup on the coffee table and folded her hands in her lap. 'But what he did has resonated through time and now it has raised its ugly head and is threatening our very existence.'

'Please tell us what it is,' Rose urged. 'Maybe we can sort it out some way.'

Sylvia sighed. 'I don't think that's possible. But I will tell you. Cornelius was a gambler. He used to go away to France and the casinos there, and also to Monte Carlo, where he met a man called Etienne Bernard.'

'In France?' Lily asked, remembering the envelope they had found.

'Yes,' Sylvia replied. 'He owned a big house somewhere in the South of France. I think it was a town called Menthon. It's near Monte Carlo. He also had an apartment in Paris. Anyway, to cut a long story short, Cornelius was at this house sometime in the early nineteen twenties playing cards. He lost heavily and to get out of that debt he signed over Magnolia Manor to this man.'

Lily gasped and stared at Sylvia. 'He – what?'

'You heard right,' Sylvia said. 'Cornelius signed away the house and gardens and farm and everything he owned to clear his debts. I have a feeling he was threatened in some way.'

'Sounds like some kind of gangster,' Rose said with a shiver.

'They were quite brutal about debts in those days,' Sylvia said. 'But that's what happened. And now his son and grandson think they own it all.'

'Oh God,' Lily whispered. 'But how come this Etienne Bernard didn't come over here and claim the house straight away at the time? Why has it taken so long? And how come his son, Grandad Liam, didn't know anything about it? How could the property even have been passed on to you when he died?'

'I don't know,' Sylvia said, looking confused. 'I don't understand all that legal stuff. I assumed the solicitor had sorted it out. The probate was quite quick and then I got possession of the bank accounts and the investment funds. It seemed all in order as far as I could tell. But we were all so shocked and I was trying to help your mother to look after you three little girls. It was a terrible time.'

'You were amazing,' Lily said. 'A tower of strength when everyone was going to pieces.'

'Well, someone had to take charge,' Sylvia remarked. 'And it helped me to keep going and make all the decisions that needed to be made. I felt Liam wanted me to somehow. Little did I know how Cornelius had behaved all those years ago.'

'How could he?' Lily asked, her voice hoarse. 'I mean, to give away the home that had been in the family for generations, just like that?'

'We don't know the circumstances, if he was threatened,' Rose said. 'Or he might have thought they wouldn't act on it or something.'

'Or he had been drinking,' Sylvia cut in. 'In any case, it happened. Then it seemed to have been forgotten. He came home and acted as if nothing was wrong. Nobody knew what he had done and then, when he died, the property passed on to his son, my husband, Liam.'

'Our darling grandad,' Rose said, her eyes glistening with tears.

'And it should have been passed on to my son, Fred, your father,' Sylvia added with a flash of pain in her eyes. 'But it went to me and then it should go to you girls.'

'But now that's not going to happen,' Lily said. 'We'll have to move out and leave it to this man. It seems like a bad dream.' She leaned forward and looked at her grandmother. 'What about the deeds? Where are they?'

'I don't know,' Sylvia replied. 'I'm not sure there are any. There are some old legal papers, but the actual deeds seem lost. My solicitor is looking for them.'

'Which solicitor is it?' Lily asked. 'The one Grandad used?'

Sylvia nodded. 'Yes, the same firm anyway. Lucey and Partners in Tralee. We've been with them for as long as I can remember.'

'So this Etienne guy – or his ancestors – think they own Magnolia Manor?' Rose asked.

'That's right.' Sylvia wrung her hands. 'I got a letter from a man called Arnaud Bernard, who is this Etienne's son, just before Christmas, telling me they had found papers that proved ownership of this property. And now he and his son are coming to see me in a few weeks. Right in time for the Magnolia party. Then I suppose we will be homeless.' She put her hand on Lily's arm. 'That's why I said you could only stay in the gatehouse temporarily. Once the new owners take over, that house will be theirs along with the whole estate.'

Lily clenched her fists. 'That is not going to happen. We're going to fight this.'

'How can we stop them?' Sylvia asked in a small voice. 'I'm sure they have proof of ownership that we won't be able to dispute.'

'How do you know?' Rose asked. 'Let them show what they have before we start to panic. It could be just some kind of letter or an old IOU.'

'I'll have to find out about land ownership in legal terms,' Lily muttered to herself. 'I haven't dealt with that sort of thing much.'

Rose turned to Lily. 'Yes, of course. We have to find out where we stand legally. That's your department, Lily.'

'I know. I'll look it up,' Lily promised. She turned to her grandmother, who seemed calmer. 'Do you want us to stay with you tonight, Granny?'

'Yes, I'll sleep here tonight if you want,' Rose offered.

Sylvia straightened up and looked suddenly more cheerful. 'No, I'm fine. Very sweet of you, but let's continue the way we are. We must not let those people beat us. I feel much more hopeful now that I have shared everything with you. Well,' she added, looking a little coy, 'not quite everything, but the most important part. We'll find a way to keep our lovely home. Lily, I expect you to find out the legal details and, Rose, you will have to help me write a letter to this Arnaud Bernard. You're very good with words.'

'I'll do my best,' Rose promised. 'I'll come over tomorrow and we'll do it together.'

'Excellent.' Sylvia looked at the tiny gold watch on her wrist. 'And now I think I'll go to bed. There is a movie on RTE I want to see so I'll get into bed and watch it on my TV in the bedroom. I know it's only nine o'clock, but I'm tired after the bingo last night that ended quite late. Don't worry about me. I have the dogs to keep me company. Don't I?' she asked Princess and stroked the dog's head.

Princess wagged her tail as if to agree, which made them all laugh.

The feeling of togetherness made them all suddenly hopeful; Sylvia looked calmly at Lily and Rose as they kissed her goodbye.

'Sleep tight, girls. Don't stay up too late now.'

'We won't,' Rose promised. 'I'll be here tomorrow and we'll put that letter together. And then we'll make plans for the Magnolia party. We'll make it the best one ever.'

'We will,' Sylvia agreed with a determined look in her eyes. 'We have to show them the Fleury spirit.'

'The Fleury spirit,' Rose said as she and Lily walked back to the gatehouse. 'Granny certainly has it. But do we?'

'Of course we do.' Lily stopped on the gravel path and looked up at the moon, breathing in the cool, fresh air. 'When I'm here, I feel I do. But not so much when I'm somewhere else.'

'I know.' Rose stood beside Lily and looked around. 'The garden is so still. It's as if it's waiting for something. The trees and bushes and plants all seem so part of us – or are we a part of them? Do you know what I mean?'

'Yes, I do.' Lily started to walk again. 'We have to find a way to stop them.'

'You mean the Bernards?' Rose fell into step with Lily. 'I can't wait to meet them and tell them what I think of them waltzing over here and telling us to move out. They have a fight on their hands if they take us on.'

'It'll be a legal fight,' Lily said. 'And one we can't be sure to win. We could take them to court, but that will cost a lot of money we don't have. And then we could lose and have to pay their legal fees as well. But we have to do our best. I'll contact that Lucey firm tomorrow and take it from there. Get all the information I can and...' She paused as something hit her. 'What was that Granny said? She hadn't told us everything?'

'She said she hadn't told us all of it. Only the most important part,' Rose repeated.

'So what hasn't she told us?' Lily muttered. 'I wonder if that's something else we have to get out of her. I have this feeling...'

'What feeling?' Rose asked.

'That Granny has done something she shouldn't have,' Lily said slowly. 'But what?'

12

Lily woke up early the next morning, still considering the disturbing thought that Sylvia was hiding something from them. And the more she turned it over in her mind, the more she became convinced that whatever it was might be illegal in some way. It was the only reason she could think to keep it a secret, what with the threat of losing the manor hanging over their heads. But what had she done? Lily only knew she needed to get out of bed and do something to clear her head.

She checked the time on her phone and saw it was seven o'clock. Would she have time to exercise before heading in to work? A short run around the gardens would be quite okay. She knew that if she took the path around the perimeter, down along the shoreline and then up to the house and around the greenhouses it would be about two kilometres. If she did that twice, it would be a good workout, and she'd still have the time to pop in to Granny to say good morning and see if she was okay. She knew there was no use asking Sylvia to reveal what she had hinted at the night before – she didn't take kindly to being pressured. Lily would have to wait until later to try to find out her granny's secret.

Lily's phone pinged with a message.

Hi Lily, Brian from the pub here. Didn't want to wake you with a phone call so I waited until now. I'm back at work so if you call into the pub at lunchtime, I'll tell you about my granny. Cheers, Brian

She had nearly forgotten about the arrangement, but now it all came back to her. She would certainly call in and talk to him. He might be able to tell her something that would bring her closer to finding out what had happened with Cornelius, even though she now knew most of it. But you never knew... She quickly texted a reply back to say she'd be there.

Dressed for her run, Lily tiptoed down the stairs carrying her shoes, careful not to wake Rose. She knew her sister didn't like getting up early and would be like a bear with a sore head if she was woken up from her slumber before at least eight.

Once outside, in the light of the rising sun, Lily put on her trainers, checked her watch and set off at a gentle pace, planning to increase her speed once she felt warmed up. The rosy light, the earthy smell of green leaves after a recent shower and the cool breeze gave Lily a jolt of delight and she started off on a high she hadn't expected. The path ran through the overgrown part of the garden; she had to push through foliage and dodge overhanging branches as she made her way to the shore and the track that ran along the tiny beach, past the jetty and the little bay where sailing boats and tiny dinghies lay at anchor.

As she approached the wooden jetty, she saw the outline of a man against the early morning light. He was holding a fishing rod and a small bucket. Lily came to a stop as the figure came closer. She peered at him and saw who he was. Dominic, smiling broadly as he noticed her.

'Hi,' he said. 'You're up early.'

'Yes,' she replied, feeling a little self-conscious. 'Thought I'd go for a quick run before work.'

'Nice morning for it,' he said, peering at the sky. 'It'll be raining in about an hour.'

She looked at his fishing rod and bucket. 'Any luck?'

'Nah,' he said with a crooked smile. 'I'll be getting my fish at the fish shop beside the warehouse in Dingle. They have great fish and it's not too expensive.'

'That's a good tip,' Lily remarked. 'I'll get some there for our dinner later.'

He raised an eyebrow. 'Our dinner? You have company?'

'My sister Rose is staying with me for a short break.'

Dominic nodded. 'Oh yes, I think Sylvia mentioned that. She's so happy to have you both around.'

'I know.' Lily stood there for a moment, not wanting to end the conversation. She had enjoyed talking to him that Sunday morning on the beach in Ventry. Very much. His empathy when she told him about losing her father had been a huge comfort. And then he had said he'd help her with the greenhouses. She didn't want to tell him that they might not be able to do what they had planned.

They looked at each other for a moment that was loaded with something that felt new and exciting to Lily. But she didn't want to stand there looking needy.

He looked suddenly a little shy. 'I was thinking... I've made a bit of a list of initial work we can do to the gardens... the conservatory mostly. I'll be in town during the day. Would you have time for a bite to eat around lunchtime?'

'Oh... Well, yeah. Okay. Why not?' she replied, knowing she didn't sound enthusiastic even though her heart was fluttering.

'I was thinking we could plant a few more trees, knock down one of the outhouses—'

'Knock down?' Lily interrupted.

'Yes, it would open up the space.' He laughed. Was he teasing her again? she wondered.

'Well we're not after more space; I'd suggest revamping the current buildings, but I do agree with adding to the treeline.'

'Okay, have it your way,' he replied and she couldn't help but smile. He *was* teasing her.

'I was going to that pub where you sang the other night to talk to... someone. How about there? I think they serve some kind of pub grub for lunch.'

'If it doesn't ruin your plans with that someone,' he said.

'No!' she protested, suddenly realising what she'd said had sounded like. 'That wasn't what I meant. It's the guy who works there – we have something to talk about. I don't even remember his name.'

He let out a laugh. 'I think you mean Brian. Tall with dark curly hair, teeth like a horse?'

Lily nodded. 'Yes, that's him. He said his granny knew my great-grandmother and I wanted to find out about my great-grandfather. I thought he might be able to give me some clues.'

'The dude in the painting?' Dominic asked with a mischievous look in his green eyes.

Lily laughed. 'Yeah. Him.'

'Sounds interesting. I'll stay away until you've talked to Brian.'

Lily hesitated, wondering if she should cancel that meeting. But it wouldn't make any difference if Dominic heard what the young man was going to tell her. 'I don't think he's going to say anything that's not common knowledge. I don't mind if you're there when I talk to him.'

'I wouldn't blab it around town anyway if it's confidential.'

She smiled her thanks. 'I'll let you know if it is or not. But now I really have to go if I'm to get in a bit of running before work.' Lily started to move off. 'See you at that pub at lunchtime.'

'One o'clock?' he shouted as she broke into a run down the track.

'Okay,' she shouted over her shoulder before she rounded the corner and headed up the path towards the greenhouses.

As she ran, Lily tried to gauge her feelings towards Dominic. He was quite contradictory, sometimes friendly and other times teasing her with a challenge in his eyes, and sometimes it seemed as if he saw right through her and noticed all her flaws. But then, there was his empathy and all the things they had in common that made her feel she had met a kindred spirit.

Was he just being helpful? Or did he want to get to know her? And how did she feel about that? Newly divorced, she wasn't ready for another relationship or even a flirt. Was she? She'd wanted to take a break from men and whatever dating and starting a relationship brought with it.

She did like Dominic, however, and it wasn't only because of his looks but the intelligence and gentleness in his eyes, his beautiful singing voice and his kindness towards her grandmother. She felt he would be a good friend she could trust in all weathers. But that was all it could be. For now.

Lily's thoughts were interrupted as she slowed to a walk near the back of the house. She saw her grandmother's blue Golf pulling out of the courtyard and waved. 'Hi, Granny,' she shouted as Sylvia stopped and stuck her head out the window.

'Hello there,' Sylvia replied when Lily came closer. 'What are you doing here?'

Lily panted, wiping her forehead. 'I'm running around the garden to get a bit of exercise. Thought I'd call in to see how you are.'

'I'm grand, girl,' Sylvia replied. 'I'm just off for a bit, but I'll be back around three to write that letter with Rose. Is she up?'

'Not yet.' Lily bent over and put her hands on her knees, trying to slow her breathing. 'I'll tell her when I get back to the house.'

'Take it easy, darling,' Sylvia urged. 'All that running and sweating can't be good for you. Yoga would be better.'

'I love running,' Lily said. 'It makes me feel well and it's a great way to get fit.'

Sylvia shrugged. 'If that's what makes you happy. Have a lovely day.'

'Where are you off to?' Lily asked, noticing that Sylvia was dressed in a pleated tweed skirt and matching jacket, as if she was going to some kind of event.

'A meeting and then a funeral at eleven.'

'Oh, that's sad.'

Sylvia smiled and shrugged. 'Not really. It's for old Josephine O'Malley, God rest her soul. She was ninety-eight and died in her sleep. I was in school with her youngest sister. It'll be a beautiful mass and then lunch at the Skelligs and I'll be able to catch up with a lot of my friends. That's how us old folks meet these days, at funerals.'

Lily couldn't help smiling. 'I see. So it's both sad and happy, then?'

'Mostly happy,' Sylvia replied. 'As we're not the one in the coffin. See you later, I hope. I need a little help organising the Magnolia party. It's weeks away still, but we should get started on the ballroom. We should also start planning food and flowers and all that. Do you think I should ask Dominic and his band to play? They could perform on the gallery above the ballroom. Wouldn't that be grand?'

'I think that would be fabulous,' Lily agreed, straightening up. 'I'll ask him when we meet for lunch if you like.'

Sylvia looked startled. 'You're meeting him for lunch?'

'Yeah, he asked me just now when I bumped into him down at the jetty. Just a quick bite in a pub. Nothing special.'

'He's a nice lad, but a little unusual,' Sylvia remarked.

'Lad?' Lily asked. 'He looks a little old for a lad.'

'According to his aunt, who is no liar, he's forty-two,' Sylvia said. 'To me, that's a lad. He has a nice profile on Facebook with all the stuff he does.'

'Oh. Well, I'm not on Facebook. Not on social media much actually. Rose is the Insta queen. Everything she does is out there.' Lily shrugged. 'I suppose I should be out there more.'

'I find it quite entertaining.' Sylvia put the car in gear. 'You'd better go and clean up or you'll be late for work.'

'I will. Bye, Granny.' Lily waved as the car moved off down the avenue.

When she came back to the gatehouse, Rose had just emerged from her bedroom looking sleepy.

'Have you been out already?' she asked, looking in awe at Lily. 'And running this early?'

'It was a nice morning.' Lily took off her shoes. 'I met Granny all dressed up to the nines. She's going to a funeral she said. She'll be back around three and wants you to come over and help her with that letter.'

'Okay.' Yawning, Rose shuffled into the kitchen. 'What you doing for lunch?' she shouted above the clatter of breakfast dishes.

Lily froze for a moment on her way up the stairs. 'I'm... uh, meeting someone.'

'You're in a meeting?' Rose asked.

'That's right. A lunch meeting.'

'That guy works you to the bone,' Rose remarked. 'Okay, then see you later.'

'Okay,' Lily replied with a sigh of relief. No need to tell Rose about Dominic at the moment. She wanted to keep it to herself without her sister passing comments or handing out advice. Rose was a self-appointed agony aunt and could be annoyingly accurate, except in her own relationships. Lily wanted to see Dominic without Rose looking over her shoulder. It might be the start of something or the end of it before it began. *Who knows?* Lily thought as she stood in the trickle of water from the shower in the old bathtub. *I'm not ready for anything serious, but wouldn't it be great if we could be friends?*

Lily arrived at the office at the same time as Wolfie, who opened the door for her with a flourish. 'After you, ma'am,' he said. 'You look as if you're ready for another day shuffling papers around.'

Lily laughed. 'I'm getting on top of it.'

'That's great to hear.'

They walked in together and hung their jackets on the hall-stand in the reception area. Lily was about to settle behind her desk when a thought struck her. 'Wolfie, do you have a minute?'

He stopped on the way into his office. 'Yes?'

'Just something I've been wondering about...' Lily paused. 'Well, as I'm not a lawyer, I only have a sketchy knowledge of these things.'

'What things?' he asked.

'It's about ownership of a property. How do you prove you own a place if the deeds can't be found?'

'Tricky question,' Wolfie replied. 'It would have to involve the land registry somehow. Most properties are registered these days. Depends on the age of the property. But if the land hasn't been registered, it's hard to prove ownership without deeds.'

Lily nodded. 'I see. And if the property was registered?'

'Then you can look it up on the land registry website and find what is called the "folio". This has the name of the owner and is all you need to prove ownership without deeds.' He paused, wrinkling his brow. 'But if the property wasn't registered,' he continued, 'and most older properties aren't because they've been in the same family for generations, then...'

'Then?' Lily looked expectantly at Wolfie. 'Go on.'

'Well then, the last will is what you have to look for. Properties in Kerry didn't have to be registered until 2011, which is
why a lot of people have a problem when they sell an old house.
There are no deeds and they have to register in a hurry.'

'So then there might be no deeds at all?' Lily asked.

'Exactly.' Wolfie studied Lily for a moment. 'Would you like
me to find out about a particular property for you? Just tell me
the name or address of it and I'll see if I can find it.'

Lily looked at Wolfie's kind face and felt a sudden urge to
tell him what Sylvia had revealed. Then she changed her mind.
No need to worry about this until they had to. 'No thanks,
Wolfie. You have enough to do. It was just curiosity on my part.'

He nodded. 'Okay. Let me know if you need any help.'

'I will. You have a client at ten o'clock, by the way,' she
reminded him.

'Oh yes, I remember. Thanks.'

Wolfie disappeared into his office while Lily sent him a
silent thanks for being so discreet and understanding. He must
have known her question had to do with Magnolia Manor but
hadn't mentioned it or asked for details.

The morning was taken up with the continued sorting and
organising of documents and files, a tedious job but satisfying as
Lily could see that it would work perfectly now that it was
nearly complete.

Even though this was all-absorbing and quite enjoyable for
someone with her ordered mind, she kept checking her watch to
see if it was time for lunch yet. Dominic's invitation had
surprised her and she couldn't wait to find out more about him,
and discuss what to do with the gardens and greenhouse. And
then there was the meeting with the waiter, Brian, who may
have something to tell her about her great-grandmother that
could throw some light on what Cornelius had done back then.
Was it really true that he had given away Magnolia Manor to
pay his gambling debts? And, if he had, was that truly legal? It

didn't seem possible. They needed to gather any information they could before they had to face this man who claimed he was the rightful owner. Lily hoped they would be able to laugh in his face and tell him his claim was ridiculous. If only it were possible...

13

Just before one o'clock, Lily got ready for her lunch date. Not much to do other than take her hair out of the band that held her ponytail and fluff it up a bit. She looked at herself in the mirror of the tiny wash room just off the reception area. She should perhaps put on a bit of makeup, but as Dominic had never seen her glammed up, it didn't seem to matter. He would have to take her as she was, even though with her hair bouncing around her shoulders she looked, hopefully, a little softer and younger.

Lily told Wolfie she was going out for lunch and he simply nodded, seemingly absorbed in something on the computer screen. Then he looked up and studied her for a moment.

'You look different,' he said.

Lily touched her head. 'I let my hair down.'

He laughed. 'Good idea. But it wasn't about your hair. I meant the look in your eyes. You're happier than before. More light-hearted, I think.'

'Could be that I'm settling in and getting used to living here,' Lily said, surprised by his interest. It was true, she had barely thought of Simon for the last few days. 'I feel a lot better than when I arrived.'

'That's good to hear. Does this mean you'll be staying? For good?' he asked, looking hopeful.

'Oh, well for a long time to come anyway,' Lily replied. 'I like working for you.'

'Not *for* me,' he corrected. 'With me. We're becoming quite a team, I feel.'

'Oh, Wolfie, that is so nice of you,' Lily exclaimed. 'No other boss has ever said that to me. I've always felt like a lowly secretary who is there to serve the high and mighty solicitor. But now, I feel appreciated and that is truly wonderful.'

'Really?' He looked shocked. 'That's the way they treated you up in Dublin? How stupid of them. Don't they know we couldn't survive without a good assistant like you?'

'They just want to keep us in our place.' Lily smiled at Wolfie. 'You're the best boss I've ever had.'

He blushed. 'Ah shucks, I don't do much. But now you have to go or you'll be late for lunch with that person who puts a smile on your face and makes your eyes sparkle.'

'I don't know what you mean,' Lily said, trying to look bland. 'But I'll be off anyway. See you later and don't forget to call Sean Murphy about the probate thing. I wrote the number down on a Post-it and stuck it on your screen. It's right in front of you.' Then she smiled, waved and walked out, her spirits lifted by what he had just said.

What a lovely, generous man Wolfie was. She wondered idly if he had a girlfriend. She didn't know much about his private life as he kept that very much to himself. In any case he would make a wonderful husband for some lucky woman out there. But at that moment, another man was much more on her mind, and with butterflies whirling around in her stomach, she walked up the street to meet him.

. . .

Lily walked into the pub, looking around for Dominic, but she couldn't see him. The place was quiet, with only a few of the round tables occupied by people enjoying the pub grub on offer.

Lily gave a start as Brian, the young waiter, rushed to her side. 'Hi, Lily,' he said. 'Nice to see you again.'

'Hi, Brian,' she replied, smiling at him. 'Do you have time for a bit of a chat?'

'Yes. I have ten minutes or so before the rush.' He pointed at a table near the window. 'Let's sit over there.'

They walked together to the table and sat down, Lily facing the window and Brian opposite her. 'Do you want to order lunch?' he asked.

'Thanks, but I'm meeting someone later, so I'll order then,' Lily replied, glancing briefly at the view of the harbour and the inlet, where a small boat was bobbing along the waves on its way in.

Brian nodded. 'Grand.' He cleared his throat. 'So... what was it you wanted to chat about?'

'You said your granny knew my great-grandmother,' Lily reminded him, tearing herself away from the lovely view. 'Caroline Fleury?'

'Oh. I remember now. Well, yes, she did know Mrs Caroline. Mary, my granny, worked as a maid at Magnolia Manor when she was very young.'

'When was this?' Lily asked.

'Sometime in the early nineteen fifties. She would have been around sixteen then. She used to help Mrs Caroline in the greenhouse with the plants and flowers. Mrs Caroline used to say my granny had green fingers. She did too. Could make a plant grow in your ear, we used to joke.'

Lily smiled and nodded. 'I know what you mean. Some people have that gift. It appears Caroline had that too.'

'She was also good at painting and drawing,' Brian said. 'A lovely, gentle soul, my granny used to say.'

'Used to say? Is she dead?' Lily asked with a sinking heart. She had hoped she would be able to interview this old lady to find out more.

Brian suddenly looked a little sad. 'No, but she's in a nursing home. She's in her nineties and very frail both in body and mind. Doesn't remember much any more. I visit her once a week. Sometimes she doesn't remember who I am, but I still go. I remember her kindness to me as a child, and when I sit with her and hold her hand, I think she can feel that I love her.'

'I'm sure she can,' Lily said, touched by the emotion in the young man's eyes.

Brian sat up. 'Yeah, well... No need for you to be sad. I thought I'd tell you all the things she told us when she was a bit younger. About her memories of Mrs Caroline. Such a kind lady, she said, gentle and sweet. The two of them shared this love of plants and flowers. My granny had a little painting of the garden Mrs Caroline gave her.'

'How lovely.' Lily looked at Brian thoughtfully. 'Where is that painting now? Who has it?'

'It's hanging in her room in the nursing home.' He paused. 'Maybe... if you don't think it would be too weird, you could come with me when I visit her and take a look at it?'

'Oh, I would like that,' Lily said, smiling at Brian. 'How kind of you to suggest it. I'd love to meet your granny.'

'She might be a little... off,' Brian warned. 'Like she says strange things and mixes people up. Depends on how she's feeling at that moment. Sometimes her mind is crystal clear and then she suddenly loses her concentration.'

'Oh, that's understandable. Quite common with someone so old, I'd say,' Lily pondered.

'Exactly.' Brian looked relieved. 'So if you like, you could come with me next Sunday to see her?'

Lily nodded. 'That would be great. We could go in my car, if you like.'

'Brilliant. Maybe you could pick me up from here at eleven o'clock?'

'No problem.'

'See you then.' Brian got up. 'Must get back to work. And your date has just walked in, I see,' he added with a little smile.

Lily looked up with surprise and noticed a sudden stir through the pub as Dominic walked in.

'Oh, eh, he's not...' Lily started.

But Brian had walked off.

Dominic sauntered across the room with a presence Lily hadn't noticed before. It was as if the room had brightened suddenly. But he did have a natural charisma; it was just there like an aura around him. He smiled and shook people's hands on the way to Lily's table. Then he was at her side and beamed her a smile.

'Hiya, Lily. You're here already.' He pulled out a chair and sat down.

'Yes, I came early so I could speak to Brian before we ate.'

'And did you?'

'I did. So all is well and we can order lunch.'

'Perfect.' Dominic glanced at the bar and another waiter ran up to them within seconds.

'Hi, Dominic, what can we get you?'

Dominic looked at Lily. 'What would you like?'

'Nothing much,' Lily replied. 'Just a sandwich will do.'

'Two hot ham and cheese paninis,' Dominic ordered. 'And two glasses of lager. That okay?' he asked Lily.

'Perfect.' She smiled. 'How did you do that?'

'Do what?'

'Get the waiter to rush over the minute you sat down. I usually have to wave and shout like a lunatic to get any kind of service.'

He shrugged. 'Don't know. It just kinda happens.'

'It's a rare gift.'

'I know,' he said with mock modesty.

Lily laughed. 'You must give them some kind of look that makes them jump into action.'

'Like a laser beam?' he suggested, waggling his eyebrows.

'Sounds dangerous.'

'Like something from *Star Wars*,' he said. 'Wouldn't that be cool?'

'It would,' Lily agreed. 'I love those movies.'

'Me too.' He smiled and shook his head. 'This will date me, but we rented it on VHS as a kid and I thought it was the best thing I'd ever seen. I wanted to be an astronaut after that.'

'So you could fly into space?'

'Yeah, something like that.'

'But instead you became a... what?' she asked. 'Handyman, carpenter? Have you always done this type of work?'

'Not really. I studied engineering at Trinity.'

'Really?' Lily looked at him with interest and was about to ask him what kind of engineering, but their order arrived and they both started to eat hungrily. 'Nice sandwich,' Lily said when she had eaten half of it.

'Yeah, they do great food here.' Dominic took a swig of beer. 'So,' he said, studying her intently. 'Tell me what a hot-shot legal secretary from Dublin is doing working for Wolfie Quinn? Isn't that a bit of a step down?'

'Not exactly.' Lily put her sandwich on the plate. 'I feel it's a step in the right direction. Dublin was getting hectic and, well, after my divorce I needed to get away. I've always loved Dingle. It's in my blood. I'm ready to downsize and live a simpler life.'

'Life is never simple,' he argued. 'But I know what you mean. I've done the city thing too and then felt like I was stuck in some kind of vicious circle of work, eat, sleep and nothing much else.'

'Oh?' Lily looked at him with interest. 'You were working in Dublin?'

'No, London. As I said, I have a degree in engineering from Trinity but I got a job with a firm in London. Quite high-profile and well paid. But it wasn't right for me. And then...' He paused. 'Something bad happened that made me want to come home, if you know what I mean.' There was brief flash of pain in his eyes, but then it was gone as quickly as it had appeared.

'Of course,' Lily said, wondering what had happened to him.

'So I quit after three years,' he continued. 'And moved here and set up my workshop doing all kinds of jobs. But then it was also the music scene that had pulled me back home.'

'You're very talented.' Lily tried to digest all he had told her just now. He had a degree in engineering from Trinity College and had had a high-profile, highly paid job in London. Then he had given it all up to live on the Dingle Peninsula doing odd jobs for people and singing in the local pubs... That was a lot more to give up than she had. 'So you like the simple things in life?' she asked.

'Nature,' he said. 'That's my thing. The ocean, the mountains, the air, the light on the water in the early morning, my dog and my work. And the music. I don't need anything else.'

'Or anyone?' She couldn't help asking. She was dying to know about his love life. Such a good-looking man couldn't possibly be immune to women.

He smiled. 'Well, that is another story. Not one I care to share at this moment. But I've had my ups and downs when it comes to relationships. You don't get to my age untouched. Except if you live like a monk. I'm still looking and hoping to find my true significant other.'

'Aren't we all?' Lily said airily. 'It's very hit and miss, isn't it?'

'A lucky dip, I suppose. So far for me, no luck.'

'Thought I had found it for a while,' Lily said with a sigh. 'But I was barking up the wrong tree.'

'Mr Right turned out to be Mr Wrong?' he asked.

'Something like that.' She picked up her glass and took a sip.

'Must have been rough,' he said. 'The divorce, I mean.'

'Yes it was,' she replied. 'It seemed to happen so fast. One minute we were in a church in front of our friends and family promising to love each other till death did us part, and then, two years later, he announced he was leaving me as it wasn't "working" for him. I thought we could talk, get help or maybe just take a break for a while, but he wanted to be shot of me.'

'I'm so sorry,' Dominic said with empathy in both his voice and eyes.

'Thanks. But it's helped me a lot to come back here.' Lily sighed. 'Can we talk about something else now? I'm sorry I brought it up.'

'You don't have to apologise. So,' he said after a while, 'did you find out anything from Brian?'

'Not really. I might later on. His granny knew my great-grandmother and I'm going to meet her to see if she remembers anything.'

'Don't tell me if you don't want to.'

'I don't mind,' Lily said. 'You're involved with Magnolia Manor and my grandmother, so I feel you're part of the place in an odd way.'

'I suppose I am,' he said. He ate the rest of his sandwich in one gulp and wiped his mouth with the napkin. 'I do like the place. I find it fascinating with all its history, the gardens, the shoreline, the boathouse... I've done a lot of work there during the past few years. I would love for it to stay the same forever. It's so part of the landscape and the history of this area.'

'It can't stay the same,' Lily protested. 'It has to evolve and become something better, more modern, but without ruining it. That's what my sisters and I want to do. We want to let the house live again and not stay like some mausoleum that will crumble and die.'

Dominic's eyes lit up. 'What exactly do you want to do, if you don't mind me asking? You told me about your plans for the greenhouse and the garden centre but not about the house.'

'We want to restore the house from top to bottom,' Lily explained. 'Do everything up and modernise the areas that need it. Replace the old plumbing, rewire the whole house and get it all back to its former glory. What we're planning would cost a lot of money, but we could get investors or partners to help us... It was once such a beautiful house.'

'I know it was. Go on,' he urged with a strange expression.

'We thought, once it's all finished, we'd live in it and use it for a wedding venue. Not as a hotel, but as a place for receptions. The ballroom would make a fantastic reception room where there could be dancing, with a live orchestra in the gallery. The grounds would be amazing for photographs once they were tended.' Lily shook her head and sighed. 'I know it sounds like a mad idea. It would cost millions. I mean we'd have to hire a structural engineer and an architect and all kinds of builders and experts...' Her voice trailed away as she thought of how much work it would all entail.

Dominic looked at her thoughtfully for a moment. 'Yes, it's quite a tall order to do all that. But not impossible.'

'Why not? I mean how do you know?'

'Because...' He paused. 'I'm actually a structural engineer.'

Lily blinked. 'Really? So...' She suddenly had so many questions but didn't know where to start. 'Are you saying you'd help us?'

'No, I don't think I'd want to get into such a huge job. But I can tell you that the structure is sound enough.'

'How do you know that?'

He suddenly looked a little awkward. 'Never mind how. I just do. In any case, I think you could get a grant to do it up. To make it more energy efficient if nothing else. And then take a loan between the three of you for the rest.'

Lily nodded. 'Well, that sounds as if it could be doable. But we wanted to convince Granny to agree to this plan first. I'm not sure how she would feel about it. And please don't tell her what I just said. We might have to give up the whole idea anyway.'

'It will be yours one day, I suppose,' Dominic remarked. 'And then you can do whatever you want.'

'Well that's a day we don't look forward to. It would mean Granny will have passed away. But we were hoping she'd join us in our project. That was before we knew about—' She stopped, feeling she had said too much.

'About?' Dominic asked.

'Well, it might not be ours for long,' Lily said. 'There's something going on that I can't tell you about. We could lose it all if...' She stopped, torn between the desire to tell him about the threat to their ownership of the manor and the feeling it wasn't her secret to tell. 'Sorry, I can't say any more right now.'

Dominic suddenly took Lily's hand in a tight grip. 'It's fine. I don't need to know. I see you're upset about something though. If it's about the house and whatever is troubling your grandmother, it has to stay in the family. Don't tell anyone unless you want to.'

'I don't think I can, yet.' Lily felt tears well up as she looked at Dominic. 'Thanks for being so understanding.'

He let go of her hand. 'No problem. I can understand you're worried about whatever is going on and the effect it might have on your granny. But she is a tough old boot, you know. That generation have been through a lot, so they're more weathered than us little snowflakes.'

Lily smiled and nodded. 'That's for sure. They seem to be better at taking stuff on the chin.' Her phone suddenly pinged and she glanced at it. 'It's Nora. She wants me to call her. It seems urgent.'

Dominic got to his feet. 'I have to go anyway. I have a job in the restaurant above Inch Beach. Their light fittings are on the blink. I'll bring Larry and give him a run. He loves that.'

'I can imagine. He's a lovely dog.'

'He is. But he's quite needy, being a rescue dog. Bye for now, Lily. Nice to talk to you. I'll get the bill on the way out.'

'You're always paying for my food,' Lily said in a light tone. 'Next time it's on me.'

'It's a deal,' he said and started to move off. 'See ya, Lily.'

'Thanks for lunch.' She watched him talk to the waiter on the way out and then he was gone. She picked up her phone and called Nora. 'Hi, what's up?' she asked.

'I'm at the house,' Nora said in a hoarse voice. 'Sylvia told me about the deeds and I thought I'd take a look around and see if I could find them. You have no idea what I've found instead. Can you come here straight away?'

'What? Why?' Lily stammered. 'I'm not sure I can come right now. I have to get back to the office. Is it important?'

'Yes,' Nora urged. 'It's... it's terrible. Please, Lily, come as soon as you can!'

14

Her heart pounding, Lily ran down the street to the office. Once inside, she knocked on Wolfie's door but there was no answer. She peered in but found the room empty. He was probably also out for lunch somewhere. No time to do anything but to scribble a brief Post-it note and stick it on the computer screen. *Emergency at home, must go, back asap.* A text message would probably have been the better option, but she saw he had forgotten his phone on the desk, so this would attract his attention as soon as he came back. Then she went outside, got into her car and drove as fast as it was legally possible to Magnolia Manor, arriving at the front of the house in a shower of gravel.

Lily was just approaching the big front door when it opened and Nora peered out. 'Thank God you're here,' she said in a shaky voice, pulling Lily inside. 'Come in and take a look.'

'At what?' Lily asked as she followed Nora through the big hall and down the long corridor.

'At this,' Nora said and flung open the double doors to the dining room.

Lily stepped inside and looked around. 'What happened?'

she said in shock, looking at the bare walls. All the paintings were gone. The collection, which had consisted of very old Dutch still lifes, portraits by well-known Victorian artists and watercolours by Irish painters, had disappeared. All that could be seen were the outlines on the wallpaper where they had hung. And not only that, some of the furniture was missing as well. 'The Regency sideboard,' Lily said. 'And the Georgian side table, and the bookcase.'

'Exactly,' Nora said, looking shocked. 'Anything of value, except the dining table and chairs, have been removed. There's stuff gone from the drawing room too. The two leather armchairs, the little sofa and the painting that used to hang between the windows. Gone.'

'Has Granny sold them?' Lily asked. 'Has she been that short of money?'

'I don't think so,' Nora replied, looking confused. 'I mean, she's been buying things and going to restaurants with her friends and so on. I think she would have told me if she had that kind of problem. Don't you think?'

'Yes, she would. You're the only one who truly knows what's going on with her,' Lily said as her knees felt suddenly weak. She sat down on one of the dining chairs and stared at the blank walls, thinking hard.

'Not lately,' Nora replied. 'There is a lot going on that she seems to keep to herself. She told me the deeds were missing but not why or where they could have gone.'

'Is it something to do with property tax?' Lily pondered. 'Or is Granny trying to raise money for the Magnolia party? She said it had to be the best ever if it's the last one she'll ever host.'

'I know,' Nora agreed. 'But she said she had a slush fund for the party and she wants to spend it this year.'

'I can't bear it.' Lily started to cry, feeling utterly hopeless. 'Granny just told us about that letter that had so upset her. I feel I need to tell you as you are so part of the family.'

Nora sat on the chair beside Lily. 'You know I'll keep it to myself.'

'Of course. I know that.' Lily went on to tell Nora about the letter from the Bernard family and how they were claiming ownership of Magnolia Manor.

'Oh my goodness,' Nora said, appalled. 'I had no idea. No wonder Sylvia was so upset about the deeds being lost.'

'We all are,' Lily said. 'It's so sad to think we won't own this house any more, that someone else will come and live here and maybe tear it down and build some modern apartment block or something.'

'It's a horrible thought,' Nora agreed. 'And just now when you have come here and started to feel so at home. But who removed all these things?'

'That's what I want to know,' Lily replied. 'Someone – and I think Granny – has had it all taken away. But who did it for her? And when?'

'I don't know anything about that,' Nora stated as she sat there still looking around in shock. 'If she had it moved, it must have been when I wasn't here. Late at night, or during the weekend, I suppose.'

'We have to talk to her,' Lily said, dabbing her eyes with a tissue. 'When she comes back from the funeral lunch.'

Nora nodded. 'Good idea. I think you need to lay all the cards on the table. Sylvia has been a little too secretive with you. But,' she added, 'it has nothing to do with me. I can't get involved.'

'Of course not,' Lily said, getting up. 'It's our mess and we'll sort it.'

'You have my support, of course,' Nora promised, standing up. 'As always.'

Lily gave Nora a hug. 'Darling Nora. What would we do without you?'

'What would I do without *you*?' Nora countered. 'You're all like daughters to me. I'll always be here for you. Now, please don't give up. You have to be strong for Sylvia. She needs you, whatever she says to the contrary.'

'You're right.' Lily let Nora go. 'That cheers me up a little. I'd better go back to the office for a bit. Rose should be helping Granny with that letter soon.'

'Is there anything I can do?' Nora asked.

'Not at the moment. Best not to say anything to Granny until I've had a chance to ask her about it,' Lily warned.

'I'll make you something for supper,' Nora offered. 'You could have it in the kitchen with your granny when you've finished talking to her.'

'Not sure we'll feel very hungry,' Lily muttered. 'But thanks, Nora, you're a star.'

'I'll make an Indian curry,' Nora said. 'Sylvia loves that.'

'So do we,' Lily said. She zipped up her jacket. 'I'll go back to the office for a while and then I'll be here a little later on. Let's keep this to ourselves for now. I won't even tell Rose.'

Nora nodded. 'Grand. I'll get going on the curry.'

'Brilliant.' Lily walked to the door. 'See you later. And, Nora, thanks for supporting us.'

'Happy to help,' Nora said. 'So glad to have you girls back here. It's like the old days.'

'In a way,' Lily said in a sad voice. 'I wish it really was all back to what it was.'

'Those were the good times,' Nora said wistfully.

'When we were younger and more hopeful,' Lily said. 'But hey, we'll get out of this. Somehow,' she added, not feeling very hopeful at all.

Much later, after what felt like a very long afternoon at the office, with a last effort to get the filing system sorted out, Lily returned to Magnolia Manor, entering through the kitchen door. The dogs lying around the Aga in the kitchen didn't bark but simply wagged their tails and went back to sleep. Lily patted Princess on the head and continued into the study, where she found Sylvia and Rose at the desk.

Rose turned around when Lily came in. 'Oh great. We've just finished writing the letter.'

'Not that it will do much good,' Sylvia remarked. 'But we had to try. Rose was a great help.'

'Can I read it?' Lily asked.

'Of course.' Sylvia handed Lily a sheet of paper with a short letter typed on it.

Dear Mr Bernard,

My granddaughters and I understand that you are claiming ownership of our property, Magnolia Manor, on the basis it was given to your grandfather as payment for debts incurred by one of our ancestors in the 1920s. We are contesting your claim unless you can present the deeds to the property with your name on it. Our solicitor, Mr Lucey in Tralee, will also be in touch, but I thought I'd contact you directly to tell you that we intend to fight your claim as strongly as we can and will take this to court if you persist. If you try to enter the property during this process, you will be legally charged with trespass.

Yours sincerely,

Sylvia Fleury

'Hmm, okay,' Lily said, handing back the letter. 'I suppose that's fine.'

'You don't seem that impressed,' Rose said.

'I'm not sure you should be sending it at all. It might be better to let our solicitor handle it, now that I think about it. And why did you say we'll take them to court? Didn't I tell you it'll cost a huge amount of money?'

'Yeah, but threatening to do it might give them a fright,' Rose insisted.

'I suppose it might. Except if they're rich, that won't stop them. But it's okay. Send it. Better to let them know we're not taking this lying down. But please send a copy to your solicitor as well, Granny. Or email him one. He should know about this.'

'Good idea.' Sylvia put the letter into an envelope. 'I'll post this tomorrow.'

'Good.' Lily sat down on the sofa. 'So,' she said. 'Now that's done, I need to talk to you about something. And I want you to tell me the truth, Granny.'

'The truth about what?' Sylvia asked.

'What's going on?' Rose asked, looking confused. 'We know about the deeds and all that.'

'It's about all the things in the house that are missing,' Lily interrupted. 'The furniture in the dining room, the paintings and the oriental carpet in the drawing room. I'm sure there's other stuff too, but I haven't been upstairs since I've been here.'

'What?' Rose exclaimed. 'Those things are missing? Why didn't you tell me?'

'I only just found out,' Lily said and looked at her grand-mother. 'So, what happened, Granny?'

Sylvia's face was suddenly white and she gripped the armrests of her chair. 'You mean... You've been snooping around? I *told* you not to go into the rest of the house!'

Rose put her hand on Sylvia's arm. 'Granny, Lily wasn't snooping. She probably just wanted to look around.'

'For the deeds,' Lily said, deciding not to involve Nora. 'Only I have a feeling there are no deeds at all. The property might not have been registered, you see. But we'll sort that out later. Okay,' she continued, 'so you told us you had closed up most of the rooms and not to go in there but... I had a feeling something was going on.'

'Going on?' Sylvia said.

'Granny,' Lily said sternly. 'We need to know. Please don't accuse me of snooping. You have been hiding all this, but we have a right to know. How can we be a team if we don't know everything? So please answer this question. Have you sold all those things?'

Sylvia sighed deeply. Then she looked back at Lily with sad eyes. 'No, I haven't sold anything. I have had it put away in a safe place. It's your inheritance and I didn't want that man to lay his hands on any of it. The lovely furniture, the beautiful paintings, the carpets, not to mention the family jewellery. I couldn't bear the thought of anyone but you girls getting it when I die.' She let out a deep sigh. 'I'm sure you're going to say it's against the law to do what I did. That's why I didn't tell you.'

'Oh.' Lily thought for a moment. 'Well, I don't think it's illegal, actually. I mean, that man is claiming ownership of the property, the house and grounds. But I don't think he's entitled to the contents unless Cornelius gave that to him as well.'

'Some of those things were bought by your grandfather Liam,' Sylvia said, 'and also by your father, so that was a long time after Cornelius gave the house away. But in his will he said he bequeathed everything to Caroline and then, when she died, she left it all to her son, your granddad. Who gave it all to me.'

'I see.' Lily nodded. 'That's good to know. We will ask your solicitor for a copy of the will. It might be enough to prove your ownership if there are no deeds. In that case, I think it's all okay. And maybe it was a good idea to remove it, actually.'

'Some of the jewellery is very old,' Sylvia cut in. 'From the early eighteen hundreds. It has been handed down through the generations. Very valuable.'

'I know. It's all lovely,' Rose said with a wistful sigh. 'And I was looking forward to wearing some of those gorgeous pieces.'

'And so you shall,' Sylvia said, looking at Rose, her eyes shining. 'At the Magnolia party. You will all wear something from the collection.'

'How wonderful,' Lily said, feeling a surge of love for her grandmother. 'I hope Vi will be able to come too.'

'If she gets that part, she will,' Rose stated. She turned to her grandmother. 'So where are all the things you had removed?'

Sylvia shook her head, her mouth pinched in a thin line.

Lily let out a disappointed sigh but decided to let it go. She didn't want to push her grandmother. 'Never mind.' She patted Sylvia's hand. 'Let's go and have supper. Nora made her famous curry.'

'Oh fabulous. Can we eat now?' Rose asked, getting up. 'I'm starving and the thought of Nora's curry is making me even more hungry.'

'I can smell it from here,' Lily said, laughing. 'The best remedy for stress.'

Sylvia handed Lily the letter. 'Could you get a stamp for this and then post it tomorrow? But make a copy and send it to Mr Lucey. It's too late now.'

Lily took the letter and put it into her handbag. 'I'll look after it.'

'Thank you, sweetheart.' Sylvia rubbed her hands together. 'And now, dear girls, we'll eat and I'll even open a bottle of wine. I think we need to relax after all this.'

Rose stretched her arms over her head. 'Oh yes. I've been feeling so tense. Let's relax and not worry about a thing for a while.'

Lily agreed, even though she knew she wouldn't stop worrying until all the problems had been resolved. The owner-ship of the house, the missing deeds and the removal of valu-ables from the property played on her mind all through the evening. Rose and Sylvia didn't know how serious this could be and she decided not to tell them. She'd consider each problem and try to assess their legal situation. She knew Sylvia was worried, despite appearing brave and positive. Rose wasn't happy either. To Lily, however, there was one bright spot on the horizon. Her budding friendship with Dominic.

15

The next few days flew by as Lily was so busy at work, but by the weekend she was able to look forward to a little free time with Sylvia. Rose had returned to Dublin but would be back for the Magnolia party, which was only two weeks away. The tree from which the manor took its name already had big buds ready to burst into bloom – perfect timing as usual. The weather was turning milder and there was a definite feeling of spring in the air. Lily had been looking forward to her visit to Brian's grand-mother, but he rang to say she was feeling poorly so the visit would have to wait. He'd call when she was feeling better and would be more alert. Lily was disappointed but she hadn't really expected to learn much from the visit anyway. Hopefully the old lady would feel better soon.

On Saturday they would do the final planning for the party and then on Sunday take a break before they got stuck into all the preparations. Lily suggested a drive around Slea Head to Nora and Sylvia, with lunch in a little pub overlooking the ocean near Ballyferriter. But Sylvia said she would be busy visiting an old friend on the other side of the peninsula and would be away all day. Nora, on the other hand, loved the idea, but suggested they take out the bikes from the shed, clean them up and ride them around the coastal road instead of driving.

'That way we'll see the beautiful views much better,' she declared when she called in for a cup of coffee in the gatehouse kitchen on the Saturday morning. 'I want to start cycling again like I used to. A great way to keep fit.'

'Great idea,' Lily replied, delighted by the prospect of spending the day with Nora. 'I had forgotten about our bikes. I haven't cycled for a while but I'm sure I'll get the hang of it very quickly.'

'Of course you will,' Nora declared. 'I just heard the forecast and it's not going to rain tomorrow. Might be a bit windy but isn't it always?'

'True.' Lily began to look forward to their outing the following day. 'It'll be fun to do something like that together.'

'Yes,' Nora said. 'And we can have a good old chat about everything and maybe see if we can figure out where those deeds might be. Two heads are better than one, don't you think?'

'Oh yes,' Lily said and started to tidy up the breakfast dishes. 'I hope we can get the bikes ready.'

'I've already asked Martin to check the tyres on my bike. I'll ask him to do yours as well if you like,' Nora offered, picking up her phone. 'Dominic could help him. He's around today doing all kinds of jobs.'

'Dominic?' Lily said, her heart doing a funny skip. 'Don't worry about calling, Nora. I'll go and see Martin myself and take a look at my bike at the same time. I haven't seen him since I arrived. Has he been away?'

'Yes, he took a break from work to go fishing in Galway with his cousins up there. It's a yearly thing. He'll be delighted to see you. But don't forget that we promised to spend the afternoon helping your granny with the planning and making lists,' Nora reminded her.

'I won't forget,' Lily promised and went into the kitchen to put the dishes in the sink. Then she walked out of the house after having glanced in the hall mirror on the way out. She looked okay if a little uninteresting in her jeans and grey hoodie and her hair in the usual ponytail. But what did it matter? Dominic might not even be there and she'd just have a chat with Martin about fixing her bike.

Lily took the path through the garden to get to the bike shed. The rain had just stopped and she breathed in the warm smell from the plants and shrubs. Big drops of water dripped from the leaves over her head and the dappled sunlight through the new foliage was lovely. It was a little like walking through a garden in a fairy-tale and Lily slowed her pace, thoroughly enjoying the beautiful morning. She had forgotten how magical the gardens were, but now all the memories of playing here as a child came tumbling back. The three little girls used to get lost in the fantasy world the subtropical gardens provided. They had played Tarzan and Jane, hide-and-seek, done treasure hunts and all sorts of other games. It broke her heart to think she might no longer be able to walk here, or live in the gatehouse that she had planned to turn into her new home while the big house was being restored.

She reached the bike shed that stood behind the greenhouse. The door was open and Lily could hear someone tinkering with something inside. She peered in and found Martin oiling the chain of Rose's pink bike. Her own blue one leaned against the wall.

'Hi, Martin,' Lily said, kissing his cheek.

He looked up from his task and smiled. 'Hi there, Lily. Long time since I saw you.'

'I know.' Lily smiled and shook her head. 'My life's been a little crazy this past year.'

'So I heard,' he replied. 'So sorry about your divorce. How are you now?'

'Much better,' Lily replied. 'Especially now that I'm here.'

'That's good news. Have you come to check on your bike? I've nearly finished Nora's machine and it's ready to go except for the tyres. Dominic has gone to get new ones for you both. It won't take me long to fit them and then you'll be able to go off on your skite tomorrow.'

'Fantastic.' Lily walked further into the shed, breathing in the smell of oil and tar. She smiled at Martin, thinking he was so reassuringly the same as he had always been, even if a little older. Tall and angular with thinning grey hair, he had a lovely smile and had been such a comfort to them all when tragedy had struck. She remembered tucking her small, cold hand into his big warm one as they walked down the garden path the day after the funeral. She had been so lost and lonely among all the adults who were grieving, nobody paying attention to the children. But Martin had been there like a big, comforting presence, not saying much, just making them feel secure in the pain and confusion after the loss of their grandfather and father. She felt a surge of love for this kind, unassuming man who was still there for them whenever they needed someone to lean on. He was the manager of the largest supermarket in the town but still found time to help out whenever he was needed. Together with Nora they were a huge support to Sylvia.

Lily watched Martin expertly fix the chain on the bike. 'You're so good at this,' she said.

'I like tinkering with bikes,' Martin said. 'They are such amazing machines when you think about it.'

'Oh yes,' Lily agreed, taking a rag from a peg. 'I'll clean up mine before you start on it.' Lily started wiping the bike. 'I might use this instead of the car on nice days. It'll make me fit and I won't pollute the environment.'

'That would be grand.' Martin put the bike he had been working on against the wall.

'Martin,' Lily started, 'I was wondering if you know anything about what Granny's been up to? I'm sure you know how worried she's been and everything. And now we've discovered she removed some of the valuables from the house to some secret place she won't tell us about.'

Martin looked thoughtful. 'I didn't know anything about that. Must have been during the Christmas holidays. Of course Nora and I are concerned about Sylvia. She has been quite frantic lately. And now she is all up to ninety about the party. But we are trying to help her as much as we can. Once the party is over she might calm down a little.'

'I hope so.' Lily rubbed the saddle on her bike. 'But then there are those dratted deeds that are missing and the threat of losing the house. We have to sort out the legal angle and see if we can get the lawyers on the case to stop those awful people.'

Martin put his hand on Lily's arm. 'I'm sure it will be all right in the end. Just try to calm Sylvia down. Her health is robust but, at her age, she shouldn't have to worry in this way.'

'No she shouldn't,' Lily said with feeling. 'It makes me so angry to think about it. Thank you so much, Martin, for all you've done for Granny.'

'Ah sure, we're family,' Martin said with a fond smile. 'Not by blood, but by our hearts. The Fleurys have been very good to us.'

'That's a lovely thought,' Lily said. 'Family by heart. You're a true star, Martin.'

Martin's face turned pink. 'Ah, thank you, Lily. But I have to leave now. The shop will be getting busy. I'll be back this evening to put the new tyres on the bikes and check that they're in good working order.'

'Okay.' Lily smiled at Martin. 'See you later, so. Thanks a million for doing up the bikes.'

'No bother,' Martin said. 'Happy to help you girls get back into it.'

When Martin had left, Lily finished cleaning the bike and was about to leave the shed when a big white dog trotted in wagging his tail.

'Hello, Larry,' Lily said, patting the dog on the head. 'Where is your master?'

'Right here,' Dominic said as he carried four bike tyres into the shed. 'Where's Martin?'

'Gone to work,' Lily replied. 'But he'll be back later to put on the tyres.'

Dominic put the tyres on the floor. 'Okay to leave them here?'

'Yes, I suppose so. He's going to get the bikes ready so Nora and I can go on a trip around Slea Head tomorrow.' Lily stood there feeling both awkward and happy to see Dominic again. Despite being dressed in baggy paint-stained jeans and a black sweater with holes, he managed to look annoyingly handsome. 'Eh,' she started. 'Would you like some coffee? I was about to go up to the house to make one with Granny's new Nespresso machine.'

'Yeah, that would be great,' Dominic replied with a crooked smile. 'I wanted to talk to you anyway. About your plans for the house. I've been thinking about it a lot. Not that I'm dressed for the manor.'

'That doesn't matter. Granny's out so we'll be on our own,' Lily said and then blushed. That had sounded like some kind of invite, which she hadn't meant at all. 'I mean...'

He grinned. 'I know what you meant. I'd love a coffee and promise not to read anything at all into what you just said.'

Lily didn't know whether to laugh, cry or just run away. Why did she often end up feeling like a schoolgirl during their conversations? He was so easy to talk to and seemed interested in her, which was a huge boost to her dented confidence. But it annoyed her that she became so flustered when he teased her. The invitation to coffee had come out so naturally because she liked being with him. She hadn't meant anything by the comment of them being alone. But then the thought of them being alone... She shook her head as if to dislodge the idea. 'Oh never mind,' she finally said and walked out the door of the shed.

He caught up with her outside, Larry trotting beside him. 'Great weather we're having.'

Lily laughed and looked up at the grey clouds rolling in. 'Not really. That's a heavy shower waiting to happen.'

'Let's get inside, then,' he urged as raindrops suddenly smattered against the leaves.

They raced up the path and around the house, arriving at the back door, breathless and wet.

Lily took a towel from a hook inside the door and handed it to Dominic. 'Here, use it to dry Larry. He's wetter than we are.'

Dominic rubbed Larry's back with the towel. 'Do dogs get preferential treatment around here?'

'No, but I didn't think you'd like to use a dog towel,' Lily argued. 'Granny's dogs must be out with Nora so you can let Larry into the kitchen to sit by the Aga while I get you a towel.'

'It's okay. I'm not that wet.'

'Okay, neither am I,' Lily said and led the way into the kitchen. 'Sit down and I'll make you a cappuccino. Or do you prefer your usual Americano?'

'A cappuccino would be great for a change.'

'Coming up.' Lily busied herself making coffee and frothing milk while Dominic sat at the table. Then she put a cup in front of him and settled opposite with her own.

Dominic took a sip. 'Nice,' he said.

'Yes, that machine makes a great cappuccino.' Lily skimmed some froth off her coffee with a teaspoon. 'Nora gave it to Granny for Christmas. She loves it.'

'I know.' He put down his cup and looked at Lily. 'So how are you settling in?'

'Very well,' she replied. 'It's a bit hectic at the moment because I'm organising Wolfie's filing system, which seems to be taking forever, but once that's done it'll be much easier. It's nearly all done.'

'You're beginning to feel at home in the gatehouse too, I've noticed.'

'Yes, I suppose I am,' Lily said. 'My sister Rose was here for a visit which was nice, but...' She stopped, not sure if it was a good idea to reveal all that was going on.

'But...?' he asked, sounding concerned. 'You're looking a little worried. Is everything all right with your grandmother? She's not unwell or anything?'

'No, it's not that. It's about something else. Something that...' Lily stopped again. 'It's about the house and the whole estate,' she finally said, feeling she needed to talk to someone about it. Her grandmother liked and trusted Dominic so he would be a good person to confide in. 'We might lose it, you see.'

Dominic looked startled. 'Lose this place? How?'

'Well, it's all my great-grandfather's fault. I wasn't going to tell you but I'm sure it will all come out soon anyway,' Lily said and went on to tell Dominic the whole story.

His eyes widened when she had finished. 'Wow. I had no idea this was going on. So that's why...'

'Why what?' Lily asked.

'Why she's been looking so down,' Dominic replied, looking suddenly awkward. 'And why she was so mad at the dude in the painting and had him removed from the house. And also why...' He paused, looking at Lily with probing eyes. 'But are you sure about this? I mean that French guy might be wrong. And if he doesn't have the deeds, then what happens?'

'We don't know if he has them or not,' Lily said, puzzled by the expression in Dominic's eyes. It was as if he knew something he wasn't going to share with her. Then she dismissed it. She was just hypersensitive. 'All I know is that they're missing,' she pressed on. 'Granny's solicitor doesn't have them and they're not in the house as far as we know. And on top of all that, Granny has removed anything valuable from the house, which I'm not sure is quite legal. She said it's in a safe place but refused to tell us where that is,' Lily ended, feeling miserable. 'It's all so sad and heartbreaking. Poor Granny. Where is she going to go? She loves this house and so do we. We had such great plans, but now...' Lily's eyes filled with tears and she couldn't stop them running down her cheeks. 'I'm sorry,' she whispered and got up to get a piece of kitchen paper from the roll on the shelf beside the Aga.

Dominic rose and went to her side. He stood there, looking at Lily with great sympathy and then he put his arms around her. 'Don't cry,' he said into her ear. 'I'm sure it will be all right.'

'How?' she asked, dabbing at her eyes. His arms felt so comforting and his eyes were so kind it made her cry even harder. She wanted to stay there and put her head against his chest and keep crying, but she pulled herself together and stepped away from him. He was only trying to comfort her and that made it a lot worse. 'Please don't be so nice,' she said, dabbing her eyes. 'It makes me feel even sadder. I know it's not going to be all right. It's going to be horrible. We'll lose the house...'

He suddenly grabbed her shoulders in a tight grip. 'Stop it,' he ordered. 'This isn't going to help you. I know the thought that you might lose this place that is so dear to you is awful. But it hasn't happened yet and it probably never will. I find it hard to imagine that some old story about a debt that happened a hundred years ago will mean that someone with some old letter or whatever can actually be declared the owner. You have to fight this with every legal weapon you have. Those deeds have to be somewhere.'

Lily blew her nose and tried to come to her senses. 'I'm not sure we'll find the deeds. But you're right. We have to try and fight this.'

'Yes, you do,' he said letting go of her. 'I think you should get going on your plans. I was going to offer to help you with a structural survey and, while I do that, I could look for the deeds. You never know. They might be tucked in behind a wall or something. No better way to search than to look into every nook and cranny.'

Lily looked at him in awe. 'You would do that? For me?'

'For all of you,' he said, looking suddenly shy. 'For the beautiful house that deserves to be restored to life again and be as stunning as it was in the beginning. It will sit on the hill like a jewel overlooking the bay and the beautiful landscape.'

'Gosh.' Lily was amazed at the passion in his voice. 'I didn't know you felt so strongly about the house. But thank you. And yes, I accept your offer. I have no idea how we're going to explain it to Granny though.'

'Leave it to me,' Dominic said with a smile. 'I know what to say to make it all perfectly natural.'

'I'm sure you do.' She sighed, feeling her anxiety slowly disappearing. 'You know, it might seem strange that my sisters and I are so attached to a place that we haven't visited much in the past few years. But it has always been a home we knew we could come to if we needed it. It was going to be ours one day and we'd do something with it, or live here and try to keep it going in some way or other. Together.'

He leaned against the counter, his arms folded, looking at her with great understanding. 'Of course. I feel the same about the little house I grew up in where my parents still live. They are there and the house is the same and in my mind it always will be. It's my safe place, my home of comfort and security. In my head, anyway, even though I have my own place and my own life now. If that was to go, and when my parents eventually pass away, I will feel oddly insecure and adrift.' He drew breath. 'Sorry that was all about me.'

'That's okay,' Lily said. 'It was also about how you understand how we feel.'

He smiled. 'Good. That's what I was trying to say.' He went back to the table and drained his cup. 'I have to get going though. I've a few jobs to do and then the band is playing in a pub in Anascaul tonight.'

'Which pub?' Lily asked.

'The South Pole Inn. Tom Crean's place.'

'That's an amazing pub. I'd love to watch you play again. I'll see if Nora wants to come with me.'

'That'd be great.' He walked to the door and snapped his fingers at Larry, who jumped up and stood by his side. 'Thanks for the coffee. I'll head off now that it's stopped raining.'

'Bye, Dominic. Sorry about crying all over you. I didn't mean to at all.'

He smiled. 'Ah sure, it was just one of those things. Onwards and upwards, yeah?'

'I'll do my best,' Lily promised. 'Thank you for offering to help with the survey too.'

'That will be a huge pleasure. All is not lost yet,' he said. 'Hope to see you tonight. We start playing around eight.'

'I'll be there,' Lily said as he walked out, Larry at his heels.

She sat down at the table again, her legs wobbly. She finished her cappuccino, staring out the window, breathing in the smell of coffee, wood burning in the stove, herbs and spices from a casserole waiting to be heated for dinner, thinking about what had just happened. Dominic had been so sweet and understanding and what he said was so true. This house, like all childhood homes, was a haven and a secure place she had thought would always be there. A port in a storm, a kind of womb where Granny would always be waiting and ready to care for her girls.

Lily was supposed to be an adult, responsible for her own life, but here at Magnolia Manor she was allowed to be a child again. It had seemed silly to feel like that, until Dominic had confessed that he felt the same about his childhood home, and now she knew she wasn't weird or childish. Or alone. But oh, if they lost Magnolia Manor... Lily clenched her fists. No, that must not happen. She would have to do her utmost to make sure it didn't. And now that she had Dominic to help out, it might still all be possible, if the deeds were found and the claim by the Bernards could be rejected. She could nearly see the house, restored and shining, the glasshouses repaired and her little garden centre nestled in the lush vegetation... It was a dream, but maybe, one day, it would come true.

16

When Nora heard about the event in Anascaul at the famous South Pole Inn for a trad music evening, she was keen to come with Lily. The pub had been built by Tom Crean, the hero of the Antarctic expedition at the beginning of the last century, and was a popular tourist spot. 'Fabulous pub,' Nora said as they were walking back from the shed with their now-restored bikes just after lunch. 'Great food and now music, of course I'll go with you. It will be a lovely break from all the work with the party planning. What's the name of the band?'

'The Fiddler's Elbow,' Lily replied. 'Dominic's band.'

'Even better,' Nora said. 'I could do with a night out and Martin wants to watch some boring old documentary on TV tonight.'

'Pity we can't cycle there,' Lily said, 'but we don't have lights on the bikes yet. In any case there'll be heavy showers tonight before the weather clears.'

'That steep hill up to the village could be too much before we're really fit,' Nora remarked.

'Very true.'

'The ride around Slea Head tomorrow will be a good test.'

'We'll probably be very stiff and sore the day after.'

'I'm sure we will.' Nora was silent for a while. Then she looked at Lily. 'I was wondering if we shouldn't do a thorough search for the deeds in the house? They could be stuck in a cupboard somewhere you haven't looked.'

'Granny said she's looked everywhere,' Lily replied. 'If they were in the house I'm sure she would have found them. But I'm going to go through Caroline's notebook that I found in the trunk again. I just skimmed through it the first time, but maybe she wrote something about the deeds that I didn't see.'

'Caroline's notebook?' Nora stopped walking. 'That sounds interesting.'

'It was mostly full of sketches and then a little comment about someone that Cornelius used to visit,' Lily said. 'She didn't like him and was worried about what they were up to. And she turned out to be right, of course. There was nothing in what I read about the deeds, but I thought I'd look through it again to see if I missed something.'

'Let's do that together,' Nora suggested. 'Page by page. Two pairs of eyes are better than one.'

'Good idea,' Lily agreed and started to walk faster. 'We have a little time before we have to go and help Granny.'

'I'll make tea,' Nora offered when they arrived at the gatehouse.

Lily leaned her bike against the wall. 'Great. I'll get the notebook and start looking through it. Then you could have a go.'

Lily went to her bedroom and got the notebook from her handbag, then went back downstairs to sit on the sofa with it. She looked up briefly as Nora entered with two mugs of tea and then dived in again while taking occasional sips of her drink. Then she handed the notebook to Nora. 'Here, you take a look with fresh eyes. Her handwriting is quite difficult to read.'

Nora sat down and started to go through the notebook, scanning each page intently. 'Lovely drawings,' she mumbled. Then she sat up, looking excited. 'Oh, I think I've found something. Right after the notes about Cornelius and his gambling. The pages were stuck together. Look.' She held out the open book to Lily. 'There, under another little drawing of the magnolia. It looks as if it was added later. The writing is clearer and the ink black instead of blue like the other note.'

Lily put the mug on the coffee table, took the book and looked at the page. There was a lovely drawing of the magnolia tree in full bloom and then something scribbled underneath.

The document proving our ownership is behind the tree. It will only be found if you take it down and turn it around.

'What does that mean?' she asked. 'Could she be referring to the deeds?'

'I don't know,' Nora replied. 'But it has to be something that can help you legally.'

Lily nodded, still staring at the words on the page. 'Yes, that's possible. But behind the tree? And do we have to take *it* down to find this document, whatever it is? Did she bury it underneath it?'

Nora shrugged. 'I don't know. I have a feeling it means something else but what?'

'You mean a riddle?' Lily looked at the tree in the drawing. 'She must have done this when Cornelius came back from France to stop him giving the house away.'

'In the late nineteen twenties?'

'Sometime around then, or the early thirties,' Lily suggested. 'Or maybe later still. Could be after Cornelius died in nineteen seventy. She died a few years after him.'

'Still a long time ago. But what he did cast an even longer shadow.'

'All the way to us.' Lily shivered.

'It's quite eerie, really,' Nora mumbled.

'We have to have a look at the tree,' Lily said.

'There won't be any sign of what Caroline did,' Nora argued.

'I know but I just want to walk around it. Ask it a question or something.'

'That's mad.'

'I know.' Lily took the notebook from Nora. 'But maybe there are vibes. Trees are mysterious, you know. That tree has been there since it was planted by one of our ancestors.'

'It has been replaced a few times since the house was built,' Nora remarked.

'Which was two hundred years ago. Oh, Nora we can't lose the house,' Lily exclaimed. 'It belongs to us.'

'I know. But we have to leave that for now and go and help your granny with the party planning. And then we have to get ready to go to Anascaul. I'm really looking forward to the evening.'

'Me too,' Lily said, her eyes still on the pages of the notebook. 'I'll go through the rest of the notes again. Aren't the drawings amazing?'

'She was a very talented artist.'

When Nora had finished her tea, Lily closed the notebook. 'Nothing much else there. Maybe she didn't want to reveal too much.'

'Could be.' Nora got up from the sofa. 'We'd better get going. Sylvia will be waiting. And then I have to decide what to wear tonight. We don't need to dress up but I'll change into something less drab. It's been a long time since I had an evening out.'

Lily went upstairs to put the notebook away while she thought about those lines in Caroline Fleury's diary. *'Behind the tree.'* *What does that mean? Was it some kind of riddle, or a message to whoever found the diary?* In any case, it was clear that the deeds had not gone forever, so that was more than a glimmer of hope. It made Lily feel a lot better about everything and she turned her thoughts to the evening ahead. She was determined to have a good time tonight. It would be so nice to have Nora as company too. They had never been out together before and it would be an opportunity to get to know each other better as adults. Nora was in her sixties but still eager to have fun. It was a side of her Lily was looking forward to discovering.

She decided to dress up a little bit and make herself look as pretty as she could. She didn't know much about Dominic's personal life, and she wasn't planning anything, but it didn't hurt to make an effort. Just in case...

17

As Lily got ready for the night out, she smoothed her hair, expertly blow-dried by Nora, and hoped her new look wouldn't seem too contrived. She wasn't used to wearing so much makeup, but Nora insisted, saying it was Saturday night and Lily needed to be glammed up a bit. Nora was pretty glammed up herself, her light brown hair curly and her eyelashes covered in lashings of mascara, all of which made her look both years younger and very pretty.

'Come on,' she urged. 'Let's paint Anascaul red and give the beer drinkers something to look at.'

Surprised to see Nora so light-hearted, Lily stopped arguing and let her have her way with her makeup bag and the hairdryer. The result was startling to say the least. Lily stared at herself in the bathroom mirror, wondering who that glamourous woman was. Huge brown eyes, outlined in kohl, looked back at her and the red lipstick gave her lips a sexy pout.

'Oh God, I'm not sure about this,' Lily said. 'But you are like a fairy godmother with the makeup and hairstyling. Never knew you had it in you.'

'My daughter is a beautician,' Nora explained. 'She's taught me a few tricks of the trade. I've always loved making people up. You'll be the belle of the pub tonight. Now put on the red top I spotted in your wardrobe and the black jeans and your boots and we're done.'

'It's not a party in Dublin,' Lily protested, but went to her room and did as she was told. The red top was a little too dressy for a night at a pub in Kerry, but it did make her look quite glamorous, bringing out the auburn streaks in her dark hair and complementing her complexion. She put the denim jacket over the top, which toned it down a bit. But Nora was right. It was fun to dress up even if the event was no big deal; they'd have a good time listening to nice music and eating good food. It was no big deal to be seeing Dominic either, she told herself, if only to calm the churning in her stomach. But she couldn't deny her attraction to his looks and the way he was so understanding and helpful. Their shared interests and feelings about a lot of things also resonated with Lily. She often felt when they were together that they were like pieces in a jigsaw that fitted together seamlessly. Were they meant to meet like this? Was it written in the stars? But their feelings for each other had to develop slowly to give them time to get to know each other better. Though when she thought about him and the development of their friendship into something else, it was as if she was walking towards a horizon that was bright and very beautiful.

The afternoon had been busy with drawing up the final details for the Magnolia party. Sylvia wanted 'all the stops pulled out and no expense spared', so they ordered champagne, wonderful finger food and a cake replica of the manor made by a bakery in Killarney. The ballroom would be decorated with streamers and balloons and garlands of flowers. 'I want it to be a bit like a wedding,' Sylvia declared. 'With everyone dressed up and food galore and wine flowing like a river.' That had made Lily and Nora laugh, but they agreed: this would be the best party ever. It would cost a lot more than the usual affair but it would be worth it. Lily said she and Rose would help out with the costs from their savings, which Sylvia didn't quite like but she agreed to after a little persuasion. After that, Lily had hurried back to the gatehouse to get ready for the evening, and Nora had gone home to change and make dinner for Martin to heat up later.

The tiny village of Anascaul was shrouded in darkness as they pulled up outside the South Pole Inn. The main street of the village – lined with old cottages, pubs and shops – stretched all the way up the steep hill with the pub at the bottom. It was all lit up and the whitewashed building with its blue trim around the windows could be seen clearly. Lily felt a buzz of excitement as she got out of the car. It was a cold evening with stars twinkling in the black sky and the crescent of a new moon rising over the rooftops.

The South Pole Inn was cosy, with wood panelling and wide oak planks on the floor, and it smelled of delicious food. Lily and Nora found a seat at a little table near the fireplace, where a turf fire glowed warmly. As they were early, they had time for supper and ordered the lamb, which they devoured hungrily. Nora enjoyed a glass of lager and Lily sparkling water, as she was driving.

Nora looked at her empty plate. 'Did I eat all that?'

'You did,' Lily replied, mopping up the gravy with a piece of bread. 'And look at me, nearly licking the plate. So delicious, I'd nearly order another helping.'

Nora laughed. 'I'm not sure I could eat anything else after this. I'm stuffed. But oh, it was incredible. That succulent lamb, the mashed potatoes, the veggies and the gravy. True Kerry fare.'

'I know.' Lily was about to say something else, but stopped as she felt someone touching her shoulder. She looked up and discovered Wolfie standing there, a pint of beer in his hand. 'Wolfie,' she exclaimed. 'What a nice surprise.'

'Ditto,' he said. 'Thought I recognised you, even if you look a little more, eh, festive, than usual.'

Lily laughed. 'I know. It's all Nora's doing.'

Wolfie shot Nora a smile. 'Hi, Nora, you look very good too, I have to say. Haven't seen you since the harvest festival.'

'Hello, Wolfie,' Nora replied. 'Lovely to see you. Hope all is well with you and your dad.'

'All well, thank you,' Wolfie replied. He looked around the packed pub. 'I'd better get a place to sit down before the music starts.'

Lily gestured at the empty chair at their table. 'Why don't you join us? Plenty of room here.'

'Oh.' Wolfie looked from Nora to Lily. 'Well if you don't mind, that would be great.'

'Of course we don't mind,' Nora said. 'Come on, stop dithering, boy, and sit down.'

Wolfie smiled and pulled out the chair, folded his tall frame and settled beside Lily. 'Thank you. That's very kind.'

'We're happy to have the company,' Lily said. 'Nice to see you out of—' she started, but then stopped as she heard a fiddle being tuned. She looked at the area near the bar, where the musicians were settling in. She saw the fiddle player, the man with the tin whistle and the girl with the bodhrán. There was no sign of Dominic but, when they started to play the first bars of 'Grace', he suddenly appeared with his guitar. Soon his beautiful voice rang out, silencing the chatter and noise in the pub. It was a sad song and a curious choice to start the session with, but a perfect vehicle for Dominic's voice. He seemed to be completely absorbed by the song and the story that had inspired it: that of the young girl who had married a hero of the 1916 rising just hours before he was executed.

'Oh goodness,' Nora sighed beside Lily, her eyes glistening

with tears. 'What a wonderful voice he has. It brings me to tears every time.'

'He's so amazing,' Lily replied, her eyes on Dominic.

He spotted her and smiled as he sang the last notes.

'He's seen you,' Nora said. 'And he's smiling at you.'

'No, he's smiling at everyone,' Lily protested.

'Looks very much like he's smiling at you, though,' Wolfie whispered into Lily's ear. 'But that's none of my business of course.'

'Oh, stop it, you two,' Lily said feeling flustered and confused. 'Let's forget about it and enjoy the music.'

'Good idea,' Wolfie said, taking a swig of his pint. 'And the beer. You ladies want anything to drink? I think we should order while we have a chance. I see a waiter coming to take away your plates.'

'I'll have another glass of lager, please,' Nora replied.

'You know, I think I'll try that new non-alcoholic Guinness,' Lily said. 'Thanks, Wolfie.'

'Least I can do in return for inviting me to sit here,' Wolfie said. He ordered the drinks from the waiter, asking for another pint for himself.

'You're not driving?' Lily asked.

'Don't have to,' he replied with a grin. 'I live up the road here. I only have to stagger a few hundred yards to get home.'

'Oh, that's handy.' Lily realised she didn't know much about him, only that he lived with his father, but where that was she hadn't known or bothered to ask. She was about to enquire about his dad, but the music drowned out any attempt at conversation as the band played a lively jig, which made some people stamp their feet and others get up to dance.

Wolfie shot up and pulled Lily with him, their feet tapping the floor in perfect time with the music. Lily remembered the steps from her childhood Irish dancing lessons and fell into the rhythm easily, while Wolfie was surprisingly light on his feet.

They whirled around the floor, dancing until the music stopped and they collapsed, panting and laughing, on their chairs.

'Oh gosh,' Lily exclaimed, fanning her face. 'I had forgotten what fun Irish dancing is.'

'It's great craic,' Wolfie agreed, taking a huge gulp of his pint.

Lily looked at him in awe. 'I had no idea you could dance like that.'

'You never asked,' he said, laughing. 'I've been doing Irish dancing since I was seven. I even have a few medals. But I gave it up when I grew too tall. Haven't danced like that for years. It seems you never forget the steps.'

'You were fantastic,' Nora said.

'Ah, but I had a great partner,' he said, smiling at Lily. 'You're very good.'

'If a bit rusty.' Lily took a sip from her glass of Guinness. 'This is good stuff.'

They sat enjoying the music after the break, and then Dominic appeared in front of the band again.

'Thank you so much for listening,' he said into the microphone. 'I have a request. Someone in the audience wants me to sing "Shallow" from the movie *A Star is Born*. But I think I need a bit of help. Is there by any chance a lady out there who might want to help me out?'

There was silence in the audience as everyone looked around to see who might volunteer. Lily loved that song, but to sing with such a great performer as Dominic in front of everyone... She used to sing at the student parties in Dublin, but that was a long time ago.

Dominic smiled out at the bar, his sparkling green eyes meeting Lily's, making her heart beat faster. He waggled his eyebrows at her before scanning the tables once more and leaning into the mike.

'Hey, girls, please help me out,' he pleaded. 'It's just a few bars and you don't have to give an Oscar-winning performance. We're among friends here.'

Lily chuckled along with the crowd and suddenly, before she knew it, she held up her hand. 'I'll give it a go,' she called. 'I'm a bit out of practice but I think I can remember most of the words...'

Dominic's smile turned into a grin. 'Great!' he called back and waved at Lily to join him. 'Let's give it a try.'

Lily swallowed nervously as she slowly got up. What had she done? She shot Nora and Wolfie a nervous look. 'What was I thinking? I'll make a fool of myself,' she whispered at them.

'You have a lovely voice as far as I remember,' Nora said, making a shooing motion with her hands. 'Go on. You'll be fine.'

'Easy for you to say,' Lily muttered, her stomach churning once more, as she got up and walked to join Dominic.

'Tell everyone your name,' he said, handing her a mike.

'Hi there,' Lily said. 'I'm Lily Fleury and I'm very nervous. Please don't throw any food at me if I miss a note or two.'

Dominic laughed. 'Don't worry, they're a nice bunch. They'll love you. Thanks for volunteering.'

'You're welcome,' Lily said, her voice shaking with nerves. 'You might be sorry you asked me.'

'Of course I won't. So let's give this a whirl.' Dominic picked up his guitar and started to play and sing the opening lines.

Lily's voice shook slightly when it was her turn, but as Dominic smiled at her she grew more confident. When they sang the chorus, their voices blended perfectly and it was as if they had always sung together. Their eyes locked as they sang, and she felt they were perfectly in tune, both with their voices and feelings. She wondered if she had imagined it. Was there a spark between them or was it just the music?

When the song ended everyone clapped, shouted and whistled while Lily blushed.

'That went well,' Dominic said when the noise died down, and he thanked her for volunteering.

'Phew,' Lily said when she returned to their table. 'That was scary.'

'You were great,' Wolfie said, clapping her on the back.

Lily grabbed her glass of Guinness and took a deep swig. 'Thanks, but I don't think I'll make a career out of it.'

'I hope not,' Wolfie remarked. 'I need you in the office, not singing in pubs.'

Lily laughed. 'Don't worry, I enjoy the office work a lot more than singing in public.'

Wolfie smiled. 'Well that's a relief.' He finished his pint and got up. 'I have to call it a night. My dad will be getting lonely. Should have brought him but noisy pubs aren't his thing these days.'

'Tell him I said hello,' Nora cut in.

'I will.' Wolfie started to move away. 'Thanks for the company, and the dance, Lily. I really enjoyed the evening.'

'So did we,' Lily said, smiling at him. 'Thanks for the drinks.'

'You're very welcome. See you in the office on Monday. Nora, it was great to catch up with you. Bye for now.' With that, he moved off and disappeared into the crowd, his light blonde head visible above everyone else.

'Well that was a big surprise,' Lily said to Nora. 'I could never have imagined that Wolfie was so good at Irish dancing.'

'I know.' Nora laughed. 'I couldn't believe it when I saw him bouncing along to the music. But for a lot of boys around here, Irish dancing was one of the few things to do other than soccer and Gaelic football.'

'Village life is so different to growing up in a city like Dublin.' Lily smiled at Nora. 'This is such a treat and it's been great to get away from all our worries for a while. But they keep popping up in my mind all the same. Especially what

Granny is going through. We need to solve the issue of the ownership of the house and try to get our project going, but that might take time. But, oh, it would be so good to keep Magnolia and know we can always come back, if only we can solve this whole mess.' She shot an apologetic look at Nora. 'Sorry for bothering you with our problems when we're trying to have fun.'

Nora put her hand on Lily's arm. 'It's okay. It just makes me sad to see you so upset.'

Lily managed a wobbly smile. 'Thanks, Nora. You're the best.'

The music started again, this time with a medley of ballads. And then Dominic sang a song in Irish, which marked the end of the session. He shook his head at the shouts of 'encore' and the crowd gave up and resumed their chatting and drinking beer.

Dominic leaned his guitar against the bar and made his way to Lily and Nora. 'Hi there,' he said. 'Thanks for coming. And thanks for the lovely singing, Lily. It was fun to do that song with you.'

'You're welcome,' Lily said with a smile, having recovered her good humour. 'I enjoyed it too.'

'Maybe you'd like to join me another time?' he suggested.

'No thanks,' Lily replied. 'I don't really like performing in public. It's not good for my nerves. And your voice is so amazing that I feel a little intimidated. Have you ever thought of doing all this professionally? Your band is great and you seem to be very popular.'

Dominic shrugged. 'Nah, that would be too hard. We prefer to do this for fun without any pressure.' He smiled at Lily. 'How are you, anyway? Feeling better?'

Lily nodded, cheered by his sympathy. 'Much better. Thanks for being so kind to me earlier today. I think I overreacted a bit.'

Dominic put his hand on her shoulder. 'Not at all. It's understandable you'd be upset by all that.'

Nora suddenly got up. 'Must go and freshen up. I'll get you a beer while I'm at the bar, Dominic.'

'Great,' Dominic said, his eyes still on Lily. 'So your date left early?'

'You mean Wolfie?' Lily asked. 'He's my boss, not my date. I came here with Nora and he just happened to be here at the same time.'

'Oh. You seemed very close,' Dominic stated.

'I like him a lot, that's true,' Lily replied, deciding not to get into her relationship with her boss.

'Lovely to see you here with Nora,' Dominic continued. 'She's wonderful. And she's very fond of you.'

'Nora has been a true rock all my life,' Lily said. 'Always here for us ever since we were very young.'

'Like a kind of mother figure?' Dominic suggested.

'Yes,' Lily agreed. 'Our father is dead and our mother has started afresh with her second husband. She's not in touch that much any more.'

'But you have your grandmother,' Dominic argued. 'I have a feeling she'll be around for a long time.'

Lily laughed. 'Oh yes, I'm sure she will. She's a true life force. But I wish she wasn't so frantic. She seems to be at every bunfight in town, and every club and group that will accept her as a member. I don't know why she does it, to be honest.'

'I think I do,' Dominic said, looking up as a waiter put a pint of lager on the table. 'Thanks, mate.' He took a swig of beer. 'Ah, that's better. Singing is thirsty work.'

'I bet.' Lily looked at him for a moment. 'What's the reason then? About Granny and her activities, I mean. Why is she so busy?'

'She said to me yesterday that she's networking all over town,' Dominic replied. 'And that you're not the only one who has great plans for Magnolia Manor. But it will take some plotting and scheming to get it started. Her own words.'

'To get what started?' Lily asked, mystified.

'Whatever she wants to do.' Dominic grabbed his pint again. 'What is that?'

Dominic shook his head before he took a sip. 'Not for me to say. Why don't you ask her yourself?'

Lily frowned, feeling confused. 'Why is she telling you everything?'

'She hasn't told me anything much,' Dominic protested. 'I tried to find out more about what she was up to, but that's all I could get out of her. After that she clammed up and started to talk about the repairs she wanted me to do. I have a feeling she was sorry she said anything at all.'

'Oh, I find it so irritating that she keeps all these secrets from me,' Lily said angrily. 'I try to talk to her. We finally got the huge problem with the ownership out of her, and then we discover she had all the valuables removed and had to have another go at getting her to tell us about *that*. And now we still don't know what she's planning with all this networking stuff. If that ever gets off the ground with the deeds missing and—' Lily stopped, staring at Dominic with a feeling of despair.

He took her hand. 'It must be very frustrating.'

'That's putting it mildly.' The touch of his hand felt so comforting, just like when he had put his arm around her in the kitchen earlier.

He nodded. 'I know.' He let go of her hand, drank some beer and then cleared his throat. 'I was wondering if you could come to my house tomorrow? I'm preparing a survey report for you and I thought we could discuss the details. I've discovered lots of little things while going through the house.'

'Already?' Lily said, surprised. 'I mean, we only talked about it earlier today.'

'Oh I've been through the house and up in the attics quite a few times doing stuff for Sylvia,' he replied, looking a little awkward. 'As a structural engineer, I couldn't help noticing what was wrong up there. I need to take a closer look, of course. But right now we can already discuss some of the things I remember. We could lay out a plan.'

'That would be great,' Lily replied, her heart beating faster at the prospect of spending time together, even though the invitation was about the survey. 'Tomorrow you said?'

'Yes. I was thinking tomorrow afternoon on the way home from your bike tour with Nora. You could come down my way from Slea Head. I'll make you both a bite to eat.'

'Okay. I think we should be ready for something to eat by then. And Nora knows all about what I want to do and is on my side, so no problem there.'

'Great. You could text me when you're nearby so I can have something ready.' He rose from his chair. 'I'll be off so. See you tomorrow.' He flashed her one of his charming smiles before he walked off.

Lily nodded and waved goodbye. 'Looking forward to it.'

'So...?' Nora asked when they were on the way home. 'How did it go? Did he ask you for a date? You were looking quite intense there when I came back.'

Lily blushed. 'Yes and no.'

'What do you mean?'

'He asked me to come to his house tomorrow evening.'

'Oh? Well that's lovely,' Nora said. 'I thought I'd give you a chance to be alone and I ordered a beer for him so he'd stay put for a while. And it worked!'

'No, it didn't.'

'What?'

'The invitation was for you as well, after our bike ride. And we're going to talk about my plans for the manor, so it's all business. He's doing a structural survey. And he's also going to see if he can find the deeds, or any kind of document, while he's up in the attics.'

'I see. Well isn't that kind of him? That will be a lot of work on top of all the other jobs he does. Good idea to have a detailed survey when you lay out the plan to Sylvia. If he finds those papers Caroline mentioned, that'll be an extra bonus, don't you think?' Nora said hopefully.

'Yes,' Lily said, looking out at the winding country road lit by the headlights. 'Of course it will.' But she couldn't help letting out a sigh. 'You see, I think he's more interested in the house than me. He says he loves it and wants it to live again. So who am I to argue? We need his help. And we'll get to see inside that cute house by Ventry beach I always wanted to live in. You know the one I mean?'

'Oh yes, that's a house I'd love to see. I remember how you used to make up stories about it when you were a little girl.'

'It was like a house in a story to me. It'll be so interesting,' Lily remarked as they were at the crossroads. 'Houses can tell you a lot about people.'

'I bet it's something bohemian and a bit messy,' Nora suggested. 'With books everywhere and a saggy sofa and a doggy bed in front of a big fireplace with logs blazing.'

'Very likely,' Lily agreed, trying to imagine Dominic in such a house. It could feel very romantic with those views across Ventry Bay and the beach. She knew she shouldn't feel upset that he had only invited her for the work on the house, but part of her wished it had been for other reasons. *Ah well,* she thought. *It wasn't meant to happen. But it's nice that he's willing to help me with my plan. I have to stop imagining that he's interested in me.*

But despite trying her best not to fantasise about their relationship, she couldn't help hoping it would develop into something more.

18

Lily and Nora had a wonderful cycle tour of Slea Head that brought them around sharp bends along the coast, with stunning views of the ocean, and the headlands with cliffs plunging into the sea and waves crashing against the rocks sending spray high in the air. It was a glorious morning with clear blue skies and a cool breeze, the kind of day that made Kerry look like paradise on earth. The green fields were dotted with sheep and newborn lambs gambolling around.

'Is there anything cuter than a newborn lamb?' Lily asked as they stopped to look at a flock of sheep. 'And just listen to them calling for their mothers. Makes you want to get one as a pet.'

'They grow up to be big dirty sheep,' Nora protested with a laugh. 'But I agree, they are adorable.'

'All babies are.' Lily looked at Nora. 'Do you think I'll ever have any?'

'I'm sure you will,' Nora replied.

'I hope so,' Lily said with a wistful little sigh. 'All I need is to find a nice man who wants the same thing and I'm away.'

'Your granny would love it.' Nora leaned on the handlebars

and stared out across the sea. 'I was hoping Martin and I would have more, but it didn't happen.'

'But you have a lovely daughter,' Lily said. 'And you'll have grandchildren one day.'

'Oh, I hope I will,' Nora said. 'But let's not dwell on all this. It's a lovely day and we're here at what must be one of the most beautiful places on earth. It's impossible to feel sad on a day like today.'

'That's very true.' Lily jumped on her bike and started to pedal away. 'Come on,' she called over her shoulder. 'Let's continue. We can have our sandwiches in Ballyferriter and get a beer at the pub with the stupendous views. It's warm enough to sit outside.'

'Great idea.'

They soon reached the outskirts of Ballyferriter, a little village on the edge of the coast, and found the pub along the roadside. It was a long time since Lily had been there, but she found to her delight that it looked the same. The village was nestled in a stunning green valley between the majestic hill of Cruach Mharthain to the south and a ridge of jagged peaks to the north – Ceann Sibéal and the Three Sisters. To the east, Smerwick Harbour overlooked a two-mile stretch of white sandy beach called Béal Bán. To the west, the Atlantic was faced off by high rocky cliffs and tiny coves and beaches. All of this was even more stunning in the early spring sunshine.

After ordering beer and crisps, which Lily managed to do in Irish, they settled on the rough bench outside and enjoyed the view, the sandwiches they had brought, the cool beer and each other's company. It was a blissful moment that made them forget all their problems and worries; Lily closed her eyes to the warm sunshine, listened to the waves crashing against the rocks below the road and felt herself relax. Nothing seemed to matter at that moment, and she even forgot the niggling little doubts about Dominic.

'Que sera sera,' Nora mumbled beside Lily. 'Let's just let it all happen.'

'Yeah. I want to let go of everything right now.' Lily opened her eyes and put on her sunglasses, smiling at Nora. 'We're lucky, really, aren't we?'

'We sure are. Remember what your granny says about worrying about the future?'

'Today is a gift, that's why it's called the present,' Lily declared.

'Exactly. There is only now, and now is pretty good, I feel.'

'And hey, did you hear me in there?' Lily asked. 'I ordered the beer and crisps in Irish.'

Nora patted Lily on the back. 'I was very impressed.'

'I should brush up my Irish,' Lily remarked.

'If you're going to stay here, I think you should. You'd be surprised how many people around here are fluent.'

'I know. I'll try to find a course. Or something online.' Lily took a last swig of beer. 'But maybe we should move off? I want to cycle back slowly towards Ventry. I don't want to arrive to Dominic's exhausted.'

Nora jumped to her feet. 'You're right. Can't wait to see that house.'

'Neither can I,' Lily confessed, feeling excited at the prospect of seeing Dominic's home for the first time. Not to mention the prospect of seeing him again too.

After a long slow cycle, they arrived in quite good form at Ventry beach. Parking their bikes at the little gate that led to the garden beside Dominic's cottage, they made their way down a narrow path lined with camellia bushes in full bloom.

'Lovely little garden,' said Nora.

'Gorgeous,' Lily agreed as they came to the house standing on a grassy plateau overlooking the bay. The house was whitewashed with a slate roof and it had a huge picture window at the front. The door was painted blue like the ocean and was flanked by two large shrubs in wooden tubs.

'Kerry roses,' Lily said. 'Must be gorgeous when they're in bloom.'

Nora nodded and pressed the doorbell, the sound of which resulted in frantic barking inside the house.

'Larry!' Lily said as the door opened and Dominic stood there, holding an excited dog by the collar.

'Hi,' he said and stepped aside. 'Please come in. I'll just shoo Larry out. He can come in later to say hello.'

Larry bolted out the door and Lily and Nora went inside. They walked into the living room and stopped dead, both taken aback by the room in front of them. This was far from the bohemian, messy place they had expected.

'Oh my Lord,' Nora whispered. 'What an amazing room.'

Lily was speechless as she looked around, feeling as if she had stepped into some kind of twilight zone. Whatever she had thought Dominic's home would be, this was the complete opposite. 'It's all open plan,' she managed when she had found her voice.

'And high tech,' Nora mumbled.

In a way it was. But the sleek modern room wasn't in any way soulless. The bleached wooden floorboards, steel and black granite kitchen area, an oval dining table with four white chairs and a long bench with light blue upholstery formed a perfect backdrop to the large picture window that overlooked the ocean. The sky and the sea seemed to invade the room in such a way Lily nearly felt as if she was floating when she looked at it. Seabirds hovered just outside, peering in at them through the glass. She turned and noticed that the walls were hung with old musical instruments such as a banjo, a guitar, an old violin and a flute, instead of paintings. There was a large computer screen on one of the walls and a synthesiser below it.

'Oh wow,' she whispered. 'This is where you get your inspiration.'

'Do you compose music as well?' Nora asked.

'Yes,' Dominic replied. 'I'm working on a song at the moment. When it's ready I'll include it in my repertoire. But it's just a hobby.'

'I'm looking forward to hearing it,' Lily said.

'When it's ready,' he repeated, laughing. 'I'm doing it slowly. But please, sit down. You both must be hungry and thirsty after your long cycle.'

Lily became suddenly painfully aware of her sweaty face and wind-blown hair. 'I'd love a glass of water. And maybe I could use the bathroom?' She looked around.

'Through there,' Dominic said and pointed at a door beside the kitchen area. 'Up the stairs and the first door on the left.'

'Thanks.'

'You want the water first?' Dominic asked, going to the sink and filling a glass from one of the taps. 'It's filtered,' he said as he handed the glass to Lily. Then he turned back to the tap and filled another for Nora.

'Brilliant,' Nora said and drank thirstily. 'Tastes great,' she said when she had drained the glass.

'It really does,' Lily agreed.

He nodded. 'It makes such a difference to filter out the metals and impurities. I designed this system myself and I've applied to have it patented.'

'Oh, I see.' Lily handed him back the glass. 'Being an engineer, you'd know how to do all that.'

'I like tinkering with all kinds of things. It's quite creative,' he said. 'I've done this whole house myself.'

'Amazing,' Nora said, looking at Dominic with new respect over the rim of her glass.

'Not really,' he said modestly. 'It's just stuff I enjoy. I'll put on the kettle and make you both some tea. I got a few pastries from the bakery here as I remembered you like those, Lily.'

'Oh, great. I'll just go freshen up.'

She opened the door Dominic had shown her and started to climb the stairs to the upper floor, which seemed to have been created under the eaves. It was a little cramped but the dormer windows had lovely views up the hill. She walked into a bathroom, which was a wet room just as state-of-the-art as the main room downstairs, even though very small. It was tiled from top to bottom in sand-coloured tiles and the shower had rows of buttons and taps. Some kind of power-shower, she deduced as she rinsed her face and hands at the large sink. She patted her face dry with a towel and stared at her image in the mirror. Her face was red and shiny, her hair ruffled by the wind. But what did it matter? She didn't have to try to impress him today. It was just a business meeting after all. Her feelings for Dominic would have to take a back seat for now.

She left the bathroom and was about to return downstairs when she spotted a framed photo on a little table under the mirror on the landing. Lily looked at it and froze. *Oh no...* she thought, staring in shock at the face of a pretty young woman with long blonde hair and beautiful blue eyes. She looked as if she was very fond of whoever was taking the photo.

Lily stood on the landing, trying to steady her shaking legs as it slowly dawned on her what it meant. Dominic had a girlfriend, a stunning beauty judging by the photo. Which confirmed that whatever she had read into his kindness towards her only existed in her imagination. He wasn't interested in her at all.

Lily looked at the photo again, trying to take it all in. But then her gaze drifted to a pile of letters on the little table beside it. Letters from *her*? She knew she shouldn't snoop but couldn't help herself. She took a step closer and, without touching anything, looked at the envelope on the top of the pile. Then she saw that it was a business letter with a window. Something to do with engineering or structural surveys, she supposed. Curiosity getting the better of her, she looked at the name of the sender. Her eyes widened in shock as she read: Arnaud Bernard & fils. Lily clapped her hand to her mouth. *Could it mean...?* She felt suddenly sick as she realised what it meant. Dominic was working for *them.* The woman in the photo paled to insignificance as she stared at the letter. What was Dominic up to?

Lily managed to get through the next hour, drinking tea and chatting, sitting on the blue bench by the window with Nora and Dominic as if nothing was wrong. She looked at the rough sketches he had drawn up, trying to focus on what he was saying to her and what he had noticed during his trips up to the attics in Magnolia Manor. He looked up and smiled at her occasionally as he pointed out different things in the report, but she pulled herself up and pushed away all the emotions. This was important and she was lucky to have such a skilled engineer to help her, even if he was communicating with the Bernards. Never mind her feelings about him and her dismay at finding that letter on the landing. Magnolia Manor was more important than some romantic notions. If Dominic was working for the Bernards, she could still use his expertise and get the survey done. It would be a great help with their plans for the house. She turned her attention to what he was saying, pushing away everything else.

'The flashings around the chimneys need to be seen to,' Dominic explained. 'And the rafters in some areas of the roof need to be replaced. There is a little woodworm in some of the large beams but that can be dealt with and should be before it spreads.'

Lily nodded. 'Okay. What else?'

'The roof is made up of natural slate and some of it has to be replaced fairly soon,' he replied. 'There are some serious leaks into what used to be the servants' quarters, but I have to take a closer look and draw up a detailed survey so you can calculate costs.'

'That would be great,' Lily said. 'A huge help, I have to say. And it's great that you have done so much already,' she added, just to see what his reaction would be.

'I like to work fast,' was all he said. 'It's important to have all the facts.'

Nora nodded in agreement, then the conversation turned to the Magnolia party and the arrangements for it. Nora asked Dominic if his band would be available to play at the party. But he had a better idea.

'I don't think the band members are free that day. But in any case, I think it might be better if you had someone playing the harp to provide nice background music. The band would drown all conversation and everyone would be forced to listen, but with some gentle harp music, that won't be a problem.'

'That's a brilliant idea!' Lily exclaimed, feeling excited, despite what she felt after the discovery on the landing. 'Perfect for the mingling and sipping champagne while we listen – or not as the case may be. It will create a lovely, dreamy atmosphere. Do you know anyone who might be available?'

'Yes,' he said. 'I know a girl who plays the harp beautifully. She even won a prize at the Galway Fleadh Cheoil. I'll give you her number and you can ask her yourself. She lives in Tralee.' Dominic went to a drawer and pulled out a card, which he handed to Lily. 'Here. Give her a call tomorrow and see if she's free.'

'Great.' Lily stuffed the card into the pocket of her jeans without looking at it. 'Thanks, Dominic. Will we see you at the party?'

'Of course,' he replied with a smile. 'Wouldn't miss it for the world. I think half the town are going.'

'And the other half will be wildly jealous,' Lily added. 'But we can't invite everyone. Just people who have some kind of connection to the house and family.'

'And I have both,' Dominic said with a glance at Nora.

'You sure do,' Nora agreed. She looked out the window and jumped up. 'Gosh, it's getting late. We'd better get home before it's too dark. We don't have lights on our bikes yet.'

'You're right,' Lily said, getting up, grateful for a reason to leave. She was beginning to feel uncomfortable, both the beautiful face in the photo and that letter from the Bernards still vivid in her mind. 'Thanks for the tea and cakes, Dominic. And for showing us your amazing house.'

'It was lovely to have you both here,' he said as he saw them out. 'Call in again if you're passing.'

'We will,' Nora said, walking ahead to get her bike.

Lily was about to follow, but Dominic took her arm gently and pulled her back. 'Are you okay?' he asked, looking into her eyes. 'You were so quiet in there. Not your usual chatty self. Is all the worry about the house and your granny getting to you?'

'I was just tired after that long bike ride,' Lily said pulling away from his grip. She avoided meeting his gaze, feeling awkward. He was being kind, but she was still upset about the letter she had seen and she didn't want it to show. 'I'm not as fit as I thought.'

'I see,' he said, not looking convinced. 'Okay, if that's what it was, I get it.'

'I am a little worried about all the other stuff, of course,' Lily admitted. 'But now that we're trying to solve it together, I feel better. My sisters will be here for the party and that will make Granny very happy. So we're just going to concentrate on making it spectacular.'

'Okay. Well, I'm helping to put up the decorations.'

'That's great.'

'So I'll see you around,' he said after a moment's tense silence.

'Yes. See you,' she said just as Nora called asking what was keeping her. 'I have to go.'

'Safe home,' he said. 'Text me when you arrive.'

She searched his face, confused by both the request and the look in his eyes. 'Why?'

'Just to make sure you got home safe and sound. You'd better get going or you'll have to ride home in the dark.'

Lily nodded and walked away, leaving him still standing outside the door. She didn't turn around so she couldn't see his expression, but then she heard the door close and felt a sense of relief as they got on their bikes and cycled home in the gathering dusk. She had no idea what was going on in his mind, but now she'd seen that photo and realised there was someone else in his life, she now knew those vibes she thought she'd been feeling between them had only been in her imagination. And then that letter... What was he up to? Was he playing some kind of double game? Pretending to help her while he reported back to the Bernards? She should have asked him but was afraid he'd just tell her a lie. And she'd had enough of lies with Simon. She had to shake off the disappointment and carry on, concentrate on what was going to happen to Magnolia Manor instead. There was a lot to do if they were going to save the house and keep it in the Fleury family. Above all, they had to be careful and not tell anyone what they were doing. Least of all Dominic.

19

Sylvia woke up early after a night of tossing and turning, trying to get some sleep. But she couldn't relax as the email she had received last night kept popping into her mind. It was from Arnaud Bernard, telling her he would arrive the day of the party and that he had something important to discuss with her.

Sylvia had stared at the message, wondering what he meant. And why did he have to come that day of all days? He couldn't know about the party so it was simply a terrible coincidence, but what was she to do? She felt as if dark clouds were gathering over the house and that the dreaded family were arriving like a horde of invaders to throw the Fleurys out of the house forever.

She was going to reply to say it wasn't a good day to come and ask him if he could delay his arrival by a few days, even a week. But then she changed her mind. Let him come and see how loved they were by the whole community and how he would be seen as an intruder who had done this terrible thing to the Fleurys, the oldest family in the area. Let him understand what he was doing to them all, how he was breaking their hearts and wrecking the future of three lovely young women. *Oh, yes,* she thought with grim satisfaction as she slowly got out of bed, *he will discover that taking over this ancient property will not be as easy as he might think.*

Sylvia decided to keep the news of Monsieur Bernard's arrival from the girls. Why ruin the happy anticipation and dash any hope they might have that it wasn't going to happen? She would tell them at the right moment, but that moment was not now...

The preparation for the party helped Lily turn her mind away from her worries. She managed to block out her feelings of disappointment over Dominic and began to enjoy the excitement and look forward to the party. It would be amazing, even if the threat to their ownership of the manor loomed in the distance. They had tried to contact Sylvia's solicitor who had all the details of the wills, but he was off sick and his assistant had no idea where to find what they were looking for, so they had decided to leave that and worry about it after the party. The magnolia tree in full bloom outside the manor helped to keep her spirits up.

The day before the party, Lily and Rose – who had arrived that morning – got stuck in with the others to prepare the ballroom. They had worked hard all week, polishing the parquet floor, hanging the drycleaned green velvet curtains, washing the tall windows, standing precariously on wobbly ladders and enjoying the memories of the old room, of all the parties that had been held there, from birthdays to Christmases, confirmations, harvest festivals and all kinds of other celebrations. Nora had washed and ironed the huge damask linen tablecloth that was to go on the big table, which had been brought in from the dining room, and Dominic and Martin put up the garlands of flowers. All that was left to do was lay out the food and drink that would arrive the morning of the party. And to dress up, which Rose declared was 'most important'.

In the evening, when all the preparations were nearly in place, Lily was standing on a tall ladder, hanging the last garland over the window when she noticed a movement below her. She looked down and nearly fell as she spotted her youngest sister, Violet, standing there looking up, as if she had appeared by magic.

'Vi!' Lily exclaimed, steadying herself. 'You're here! I thought you were coming tomorrow.'

Vi laughed. 'Yes I was, but I thought I'd arrive earlier and surprise you.'

'You certainly did.' Lily climbed down and grabbed her sister's hands, staring at her lovely face. 'Oh how gorgeous you look,' she said, taking in Violet's hazel eyes, flawless skin and poker-straight red hair hanging down to her waist like a silk curtain. She was dressed in a navy cashmere sweater and jeans, which showed her slim figure to perfection. 'And you got the part, congratulations.'

'Thank you. It's not the biggest part ever but it's going to be great for my CV. It's a big production.' Vi pushed back her hair and looked around the room. 'Everything looks fabulous. You have really made a huge effort.'

'Granny wants it to be the best party ever,' Lily said and hugged Vi tightly. 'And now that you're here it will be. Have you seen her?'

Vi nodded. 'Yes, I popped into the study and said hi to her and Rose. They were so excited.'

'I bet they were.' Lily took Violet's hand and pulled her across the room to where Dominic and Martin were working on the big table, putting in two extra leaves. 'Hey, look who's here!'

Martin turned around, his face breaking into a big smile as he saw Vi. 'Hello, stranger,' he said and hugged her. 'You look like a million bucks.'

Vi kissed his cheek. 'Lovely to see you again, Martin.'

'And this is Dominic,' Lily said when Vi and Martin broke

apart. 'He works for Granny around the house and gardens.' Her tone was light, hiding the turmoil inside. No need to show how she felt about him.

Vi shook his hand. 'Hi, Dominic. I've heard so much about you.'

Dominic smiled. 'And your grandmother never stops talking about you.'

Vi laughed. 'I know. She thinks I'm going to win an Oscar every time I get a part in a movie. She has even planned what to wear on the red carpet because I said she'd be my date if ever I was nominated. Which will never happen of course.'

'Never say never is my motto,' Dominic declared, glancing at Lily.

'Well that's great but I'm not holding my breath. In any case,' Vi said with a shrug, 'awards don't mean a thing. But let's talk about the party. I'm so looking forward to it. I bought the most amazing dress in a little boutique in Tipperary. It's a vintage piece from the fifties. Green silk with a crinoline type skirt. Just wait till you see it, Lily.'

'Fabulous.' Lily looked at the window and the final garland she had just put up. 'I think that looks good. Dominic, could you remove the ladder, please? I'm going to the gatehouse to help Vi settle in.'

'Okay,' Dominic replied. 'We'll finish setting up the table and then we're finished. All that remains is setting up the food and drink tomorrow.'

Lily nodded. 'Brilliant. Thanks for all your help.'

'It's been fun,' Dominic said, looking pleased. 'And the room looks amazing.'

Lily looked around and had to agree. Flower garlands looped over the windows and newly cleaned curtains created a wonderful backdrop for the beautifully decorated room, with gleaming floorboards and framed prints on the walls they had put up to replace the paintings Sylvia had had removed. The table would be covered in the damask tablecloth tomorrow and all the wonderful food they had ordered placed on it, along with bottles of wine and champagne and their best Waterford crystal. It really would be the most elegant Magnolia party ever. She said a quick prayer that it wouldn't be the last.

The sisters woke up early the following morning and had breakfast together in the kitchen of the gatehouse. Vi said she had slept very well, despite having to share her bedroom with Cornelius, which made them all laugh.

'I'm sorry we didn't manage to get his portrait out of there, but there wasn't time with all the stuff we had to do before the party,' Lily told her.

'And it weighs a tonne,' Rose cut in. 'We didn't want to bother Dominic as he had so much to do up at the house.'

'It was okay, really,' Vi assured them. 'I didn't feel his presence at all because you had covered him up with a bedspread. I took a peek at him before going to bed and I could have sworn he winked at me.'

'I'm sure he winked in heaven,' Rose said. 'Or wherever he is.'

'I'd say he's there and that Caroline gave him a roasting when he joined her,' Lily suggested.

'Were they happy together?' Rose wondered.

'By all accounts they were,' Lily said, helping herself to a slice of soda bread from the basket. 'But she was worried about his gambling.'

'So much that she hid those documents,' Rose remarked and took a sip of tea. 'If she hadn't, we might not be in this fix now.'

Lily frowned. 'I know, but where did she hide them? It says behind the magnolia tree in her notes, but what on earth does that mean?'

'A riddle?' Vi spread butter on a piece of toast. 'Is it something from a poem? Or a song?'

Lily got up from the table. 'I have a feeling we'll never know. I think we should start getting ready. Who wants the bathroom first? I have to check some emails for Wolfie before I start getting dressed, and then I'm helping Granny with her outfit and her hair and makeup, so I can use her bathroom and get dressed there.'

'I'll have the bathroom now, if it's okay?' Vi paused and looked at her sisters. 'But first, I have a surprise for you.'

'You got the main part in that movie,' Rose suggested.

Vi laughed. 'No, it's not about me. It's something Granny gave me to give to you both.' Vi went to the desk in the living room and picked up two small very scuffed velvet boxes and handed one each to Lily and Rose. 'The family jewellery for you to wear tonight.'

'Oh how fabulous,' Rose squealed and opened her box, revealing a necklace of blue topazes and pearls. 'My favourite piece of all of them.'

Lily opened hers and found to her delight it contained the double rows of pearls with the diamond clasp Caroline Fleury had worn in her portrait.

'Wow, it's the crown jewels,' Vi exclaimed. 'They'll look gorgeous on you with your dress.'

Lily held up the necklace against the light, the pearls glimmering with a pinkish hue. 'The pearls are still so luminous even after all these years.'

'So beautiful,' Rose agreed. 'What are you wearing, Vi? The emeralds?'

'Yes,' Vi replied. 'Set in gold filigree. That's probably the oldest piece in the whole collection, except for the diamond necklace, but Granny's wearing that. And,' she added, her eyes shining, 'there is something else I was to tell you.'

'What?' Lily asked. 'There's more?'

Vi nodded. 'Not about more jewellery, but that it's yours to keep.'

'You mean we don't have to give it back to Granny?' Rose asked incredulously.

'No,' Vi replied. 'Granny said she wants to enjoy seeing you wearing it and not wait until she's gone. She thought it was better being used than being hidden away somewhere. I am guessing she doesn't want to have to worry about it any more.'

'How sensible,' Lily remarked, putting the pearls back in the box.

Rose started to gather up the plates and cups on the table. 'You can take the bathroom now, Vi, and I'll tidy up here.'

Lily handed Rose her cup. 'Thanks, Rose. I'll just check through Wolfie's emails and then I'll go and help Granny get dressed.'

'Brilliant.' Rose got up, smiling at Lily. 'You're a star to help Granny, Lily-lou.'

Lily smiled. 'I love doing her up. She's so pretty and feminine. And we have fun.'

'She's always fun to be with before a party,' Rose said. 'She's a real party princess.'

'Always was,' Vi said.

'Isn't it great to be here together?' Lily asked as she walked into the living room with her laptop. 'It's like the old days.'

'Better than the old days,' Vi argued. 'We're all grown up with jobs we love and we've settled into life as adults.'

Lily stopped and looked at Vi. 'Yeah, but what about you? Any men in your life right now?'

Vi shook back her red hair and shrugged. 'Men? Nah. Not really interested in them right now. I want to build my career. I need to have a strong foundation before I head into any kind of relationship. Better to invest in that than giving it up for a man.'

'Who says you have to give it up?' Rose asked.

'Oh with men, you always have to give up something,' Vi

said. 'And that's okay if you have built up a name in any kind of business. Then you're strong and can't be broken.'

'Isn't she sensible?' Rose said to Lily.

'Very wise,' Lily agreed. 'I'm with you, Vi. No men for me either right now. Not for a long time.'

Vi lifted one of her slim eyebrows. 'Really? I could have sworn there were vibes between you and what's his name – Dominic – yesterday.'

Lily felt her face flush. 'Don't know what you mean.'

'No? You must be blind,' Violet stated. 'The way he was looking at you...'

'He wasn't looking at me in any way,' Lily protested. 'You're just making it up.'

'No, I'm not,' Vi insisted. 'I know when two people are attracted to each other, I can feel it in the air. I'm an actress and I'm very tuned in to those kinds of vibes and auras.'

'Stop it, Vi!' Lily snapped. 'There is nothing between that man and me. Nothing at all and there never will be.'

'Why not?' Rose asked, raising an eyebrow slightly at Lily's reaction to Vi's teasing. 'I thought you liked him too.'

'Never mind.' Lily pulled out the chair at the desk and sat down, turning on the laptop. 'I have to do this and then go up to Magnolia. I know Granny is very nervous about her speech and the party. She needs someone to hold her hand.'

'Okay.' Rose started to gather up the breakfast dishes, looking as if she wanted to say something else but had changed her mind when she looked at Lily's stern face.

Vi went up the stairs to have her shower and Lily checked the emails, dealt with a few queries she hadn't had time to reply to the day before. Then her phone pinged with a message from Brian.

Granny still poorly but she gave me something to give to you, so I'll bring it to the party today, if that's all right?

Lily sent him a text back to say it was fine. She had invited him to the party because she felt that, as his granny had worked at Magnolia Manor when she was young, he had a connection to the house and family. Sylvia had even said she remembered Brian's granny working at the house back in the 1950s. Lily wondered what it was the old woman wanted her to have. She hoped she'd be able to visit her in the nursing home soon and maybe get some kind of clue as to where the deeds had been hidden all those years ago. Maybe she'd understand Caroline's riddle.

Then her thoughts drifted to Dominic and what Vi had said. *The way he looked at me... Did he?* she wondered. *I tried not to look at him so he wouldn't guess how confused I feel. And how I'm so worried about his connection to the Bernards. I was so attracted to him and felt such a strong connection. But now, after what I saw in his house, I'm not sure how I feel. I need answers to all my questions and he has to come clean and tell me the truth. But when?* Lily shook her head. *Not now anyway, that's not possible. It has to wait until after the party. But then I will get the truth out of him, whatever it takes.*

She closed the laptop with a bang, chiding herself for letting her feelings get the better of her again. She had to push it all away and concentrate on today. Her only job should be to support her grandmother and make the party an event that would be remembered for many years to come – even if the Fleury family were no longer in residence.

20

Sylvia sat at her dressing table in her bedroom waiting for Lily. She looked at the typed pages of the welcome speech she had written the day before and read it out yet again. It wasn't a long speech, just a few words to thank everyone for coming and to explain that this might be the last Magnolia party. Times were changing and there would soon be a new owner of the old manor that had belonged to the Fleury family for more than two hundred years.

Tears welled up in Sylvia's eyes as she read those words, and she wondered if she would be able to say them out loud without crying in front of all those people: friends and family and trusted employees who all loved Magnolia Manor nearly as much as she did. She looked around the room, at the walls hung with beautiful seascapes, oil paintings with gold frames of the house and gardens, a few little portraits and pictures of loved dogs and horses long gone to heavenly pastures. The fourposter bed she had shared with her husband, Liam, until he died, the tall windows swathed in richly embroidered curtains and the delicate antique dressing table she was sitting at. A lovely room that had been her haven nearly all her adult life. How could she bear to leave it? And how was she going to cope with this stranger arriving at the party? She pulled a tissue out of the box on the dressing table and dabbed her eyes as there was a knock on the door.

'Come in,' Sylvia called, trying to pull herself together.

The door opened and Lily came into the room carrying a white dress with a pattern of small pink magnolia flowers that she laid on the bed. 'Hello, Granny.'

'Is that your outfit?' Sylvia asked.

'Yes,' Lily replied. 'I found it in a shop near the harbour. It's perhaps a little too summery for the beginning of March, but I think it suits the occasion.'

'And it goes with the pearls,' Sylvia added.

Lily nodded. 'Yes, and Rose said the whole effect is gorgeous.'

'She is right.' Sylvia smiled. 'You are the eldest granddaughter, so it's right for you be the most elegant woman at the party.'

'No, that will be you,' Lily protested. 'Is it okay for me to change here and use your bathroom?'

'Of course.' Sylvia held out her hand, comforted by Lily's arrival. 'Come here and sit beside me for a bit. There is no rush, we can take our time to get ready.'

Lily joined Sylvia on the little padded bench in front of the dressing table and put her arm around her. 'You're sad.'

Sylvia nodded and handed Lily the piece of paper. 'Yes. It's this speech. I don't know if I'll be able to say all that in front of everyone without breaking down.'

'It's a lovely speech,' Lily said when she had looked through it. 'But Granny, it's all wrong. We haven't given up, have we? Once Mr Lucey is back at his desk we'll see Granddad's will and then we can contest this claim. I'm sure of it.'

'Do you really think so?' Sylvia asked, looking at her beautiful granddaughter. There was such kindness in those dark eyes it nearly made her cry again.

'Yes, I do,' Lily declared, looking defiant. 'So you can tear up that speech and just smile and say welcome and thanks for coming like you usually do.'

'Oh,' Sylvia said, feeling unsure. 'I suppose you're right. Or you would be if it wasn't for...' She stopped, not knowing how to continue.

'Wasn't for what?' Lily suddenly looked annoyed. 'Is there something else going on you're not telling me? Please, spit it out. I can't bear all this secrecy any more.'

Sylvia looked into those dark eyes, now no longer sad and kind, but hard and determined and slightly disappointed. 'Oh,' she said again, pulling herself up. Lily was right. They could not surrender. And in order to fight she had to tell Lily what was happening. 'He's coming here,' she said in a low voice.

'Who?' Lily asked.

'That man. Arnaud Bernard,' Sylvia whispered.

'He's coming here? When?'

Sylvia sighed. 'Today. I got an email from him last night saying he'll come here later today and that he has something to discuss with me.'

'Discuss!' Lily exclaimed. 'You mean he's going to let you know when we have to leave?'

Sylvia shrugged. 'I have no idea. That's all it said. I didn't reply. Thought it was no use asking questions. We'll just have to see what he has to say. He might tell us he's going to take us to court or something. And then what do we do?'

Lily looked thoughtful. 'Let's not panic. One thing at a time. He will probably arrive during the party and we'll just carry on until the guests have left. Then we can have a chat with him. I'm going to ask Wolfie to be present so we have some kind of legal backup.'

Sylvia nodded, feeling calmer. 'Good idea. And we might tell him we have Liam's will. And then we will tell him we're not taking this lying down and that they will *not* get their hands

on our house without a very long fight. So they can kiss whatever plans they have goodbye.'

'Oh God, I hope they're not planning to put some huge
modern block here,' Lily said. 'Not that it would happen
straight away, even if they can prove they own it. I would
imagine it would take a long time to get planning permission.
This is an historic building, after all.'

Sylvia stared at Lily, feeling a dart of hope. 'Is it?' Then she
nodded. 'Yes, of course it is. Hmm. That might be a fact in our
favour. If we tell this man and his son that it could take years to
get planning permission, they might not want this place after
all. What do you think?'

Lily looked thoughtful, a little smile playing on her lips.
'Yes, and we might even say there is a law that owners of histor-
ical buildings have to make certain repairs to stop them falling
down. Like the roof, which could run into millions.'

'That would be lying,' Sylvia said sternly.

Lily grinned. 'I know, but wouldn't it be fun to watch them
worry about how much that would cost?'

Sylvia touched Lily's cheek. 'You're still the bold little girl I
remember.' She ran her hand down Lily's silky dark hair. 'But
you have grown into a beautiful woman. I sometimes miss that
naughty little girl with the gap in her front teeth and that
cheeky smile. But then sometimes she comes back, making me
smile when I feel sad.'

'I had my teeth fixed,' Lily said, looking back at Sylvia in the
mirror. 'But that's all I've had done.'

'Teeth are fine,' Sylvia said. 'But don't touch anything else.
You're lovely as you are.'

Lily pouted her lips. 'Not even a little silicone to make this
pout permanent?'

'Absolutely not,' Sylvia exclaimed, horrified at the idea of
Lily's face being altered in any way. She had a unique beauty

with strong features that would look even better as she grew older.

'I was kidding.' Lily poked Sylvia with her elbow. 'I'm not going to do all that stuff. It hurts and is very expensive. I can think of a lot more fun things to do with money like that. Not that I have much of it yet,' she added with a laugh. Then she sat back and looked at Sylvia. 'But hey, we have to start making you stunning. You have to be the belle of the ball today. Strong, classy and stunning, that's us.'

'You girls, yes. But me? How is that going to be even remotely possible?' Sylvia asked, staring at herself in the mirror. 'This old face will never again be much to look at.'

'Oh but you're wrong,' Lily protested. 'You're beautiful, with wonderful bone structure and those lovely brown eyes. With just a little bit of makeup, and your hair done, you'll look gorgeous.'

'Gorgeous?' Sylvia said with a snort. 'I think that would be too much of a challenge even for you.'

'Of course not. Trust me, I got a few tips from Vi. And she gave me some makeup stuff to use. She's a true professional.'

'Actress, yes,' Sylvia said. 'But she's no magician.'

'Never mind that,' Lily argued. 'I want to have a go at it, so just relax. What are you going to wear?'

'A red dress I've had for ages, but I haven't worn it for a few years. It's quite simple and shouldn't look too old fashioned.'

'Red?' Lily nodded. 'Perfect colour for you. The diamond necklace will look fabulous with that. And I think I know the dress you mean. Fine wool. Very simple with long sleeves. Makes you look like Jackie Kennedy – or the way she would have looked if she'd lived to be—'

'A hundred like me?' Sylvia interrupted, laughing.

'No,' Lily protested and got up to get her tote bag. 'You're ageless, Granny.'

'I like that. Ageless,' Sylvia mumbled and leaned forward to study her face in the mirror. 'You're ageless, baby,' she said to her reflection.

'And you'll be a beauty when I've finished with you.' Lily opened her bag and took out a box that, when she opened it, Sylvia saw was full of all kinds of makeup and brushes. 'Close your eyes, Granny, and think of lovely things. Don't open them until I say so. And... relax.'

Sylvia sighed deeply, closed her eyes and started to enjoy Lily's feather-light fingers sweeping over her skin and eyelids. She forgot her sorrows and stress and slowly felt herself relax, looking forward to the party instead of dreading it. She would give that French man a piece of her mind and make him sorry he even started trying to take over her home.

When Lily told Sylvia to open her eyes, she blinked and looked at the face staring back at her with a surprised expression.

'Goodness,' Sylvia said, delighted. 'Is that me?' She didn't look that many years younger, but her skin was smoother and fresher and her eyes lovely, and there was just a hint of colour on her lips. 'I look like myself but much improved,' she finally said. 'A better version of me.'

Lily nodded with a satisfied expression. 'I didn't want to plaster you, just bring out your best features and make you a little brighter and more polished.' She took a hairbrush from the bag and started brushing Sylvia's hair. 'Now we'll just give this a little brush through and, when you've put on your dress and the necklace, we'll slip on your black velvet hairband and you're done. I suppose you're wearing black tights under that dressing gown and you'll be putting on black shoes?'

'Yes.' Sylvia got up and went to her wardrobe to take out the dress.

'Great.' Lily put away the brush and the box with makeup. 'Why don't you get dressed while I have a shower in your bathroom? Then we'll finish your hair and we'll go downstairs together. You'll want to check everything before the guests arrive. I saw the caterers' truck driving up the avenue when I got here.'

Sylvia smiled. 'Excellent idea, darling. I think Vi and Rose will be here soon, so we can go through everything together.'

Lily nodded as she stood at the ensuite bathroom door. 'Grand. It's good we're together. It's not going to be easy to face everything. What do you want to do about your speech?'

'I think you were right. Maybe I shouldn't say anything at all?' Sylvia suggested. 'Forget the farewell speech and just enjoy ourselves?'

Lily laughed. 'Party like there's no tomorrow, you mean?'

'Exactly,' Sylvia replied. 'Tomorrow is tomorrow, but today we're here and we'll have a good time and win the battle.'

Lily punched the air. 'Yes!'

Sylvia smiled, touched by the determination in Lily's eyes. 'If there is a way, we'll find it. Somehow, somewhere.'

But as the bathroom door closed behind Lily, Sylvia felt a dart of dread. Despite the gung-ho attitude and the brave words, she felt the end was near – the end of the Fleurys of Magnolia Manor. It would never be the same again.

21

Lily walked into the ballroom with Sylvia, feeling both excited and nervous. They had spent a lot of time and hard work preparing the room, and more money than usual on the buffet. But as she saw the big table, with all the food laid out and the rows of champagne flutes glittering in the rays of sunshine shining in through the tall windows, she felt it was worth it. If this was to be the last Magnolia party hosted by the Fleury family, it would be the best ever.

'Look at all the little sandwiches and finger food,' Rose exclaimed when she joined them. 'Smoked salmon, shrimp, tiny slivers of roast beef with horseradish cream, mini tomatoes with mozzarella and basil, chicken on skewers with a chilli mayo dip. So delicious.'

'And the piece de resistance. Isn't it amazing?' Lily said, pointing at the cake, a replica of the manor with a magnolia tree made of chocolate and pale pink marzipan.

'So fabulous,' Rose said. 'I'm suddenly starving.'

'Hands off until the guests arrive,' Lily warned Rose, who looked wonderful in a blue dress with tiny white hearts, which went perfectly with the lovely topaz necklace.

'Look, here's Granny,' Rose announced. 'Doesn't she look fabulous?'

Lily turned and looked at her grandmother walking towards her, very pleased with what she had achieved. Sylvia looked wonderful with just a hint of colour in her cheeks and lips. Her eyelids had a touch of brown eyeshadow and mascara, which all enhanced her looks without overdoing it. Her hair gleamed and the red dress with its classic lines suited her to perfection. Vi, walking beside her grandmother, had true star quality in her vintage green dress, the emeralds and her red hair in a chignon. Lily knew her own dress matched the pearl and diamond necklace perfectly and that her hair and makeup, after following Vi's instructions, made her look amazing.

'What a lovely bouquet of Fleurys,' Martin's voice said beside them. 'I don't know who's the prettiest, but together you are a knockout.'

'We did our best,' Sylvia said, smiling at him. 'And you have certainly done a wonderful job with the room. It looks magnificent.'

'It wasn't just me,' Martin protested. 'Dominic, Nora and your girls all helped and made it look like this.'

'They have all been fantastic. But I see that the guests are arriving,' Sylvia interrupted. 'We should stand by the door and say hello.' She clapped her hands. 'Girls, come with me and help me make everyone feel welcome.'

Lily, Rose and Violet did as they were told and stood beside Sylvia at the door, shaking hands or kissing cheeks, saying 'welcome,' and 'lovely to see you,' and 'please help yourself to food and drink.'

After about half an hour, as Lily was still greeting guests, she felt as if she had shaken hands with about two thousand people from all over Ireland, even though Sylvia had told her it was 'only around a hundred and twenty'. But her back ached and her hand felt quite tender and she was dying to get something to eat and drink. The room was now packed with people enjoying the amazing buffet and the champagne. The musician Dominic had recommended sat down on the gallery above them with her harp, and soon soft music began to waft through the ballroom. The tune was so lovely it stopped the conversations, and when she had finished everyone applauded enthusiastically. She smiled and bowed and then sat down again and played another tune, but by then the conversation was back in full swing.

Lily noticed that there were only a few people left to greet, one of which was Dominic, dressed in a blazer and light blue shirt. He was cleanshaven, which made him look years younger, and it showed off his square jaw and wide mouth as he smiled at Lily. There was an expression of delight in his green eyes as he looked at her and, before she could stop him, he had kissed her on the cheek.

'Hi, Lily,' he said, stepping back to study her for a moment. 'You look beautiful today.'

'Thank you,' she said, feeling her face flush. 'You're not too bad yourself,' she countered, momentarily forgetting her suspicions about that letter she had seen in his house.

He laughed and looked as if he was about to say something, but Brian from the pub, carrying a parcel, stepped forward, taking Lily's hand.

'I have the package for you from my granny,' he said and held it out to her. 'It's Mrs Caroline's painting. Granny wanted you to have it. She said it should be given back to the family and the time is right for you to have it, whatever that means.'

Lily took the parcel. 'Thank you, Brian. I'll open it after the party. I'm sure it's a lovely painting.'

'Granny loved it,' Brian said. 'It reminded her of happy times here. I think Mrs Caroline was kind to her.'

'I'm sure she was,' Lily replied. 'Now, you'd better hurry to help yourself to food and wine before it's all gone. I can see that everyone has piled their plates with everything.'

'I will. See you later,' he said before he disappeared into the throng.

Lily looked around for Dominic but he had gone to chat with Sylvia. Rose was already at the big table helping herself. There were no more new arrivals so she was free to mingle, and there was no sign of any strangers that might have come in unannounced. She assumed the Bernards would appear later and decided to try to forget about them for the moment. She had called Wolfie and asked him to come, but there was no sign of him either. Weak with hunger, Lily pushed through the crowd to get something to eat. On the way there, she met Nora and handed her Brian's gift, asking her to put it in the study. Then Lily continued to the buffet where she saw Vi holding out a glass of champagne.

'Here. You need this after all the handshakes.' She handed Lily the glass, then held out a plate with a small pile of the delicious food. 'I grabbed some before it was too late. Get this down before it's time to cut the cake and Granny makes her speech.'

'Thanks, Vi, just what I needed.' Lily wolfed down shrimps, a sausage roll and a smoked salmon sandwich. Feeling better, she smiled at Dominic, who was pushing through the crowd towards her.

'That seems to have hit the spot,' he said when he was beside her.

'Oh yes, it did.' Lily dabbed her mouth with a paper napkin. 'It was exhausting standing there shaking hands and saying "welcome, how nice to see you." But they are all friends of the family or people who have been kind to us, so I felt I should greet them so Granny could take a break.'

'And then your sisters escaped and left you on your own,' he remarked.

Lily shrugged. 'Yeah I know. But being the older sister, I'm used to taking charge.'

'You've spoilt them.' He took her arm. 'But let's forget about them. I'd like you to hear something nice.'

'Like what?' She looked at him, confused by his smile.

'It's outside. Come with me.' He gently guided her through the packed ballroom and opened one of the French windows.

'But I...' Lily gestured at the guests.

'They won't mind. Come on,' he urged, pulling her out to the terrace.

Lily stepped outside and Dominic closed the door behind them. Here on the terrace it was blissfully cool and quiet and the mild air smelled of damp earth and grass. Lily felt herself relax and watched the sun dipping behind the trees in the distance.

'So,' she said, looking at Dominic, remembering all her pent-up suspicions and resentments. She needed an answer and this was a good opportunity. 'I need to ask you something important.'

'*Shh*,' he said. 'Just wait and listen.'

'But I—'

'Hold on just a second,' he whispered. 'This is magical.'

Lily stood there, waiting for a few minutes while all was quiet. And then she heard it in the distance: *cuckoo, cuckoo.*

'Oh. It's the cuckoo,' she said in a near whisper. Then she heard it again and again, that gentle, soft sound that meant spring was here. 'I love that sound.'

'Me too.' Dominic's eyes were inscrutable as he looked at her. 'Even if it means a big, sneaky bird has just left its egg in a smaller bird's nest for them to bring up. But it says to me that nature is amazing and mysterious.'

'And magical,' Lily said. But she didn't mean nature, but rather this moment so full of something she had thought was lost. There had to be some kind of explanation to everything; he simply couldn't have betrayed them by liaising with the people who threatened to take over their home. It just wasn't possible.

She could see the emotion in his eyes when he suddenly leaned forward and his lips nearly touched hers before he drew back.

'I'm sorry. It was just that you looked so...'

'So...?' she asked. Then she touched his face with her fingertips, wanting to ask how he felt but unable to find the words.

'I have something to tell you,' he said, taking a step back, looking as if he regretted what could have ended in a kiss. 'Something you should know.'

'Oh?' she said, the letter with the name and address of the Bernards popping into her mind. She had forgotten, for just a moment, about the possibility of Dominic being dishonest. And then there was the photo of the woman...

They had nearly kissed a minute ago but now she had a feeling he was going to tell her he wasn't single. She had also momentarily forgotten all about the party, her sisters and her grandmother, but then there was a movement at the window and she saw Rose smiling at them, then gesturing wildly for Lily to come back in.

Lily stepped away. 'I have to go,' she said, trying to steady her heart and regain her breath. 'Granny must be ready to make her speech and cut the cake. But I... we... need to talk. You had something to tell me, you said.'

'Yes.' He nodded. 'I do. But now there are other things for you to worry about. So until we can get together again, I just want to tell you how amazing I think you are.' He reached out and tucked a strand of her hair behind her ear.

'Thank you,' she said awkwardly, not knowing quite what he meant, but enjoying the feel of his touch.

'Could you come to my house tomorrow?' he asked. 'We could have breakfast and then take a walk on the beach. And talk.'

Lily hesitated. 'That sounds great, but maybe not tomorrow. Things are a little difficult right now.'

'Okay,' he said, looking disappointed. 'Well, sometime when things settle down for you, then. Just let me know.' He stepped away. 'And now I will leave you to your duties.'

'You're not staying for the cake and the speech?' she asked, feeling instantly disappointed.

'No. That's for old friends and family. And I need to feed Larry and take him out for a bit.' He took her hand one last time. 'Goodbye for now, Lily,' he said before he disappeared into the shadows.

'Goodbye,' she whispered.

But he was already gone and she wondered if she had dreamt it all. But no, there was Rose, smiling at her from the French window she had just opened.

'Sorry to interrupt that romantic moment,' she said as she pulled Lily inside. 'But Granny is asking for you and she needs support right now.'

'Yes, of course.' Still flustered after what had happened between her and Dominic, Lily walked with Rose to the table with the cake, where Sylvia and Vi were waiting.

'There you are,' Sylvia said, looking relieved. 'I was looking for you.'

'I was just getting some fresh air on the terrace,' Lily explained, trying to regain her composure. But she was breathless and her face felt hot after the encounter with Dominic.

'Fresh air was not all she was getting,' Rose said with a wink.

'What do you mean, Rose?' Sylvia asked with a steely look.

'Nothing,' Rose replied when Lily shot her a warning glance. 'I was just messing.'

'This is not a time for messing,' Sylvia said sternly. 'Please, girls, pull yourselves together.'

Rose nodded, looking chastened. 'Sorry, Granny.'

Sylvia nodded. 'That's better.' She looked around. 'Where's Martin?'

'He went into the library to get something for you,' Vi replied.

Sylvia nodded. 'All right. We'll just wait for him, then.'

Vi prodded Lily in the side with her elbow. 'Who's that man over there?' she asked. 'The tall one with the white hair standing near the window. Looks kind of distinguished. I don't think I've ever seen him before.'

Lily looked across the room at the man Vi was referring to. Tall, with a shock of white hair and a square jaw, he was very handsome and held himself with old-fashioned elegance. He was dressed in grey slacks, an expensive-looking navy blazer, a white shirt and blue and red silk tie.

'Cary Grant lives,' she whispered to Vi. 'Never seen him before. And he doesn't seem to know anyone.' Then it occurred to her who he could be. 'Oh, no, that must be...' she started as her heart contracted.

'Who?' Vi asked.

They were interrupted by Rose clinking a fork against her glass. 'It's time for Sylvia to cut the cake,' she announced when the guests finally stopped chatting. 'And what a magnificent cake it is, you must agree. Could we have a round of applause for the Cakes and Buns Galore bakery in Tralee?'

Everyone clapped and some even shouted and whistled. Then Sylvia stepped up beside Rose and asked for silence. The applause died down and everyone looked expectantly at her.

Sylvia cleared her throat. 'Hello, everyone! I hope you're having a good time. Thank you all for coming and for making this party so extra special. I was going to make a sad little speech about it being the last party hosted by the Fleurys, but then I decided to forget about that and just have a good time.'

'Good idea!' someone shouted.

'Why the last time?' someone else asked.

'It's complicated,' Sylvia replied. 'There is a legal dispute over the ownership of our house with a certain family in France. But we're trying to stop them, and it could take a long time to solve. So we have decided to think positively and not worry too much about it until we have to. We're preparing for the worst but hoping for the best.'

'And partying!' the first voice shouted.

'Exactly.' Sylvia smiled. 'We'll enjoy the moment. And I see you've all done exactly that.' She turned to Martin, who had appeared by her side. 'And now, I'm going to cut this amazing cake. Martin, give me the sword.'

'The sword?' Rose hissed in Lily's ear. 'What sword?'

'I don't know,' Lily whispered back, as Martin handed Sylvia what looked indeed like a very old sword. 'Must be something she found in the attic.'

'Don't worry, we cleaned it,' Sylvia said in a loud voice. 'It's a ceremonial sword that hasn't killed anyone. It was part of a uniform from the eighteen twenties. And now...' The blade gleamed in the light from the chandelier as Sylvia neatly cut a piece from the amazing cake, as if she had done this all her life. 'There,' she shouted. 'The first piece. And now we'll cut the rest up with a normal cake knife. You'll all get a piece. But before that,' she said, holding a glass of champagne in the air, 'we will all drink to the Fleury era at Magnolia Manor. It might come to an end if we're forced to leave, but our spirit will remain here forever.' Sylvia's eyes were suddenly full of tears as she drank the toast, the sword still in her other hand.

'Stop!' a loud voice called out, in a foreign accent, beside Sylvia and the girls. 'It is *not* the end of the Fleurys.' They all turned to stare at the distinguished-looking older man who had managed to get to them through the throng of guests.

'What?' Sylvia stammered. 'Who are you?'

He bowed. 'Arnaud Bernard, Madame.'

'What?' Sylvia snapped, her eyes blazing. 'Arnaud...'

'How dare you come here?' Rose shouted, glaring at the man. 'Did you not get our letter? You're trespassing and I will call the Guards.' She looked at Lily. 'You call them, Lily. We will have this man thrown out of here as soon as—'

'No!' Sylvia protested. 'Stop it, Rose. I knew he was coming but I thought...' She turned to the man. 'It's not right for you to be here at this moment,' she said, her voice shaking. 'We need to talk to you, but not in the middle of our lovely party.'

Arnaud Bernard took Sylvia's arm. 'Please calm down, Madame Fleury. I have come to tell you that—'

'Leave me alone, Monsieur Bernard.' Sylvia broke away from his grip. 'I don't want to hear it. I'd rather see you in court.'

'No, no,' Mr Bernard interrupted. 'There will be no court case, Madame Fleury. If you would just listen to what I have to say, you will see that all will be well and the Fleury family has nothing to fear from us.' He paused. 'Could you put away that sword, please?' he continued, looking at it nervously.

Sylvia stared at him for a moment. Then she turned to Martin and held out the sword. 'Please take this, Martin. It's getting a little heavy.' She turned back to Arnaud Bernard, looking more composed. 'I'm listening.'

He seemed to suddenly notice all the guests now gathered around them, looking as if they found what was going on hugely interesting. 'Would it be possible to talk in private?' he asked. 'There's a lot to discuss.'

Sylvia nodded. 'We can go to my study. But I want my granddaughter Lily to be there with me. Rose and Vi, please see to the guests and make sure everyone gets a piece of cake.' She looked at Monsieur Bernard. 'Right. Let's go and have that discussion.'

'Of course,' he said, gesturing at the door. 'After you, ladies.'

Sylvia waved to the guests before she and Lily walked out of the room. 'Won't be a minute,' she called. 'Enjoy the cake.'

Lily glanced at her sisters and shot them a reassuring smile.

She didn't know what was going on or what the outcome would be, but she began somehow to see a light on the horizon. Whatever happened next, she felt in her bones that Arnaud Bernard was not, as they had imagined, the ogre who would throw them out of their home. But what had he come to tell them?

22

The study was cold as the fire hadn't been lit, but Lily quickly put a match to the pile of logs in the grate and switched on lamps while Sylvia sat down on the sofa, her hands in her lap. Her face was pale but she looked composed and ready to hear what Arnaud Bernard had to say.

'Please, sit down, Mr Bernard,' Sylvia said, indicating the chair beside her.

'Thank you,' he said and sat down, looking slightly awkward.

Lily settled beside Sylvia on the sofa and took her granny's cold hand, holding it tightly to show her support, while Arnaud Bernard turned to them both.

'As I said,' he started, 'you have nothing to fear from me. I have come with a proposition.'

'So you said.' Sylvia looked at him coldly.

Arnaud Bernard nodded. 'Please listen. As you know, this property, a very beautiful house with wonderful gardens, was once given to my father by Cornelius Fleury as payment for his gambling debts.'

'Yes,' Sylvia said impatiently, 'I got your letter telling me so.'

Mr Bernard nodded. 'Exactly. I'm sorry if it caused you pain. That letter was written by my son without my knowledge and he only told me about it later. I was going to write to apologise to you and see if we couldn't solve the problem together, but when I told my son we should give you back the house as a gift or something like that, he didn't agree. Then I had an idea that might be good for both of us.'

'Both of whom?' Sylvia asked. 'You and your son?'

'No, you and me. Let me explain.' Arnaud Bernard pulled an envelope from his inside pocket and handed it to Sylvia. 'This is my proposal that I hope you will like.'

Sylvia pulled out some sheets of papers that she studied for a while. When she had finished reading, she stared at him and said, 'A partnership?'

'Yes, that's right,' he replied. 'We could work together on restoring the house and turning it into a profitable business. We would own the property together, half and half. And we could create a limited company and develop this place into something amazing. A luxury hotel with a spa area, pool, gym and a restaurant. All five star and gold standard.' He paused and looked at Sylvia expectantly.

'Hmm,' was all Sylvia said, flicking through the papers. 'Interesting. Or it would be if you truly had a legal right to Magnolia Manor.' She fixed him with a steely look. 'But you don't, so this is all pie in the sky at the moment. A pipe dream,' she added. 'Castles in the air.' She handed Arnaud the papers and got up. 'I will think about it though. But now it's late and I'm tired and want to go to bed. It's been a very long day.'

Arnaud Bernard got up. 'But I...' He stopped, looking a little awkward, as if torn between good behaviour and a desire to fight his corner. 'Of course. I understand,' he said, politeness seeming to win. 'We could perhaps meet in the morning and discuss this further?'

'If I can get a hold of my lawyer, yes,' Sylvia said graciously.

'I will let you know. How can I contact you?'

Arnaud pulled a small case from the pocket of his blazer. 'I can give you my phone number.'

'Please give it to my granddaughter Lily,' Sylvia replied. 'Goodnight, Mr Bernard.' Then she sailed out of the room, her back straight.

Arnaud stared at the door that had just closed behind Sylvia, looking slightly shellshocked. He turned to Lily. 'Your *grand-mère* is...'

'I know,' Lily said. 'Stubborn and feisty.'

'No,' he replied with a strange glint in his eyes. 'I was going to say quite... *magnifique*.'

'Oh.' Lily stared at him for a moment. 'Well, yes,' she said, 'that too. And a little scary sometimes.'

He laughed and fished a card from the case he'd retrieved. 'She doesn't frighten me. My card with my contact details. Could you make sure Madame Fleury gets it?'

Lily nodded. 'Of course. I will put it on her desk so she sees it first thing tomorrow.'

He nodded and went to the door. 'Thank you. And now I will leave. I hope to see you soon, Mademoiselle Fleury.'

'Ah, eh, yes,' Lily mumbled as he beamed that charming smile at her. 'Goodnight, Mr Bernard.'

'Goodnight,' he replied before he closed the door softly behind him.

Lily slowly got up from the sofa, trying to take in all that had happened. Sylvia had been amazingly strong and hadn't been tempted by the offer of a partnership with Arnaud Bernard. Lily would have done exactly the same. Accepting that deal would have meant giving up and there was no way they would do that.

But Arnaud Bernard's reaction had been surprising to say the least. He seemed impressed with Sylvia and even a little smitten. Lily smiled. Granny still had what it took to attract a man, even though they were both a little older. There was no age limit to romance, and if they could resolve their differences, who knew what might happen?

Lily put Arnaud's card on the desk and picked up the parcel with Caroline's painting that Nora had put there. She'd open it when she got to the gatehouse. It would be lovely to see it.

'What happened?' Vi asked when Lily returned to the ballroom where the party was still in full swing.

'Yes, tell us,' Rose urged. 'It was good news I take it?'

'Not exactly,' Lily replied. 'A kind of stand-off situation. Arnaud Bernard offered Granny a partnership but she laughed in his face and marched out of the room. And then he stood there, staring at me, saying he found her *"magnifique"*, looking totally starstruck or something. So weird.'

'So what's going to happen now?' Rose asked.

'I have no idea,' Lily replied. 'But I have a feeling we need to prove Granny's ownership of Magnolia as soon as possible.'

'Oh gosh,' Rose said, looking alarmed. 'That sounds scary.'

'I'm sure Granny will win in the end,' Vi soothed. She looked across the room at the guests who were still eating, drinking and chatting. 'But let's not ruin the party. It was a huge success and everyone is having a ball. Why don't we join them?'

'Yeah, Lily,' Rose urged. 'Have a drink with us and then we'll mingle.'

'I'm not really in the mood,' Lily protested. 'I think I'll go home now.' The parcel under her arm felt heavy and she wanted to bring it to the gatehouse to open it in peace.

'But we want to have fun,' Vi said. 'The night is young and we thought we'd put some dance music on.'

Lily left them to it. She kissed Rose on the cheek and waved at Vi before she made her way to the door, shaking hands and saying goodbye to the remaining guests. They all thanked her and said it had been a wonderful party. Then she was outside in the garden lit only by the stars and the moon, which gave enough light to find her way along the gravel path to the gatehouse.

She was tired and felt quite overwhelmed with all that had happened today. First her encounter with Dominic on the terrace and then the offer from Arnaud Bernard that had ended so strangely. Finding the missing deeds, or a document that would prove their ownership, now seemed even more urgent. So many things whirled around in Lily's mind. The arrival of Arnaud Bernard had brought no joy to them at all. But once they found those deeds the whole problem could be solved, they could get on with their lives and look to the future. Even if her love life was still uncertain.

Lily thought about Dominic with a mixture of joy and dread. She had momentarily forgotten all her doubts about him when they stood on the terrace and listened to the cuckoo. But now it all came rushing back. She would have to ask him about that letter she had seen, and also about the woman in the photo and who she was. Most of all she needed to know if he had been scheming with the Bernards, in which case she couldn't continue to see him. She wondered if that was why he had snuck off. Was he scared she would see Arnaud recognise him? The thought hurt a lot. It all had to be cleared up as soon as possible. He had said he had something to tell her and she suspected she knew what it was. At the same time, she thought he had feelings for her, but what could the outcome be? He didn't seem to be the kind of man who'd scheme and plot behind people's backs, but she might have let her own feelings cloud her judgement.

Her experience with her ex-husband, Simon, and the painful divorce had made her distrustful of men, even though Dominic had been nothing but honest and kind to her. She looked up at the stars and wondered if they were aligned in her favour. Then she laughed at herself for having such notions. Her happiness wasn't written in the stars or anywhere else in the universe. She would just have to cope with whatever happened and stay strong. Those thoughts made her feel calmer and, as she opened the door to the gatehouse, she was only looking forward to a good night's sleep in order to face the day ahead.

She turned on the light as she came into the living room and was about to put the parcel on the desk to open in the morning when something stopped her. Why not take a look now? It would be a lovely end to the day to see one of Caroline's paintings and maybe put it on the mantlepiece for Rose and Vi to discover when they came home.

Lily tore open the brown paper and found tissue paper underneath, which came away easily to reveal a beautiful little oil painting of the magnolia tree in full bloom. The colours and light were exquisite and the delicate blossoms looked nearly real. Lily gazed at the painting in delight for a moment, lifting it free of its wrappings and holding it out to gaze at it properly. It was then she felt something behind the frame. She turned the painting around and found a thick rectangular envelope stuck to the back. What was this? A message from Caroline to Brian's granny? No, it was too bulky...

She recalled the riddle in Caroline's notebook. Could it be...?

The document proving our ownership is behind the tree. It will only be found if you take it down and turn it around.

Her heart beating, Lily opened the envelope and took out a wad of papers. When she saw what they were she sat frozen in shock, staring at the text on the first page and the handwritten note stuck to the top, trying to take in what it all meant.

23

The next morning, Sylvia woke up feeling quite wonderful. What an evening it had been and what a party. The day had started with such a feeling of gloom and then ended in a kind of victory. She had been trying to suppress her sadness and put on a happy face to look brave and strong, even though her heart was breaking. She had known this could be the last Magnolia party, a farewell to the house she had loved ever since she came here as a young bride over sixty years ago. She had nearly burst into tears as she made her speech and thought it was all over, when that man stepped in and made her that strange offer, which she had refused. The nerve of that man to come here and try to wriggle into the property by saying they could own the house between them. Well, that was not going to happen. But that offer told her Arnaud Bernard was not sure of his case. So they still had a fighting chance, and fight they would do to the bitter end, Sylvia told herself with grim satisfaction.

Hearing Arnaud Bernard suggesting the house could be turned into a hotel felt overwhelming and it had shaken her to the core. She had found it hard to forgive the Bernard family for trying to claim ownership, and right now she knew she never would. Their letter had caused endless sadness and worry from which Sylvia was still trying to recover. But Arnaud Bernard had been charming and apologetic and, she had to admit to herself, she was quite taken with his good looks and old-fashioned charm. She hadn't failed to notice the admiring gleam in his eyes either, and she wondered if she might turn that to her advantage, not for a partnership, but maybe there were other ways he could be useful...

Their conversation in the study had been laced with hostility, but she still felt the afterglow of his admiring glances and lovely voice with the French accent. She would call him today, invite him to walk in the gardens, and she would speak to him of her planned project, a dream that might be realised if she could interest him in that instead of the luxury hotel he wanted to build.

This is the start of a new chapter in my life, she thought, getting out of bed with more energy than she had had for a very long time. She'd better make herself look as good as last night, or he'd lose interest. Not in her, but in her project. She also had to get all her notes, plans and list of names together to present to him so that he saw how much work she had done already. All that was missing were those dratted deeds, but she was confident her solicitor would be able to sort it out, even if it took a long time. Looking forward to the day and what it would bring, Sylvia skipped into the bathroom feeling nearly young again.

Once dressed in a tweed skirt and navy polo neck, she added a string of pearls and brushed her hair that was still in great shape after Lily's efforts last night. Then she went into the study to call Lily, but found Arnaud's business card on the desk and decided to call him instead. Better to get him interested before he came off the boil. She picked up the phone and dialled the number on the card.

He replied at once. 'Arnaud Bernard.'

Sylvia smiled as she heard the deep voice. '*Bonjour,*' she said, her voice light. 'This is Sylvia Fleury.'

'Oh. Good morning, Madame Fleury.'

'Please,' she said. 'Call me Sylvia. And I hope I didn't appear too impolite last night. I was a little upset, you see.'

'You must call me Arnaud. I do understand that you must have been upset and perhaps a little shocked by what I had to say. No hard feelings at all.'

'That's a relief.'

'So,' he continued. 'What can I do for you? You have been thinking about my offer?'

'Yes... and no.' Sylvia paused. 'There will be no half and half ownership, Arnaud. You can put that notion out of your head.'

'Then we're still going to court? Is that what you're saying?' His voice was suddenly cold.

'Not quite. I have another idea I'd like to discuss with you. A possible solution to this problem, and another way for you to be involved with the Magnolia rebuild.'

'What idea?' he asked, his voice brightening slightly.

'It's too complicated to discuss over the phone. Could you come here this morning? It's a lovely day and we could walk in the garden and talk about it.'

He was silent for a moment. 'Well... Yes, I think that would be fine. I was hoping I could see you again, Sylvia, in slightly better circumstances.'

'Then your wish has been granted,' Sylvia said with a laugh. 'We will meet again. And we will be pleasant and polite and not discuss ownership.'

'Oh. *D'accord.* Maybe we should let our lawyers take over?' he suggested.

'Good idea,' Sylvia replied. 'I will call mine in a minute and see what he has found. I will see you later, then. Would eleven o'clock suit you? I have a few things to sort out before we meet.'

'Eleven would be perfect.'

'Excellent. See you then, Arnaud.'

Sylvia hung up with a feeling of satisfaction. He was definitely interested. Whether it was in her or in the idea, it didn't matter. Once she laid out her plans to him he might forget about claiming ownership and realise that her way was the best way for him to be involved with Magnolia Manor.

She gave a start as the phone rang. *Oh no,* she thought, her heart sinking. *He's changed his mind.* But it wasn't Arnaud on the phone.

'Good morning, Granny,' Lily said. 'I hope I didn't wake you.'

'I've been up for hours, darling.'

'Oh good. I hope you're sitting down. I have something startling to tell you.'

'Yes, yes, I'm sitting down,' Sylvia said impatiently. 'What is it? Good news or bad?'

'The best news ever!' Lily exclaimed. And then she told Sylvia what she had found behind the painting.

Sylvia nearly stopped breathing as she listened to what Lily had to say. Oh the joy! It really was the best news she had heard in a very long time.

24

There was a celebratory breakfast at the gatehouse. Lily had
fried bacon and eggs, the smell of which forced Rose and Vi out
of bed.

'I couldn't sleep,' Rose confessed as she sat down at the
table. 'I was so excited after seeing what you had found behind
that gorgeous painting.'

'The deeds,' Vi chortled, tying the cord of her dressing gown
before she joined her sisters. 'Those elusive deeds we have been
trying to find. And they were right under our noses all of last
night.'

'"Behind the tree",' Lily quoted. 'That's what Caroline
meant. Behind the tree in the painting. The deeds must have
been sent to Cornelius around the time she painted it. She must
have put them there after it was framed. We missed them in the
land registry because they were filed under the name of the
townland, not the house. Her name is on it, so she hid them
after Cornelius's death. Then she stuck it behind the painting
and gave it to Brian's granny to keep safe, and it hung in her
home since that time and then on the wall of the nursing home
for the last two years.' Lily looked at the rectangular brown

envelope, wrinkled and stained by time and damp, the papers inside containing all they needed to prove that their grandmother owned Magnolia Manor. Finding it had been like a wish come true. She hadn't believed it at first, but then she read the note in Caroline's spidery handwriting, pinned to the envelope with a paperclip.

This envelope contains all documents proving our ownership of Magnolia Manor: the deeds and a letter from Etienne Bernard returning the property to the Fleury family. I will hide them here for the time being to prevent us losing it yet again. My husband is not responsible enough and my son too young to handle the estate. May whoever finds it keep it safe and hand it to the rightful owner, which, I hope, will be someone sensible.

Caroline Fleury, Magnolia Manor, May 1959

'That letter from Etienne Bernard,' Lily continued. 'That's what really matters. It's our best weapon. All signed and witnessed and perfectly legal.'

'Handing back the property,' Rose filled in. 'Years after Cornelius gave it away.'

'Etienne must have been feeling guilty in his old age,' Vi suggested. 'But how come his son didn't know about it? Or were the Bernards hoping they could pretend the letter didn't exist?'

'I don't think he knew about it,' Lily said. 'Arnaud Bernard seems like a decent, honest man.'

'Good old Great-granny Caroline,' Vi said, helping herself to bacon and eggs from the frying pan Lily had put on the table. 'She wanted to keep the deeds safe so nobody could gamble the house away again.'

'I think that's what she intended,' Lily agreed. 'She wanted to make sure her son Liam inherited the house when Cornelius died.'

Vi held up her mug of tea. 'A toast to our great-grandmother who made sure we would be safe.'

Lily laughed and clinked her mug against Vi's. 'Cheers to that. But I think she was more concerned about her son, our darling granddad, and his little boy Fred at that time. She had no idea we would turn up later on.'

'I wish I had known her,' Rose said with a wistful sigh. 'She seems to have been one hell of a woman.'

'Mega strong,' Lily said. 'Just like our granny, even though they were not related by blood.'

'Maybe the Fleury men always picked feisty women?' Vi suggested.

'Probably,' Rose agreed. 'And I hope we have inherited that feistiness.' She turned her attention to Lily. 'So what about you, then? What happened with you and Dominic on the terrace that made you look so hot and bothered?'

'Nothing.' Lily squirmed as Rose lifted an eyebrow. 'Well, okay. Something happened. But it doesn't mean anything.' The image of the woman in the photo popped into her mind once more and she felt tears prick her eyes. And then there was that letter... She swallowed furiously, trying to compose herself but couldn't stop a tear sliding down her cheek.

'What's wrong?' Rose asked, touching Lily's arm across the table. 'Did he say something mean to you?'

'No, but...' Lily paused. 'He has a girlfriend,' she said, her voice hoarse. That was bad enough. She couldn't bear telling them about the letter and the possibility of Dominic plotting behind their backs.

'Oh no,' Rose exclaimed. 'Was that what he wanted to tell you when you went outside?'

'No,' Lily replied. 'He didn't say anything about her. Didn't mention a girlfriend. He... he said some sweet things and then he almost kissed me.'

'What?' Vi said, looking confused. 'Why did he want to kiss you if he has a girlfriend? And in any case how do you know he has one if he hasn't said?'

'I saw her photo in a frame on the upstairs landing,' Lily said miserably. 'She's blonde and gorgeous.'

'How do you know it's his girlfriend?' Vi asked. 'Could be his sister.'

'He doesn't have a sister,' Lily replied.

'Could be some close relative, though,' Rose suggested. 'Or an old friend. I think you should just ask him. I don't think he's the cheating kind. He seems to me to be a decent guy. A real true blue.'

'You've only met him a few times,' Lily argued. 'How can you know what he's like?'

'Vibes,' Rose said mysteriously. 'I can read people quite easily. I also felt the attraction between the two of you. It's like electric sparks when you look at each other.'

'Rose is right,' Vi cut in. 'You have to ask him. Not sure about the vibes Rose was talking about but he seems okay to me.' She drained her mug and pushed away her empty plate. 'That was delicious. Thanks for cooking breakfast, Lily. But now I think we should go and hand over the deeds and the letter to Granny.'

'If she's home.' Lily checked her watch and nodded. 'Yes, she should be back from mass and in the study reading the Sunday papers. We'd better catch her before she goes out for lunch with one of the groups she's involved in.'

'Networking,' Rose said with a giggle. 'That's what she calls it.'

'I know.' Lily got up and started to gather up the dishes. 'Let's do these first.'

'No, we won't,' Rose said sternly. 'Try not to organise everything for once. We need to catch Granny before she heads out, so let's jump into our clothes and go.'

Lily laughed. 'Okay. You're right. The dishes won't run away. Granny has to be given the documents. She was over the moon when I told her I had found them.'

They were ready to go a little later and, after locking the door, walked up the path together to the big house, Lily carrying the envelope with the deeds. Just as they were about to round the corner of the house to enter by the back door, Lily spotted something out of the corner of her eye. Two people walking arm in arm at the front of the house. She stopped dead and stared at them.

'Look,' she murmured to Vi and Rose. 'There she is. But she's not alone.'

'She's with the French guy,' Vi said.

'Arnaud Bernard,' Rose filled in. 'What is he doing here?'

'Granny seems to be showing him around,' Vi replied. 'And she's pointing up at the façade. But whatever. She has to have told him.'

'Let's see what's going on.' Lily waved at her grandmother. 'Hi, Granny,' she shouted. 'We have the deeds and everything else.'

Sylvia gave a start and let go of Arnaud's arm. 'Oh. Well, that's good. I've just told Arnaud about you finding the deeds and that letter.'

'Great,' Vi panted as she came to a stop in front of the couple. 'It's fabulous news, isn't it?'

'I hope you're not too disappointed, Mr Bernard,' Lily said.

He smiled. 'Yes and no. Of course it was a shock, as we had no idea my father gave the property back. But in a way I'm just as happy. The family honour is restored and we can now carry on and be involved in Magnolia Manor in a better, much happier way without hard feelings or hostilities.'

'Involved – how?' Lily asked, mystified by his good humour

and the obvious closeness between him and Sylvia.

'We will tell you in a moment,' Sylvia replied. 'But first, give me these deeds. I want to see them.'

'Here they are.' Lily held out the envelope to Sylvia.

'Wonderful.' Sylvia looked at Lily for a moment with what looked like tears of joy in her eyes. Then she took the envelope and pulled out the deeds. 'This is such a relief,' she said as she studied the first page. 'It seems like a miracle.' She put the pages back in the envelope and looked at Arnaud Bernard. 'Isn't it wonderful, Arnaud? That means we can go ahead.'

He nodded, smiling broadly at her. 'It certainly does.'

'Go ahead with what?' Rose asked suspiciously.

Sylvia smiled conspiratorially at Arnaud. 'I think we'll keep it between us for now.'

'Yes,' he agreed. 'It's better to finalise everything before we share it with your granddaughters. No need to get excited before everything is in place.'

'In place?' Lily asked, mystified. 'Granny, you have to tell us what's going on here.'

Sylvia patted Lily's cheek. 'I will in time, Lily-lou. Now let's go in and have a cup of coffee in the study. I think it's going to rain and we don't want to get wet, do we?'

'No we don't,' Rose said, folding her arms and glaring at Arnaud Bernard. 'But first I want to say that I think you had some nerve to come here and conspire with our grandmother. Are you still after Magnolia Manor, is that it? First you tried to take it over because you thought you had the right to this whole place because of that old gambling debt, and then, when that didn't work, you present some kind of plan to her so you can take over in a different way.'

'Rose!' Sylvia snapped. 'Stop this right now. I'm perfectly capable of making up my own mind and nobody can fool me into anything. I think you should apologise to Arnaud right now.'

'Not until you tell us what that plan is,' Rose countered. 'I still think he's trying to make you do something that you might be sorry for.'

Arnaud stepped forward and touched Rose's arm. 'Look here, mademoiselle, it is not what you think. I do understand how you feel after all that has happened. But you must know that nobody could make your grandmother do anything against her will. Indeed, it is she who is trying to persuade me to invest in a scheme she has been planning for a long time. She even has some other sponsors on board. It is her wish not to tell you until all is in place. That is her privilege. I cannot do or say anything to change her mind about that.' He looked at Rose sternly. 'No need to apologise to me, but perhaps to your grandmother.'

Rose stared at him for a moment and then dropped her gaze. 'Okay. Sorry, Granny,' she mumbled.

'I forgive you,' Sylvia said, stepping away as raindrops began to fall. 'Come inside, all of you, and we'll have that coffee while we wait for the rain to stop. And I think I will tell you what we're planning after all. You might even like it.'

'Can't wait to hear it,' Lily said as they all hurried towards the house.

'It had better be good,' Rose muttered under her breath.

When they had all settled in the study, and Lily had brought in a tray with coffee and biscuits, Sylvia cleared her throat. 'Now, my darling girls, you have to listen to every word I say without interrupting.'

They all looked at each other and nodded.

'Go ahead,' Lily said. 'We're listening.'

'Good.' Sylvia paused for a moment and then she began to speak.

Lily, Rose and Vi listened to what Sylvia had to say, and as the plans became clear stared at each other in shock.

'I don't believe it,' Rose said, looking appalled. 'Are you serious, Granny?'

25

'Yes,' Sylvia said, returning Rose's shocked eyes with a steely look. 'I'm very serious. This is a project that has been a dream for many years. I have been working hard to find sponsors, architects, builders and an engineer to inspect the structure of this house to see if it's solid enough. And it is, Dominic Doyle assured me.'

'Dominic?' Lily asked, even saying his name stirring up emotions.

'Yes. He's very qualified to do this,' Sylvia replied. 'He's done a full structural survey for me.'

'He has?' Lily stared at her grandmother while a lot of things fell into place. She now understood how Dominic knew all about the structure of the house in what seemed like a short time. But there was something else he had kept from her, and she needed to find out what part he had in the Bernards' attempted takeover of the manor. He had, if not exactly lied, kept the real truth from her, and she needed to know the whole story. She suddenly felt she didn't know him at all.

'Yes,' Sylvia said. 'And he said the structure is very solid. But I didn't know how to get enough funds together to even start, despite the generosity of some of my well-off friends, until right now, when Arnaud offered to be my business partner. It's a huge project that will take time and a lot of money to get finished.' She got up from her chair and went to the desk, pulling out a drawer and taking out papers and drawings that she handed around to her granddaughters. 'Here, take a look and you'll see what it is.'

Lily looked at the drawings she had been handed, trying to concentrate on what it said. 'Magnolia Manor senior service apartments,' she read out loud and then stared at Sylvia. 'What does it mean? You want to turn this place into an old folks' home?'

'That's terrible,' Rose exclaimed. 'We were thinking we would restore the house and gardens little by little and then we could live here and use it as a wedding venue. That wouldn't take all that time or even money you're talking about.'

'And I was going to suggest a garden centre and café,' Lily cut in. 'That has always been my dream.'

'We were going to present our plans to you when we found the deeds,' Vi cut in. 'And now we have, so—'

'Please,' Sylvia interrupted. 'You said you'd listen. I haven't finished yet.'

'Okay.' Lily handed the drawings to Rose. 'Go on. A deluxe old folks' home, is that it?'

'No, of course not,' Sylvia protested. 'It is *not* going to be an old folks' home. It's going to be the exact opposite. Flats for older people, yes. But it will be homes that they can live in and be independent as long as possible. And on the ground floor, there will be a library, a gym, a laundry and a small grocery shop. There will also be a physiotherapist who will be here a few hours every day to give exercise classes. All this to create a building where people who are older but still fit and healthy can remain so. The gardens will be tended to make more paths and areas for people to exercise in the fresh air. And we have plans for a garden centre in one of the greenhouses where there will also be a café and plant shop, so that goes very well with what you wanted, Lily.'

'Studio flats?' Rose asked, looking at the drawings.

Sylvia nodded. 'Yes. With a kitchenette and bathroom. Ten flats in all, as you can see.'

'But if this works, we intend to apply to build more in a separate building nearby on the property,' Arnaud cut in. 'This concept is new in Ireland, I believe, though it exists in many other European countries.'

'Yes,' Sylvia agreed. 'That's where I got the idea.' She looked at her granddaughters with a stern expression. 'You are so young and couldn't possibly know what it's like to grow old. But the older population in this country are a big group that should be catered for more widely. Many of us are fit and healthy but need a little more comfort and support from each other. Contemporaries to have a laugh with who have lived and loved and suffered through a long life. It will mean that these people will be less lonely and find new friends, and maybe even new hobbies and activities. This is a whole new area to be explored for the housing market.' She looked at Rose. 'It could be very lucrative for the right estate agent.'

Rose looked at Lily before she spoke to Sylvia. 'May I tell you what I think about this whole plan?' she asked.

Sylvia nodded. 'Yes. Go ahead. But please try to be polite and not too negative.'

'Negative?' Rose said, her eyes sparkling. 'Quite the opposite, darling Granny. I think this is absolutely brilliant.'

Later, as Lily, Rose and Vi walked back to the gatehouse, they discussed Sylvia's plan.

'Not sure I like it,' Vi said. 'And Monsieur Bernard is too involved. It's as if it's his project, not Granny's.'

'He's just like all men,' Lily remarked. 'Especially of that generation. They think women aren't capable of being in charge with stuff like that.'

Rose laughed. 'Then he will have a rude awakening when Granny gets going. It's her idea, her dream and he will just have to take it and be quiet. And pay.'

Lily joined in Rose's laughter. 'Oh yeah. He doesn't know what he's getting into.'

'Maybe he does and will love it?' Rose suggested. 'Have you seen his eyes when he looks at her? I think he's very attracted to her.'

'Could be that he loves feisty women,' Vi said. 'But,' she continued with a frown, 'flats for old people? What about our lovely manor all restored and beautiful again? I was looking forward to doing that.'

'I know that would have been more glamorous,' Lily replied. 'But Granny's project is a lot more realistic. And it might be more sensible and a better investment. I actually love the idea now that I've thought about it.'

'Me too,' Rose agreed. 'It's a chance to get in on the ground floor of something that will keep growing.'

'Yeah, maybe,' Vi muttered. 'But I thought we were agreed that we'd push for the restoration idea. But all you two did was smile and agree with everything.'

'What else could we do?' Rose asked. 'I know you were dreaming about standing at the top of the steps of this gorgeous restored manor house in some outfit looking glamorous, which would be great for your image. "Violet Fleury at the opening of the newly restored Magnolia Manor, which used to be her family home,"' she quoted. 'Very Instagrammable, or maybe even *Hello!* magazine. How fabulous.'

'Oh come on, Rose,' Lily chided. 'That's mean.'

'But true,' Rose said.

'And you don't post anything at all on your Insta page?' Vi asked. 'You record every single thing you do several times a day.'

'That's marketing,' Rose argued. 'Your stuff is all about you.'

Vi shot Rose an angry look. 'Yeah, well, whatever,' she said and started to walk ahead. 'In any case I'm out of here,' she said over her shoulder. 'I have to go back to work. We start rehearsals in Tipperary tomorrow, so I'll be leaving tonight, or even straight away so you won't have to listen to me any more.'

'Oh please!' Lily exclaimed and started after her. 'Don't go off in a huff, Vi.'

Rose put her hand on Lily's arm. 'Let her go. You know what she's like when she gets sniffy. She'll calm down and we'll make up later. I think she deserved to be pulled up.'

'Yes, but not like that,' Lily protested.

Rose shrugged. 'Maybe. But I was annoyed.'

'I'm going to leave you both to sort this out,' Lily remarked. 'And I hope Vi won't leave feeling sad.'

'Okay.' Rose looked suddenly contrite. 'Maybe I was a bit unfair. I'll go and say sorry before she leaves.'

'Good,' Lily said, her thoughts drifting to another matter. She wondered why Dominic had kept his involvement in Granny's plan a secret. He could at least have told her when they were having one of their long talks. And what about his involvement with the Bernards? Had he been trying to fool Granny for his own gains? There was something that didn't feel right. Maybe that was what he had wanted to tell her on the terrace... Then there was also the issue of the woman in the photo. So many questions that needed to be answered. She suddenly regretted that she had declined his invitation to break-fast. She hoped they would have a chance to talk soon, even if it turned out to be upsetting. She wanted to know the truth about his feelings for her, and what that letter was all about. Could she cope if she didn't get the answer she wanted? Well, she would have to in order to move on. If he had been dishonest she couldn't have anything to do with him. She just had to know. Rip off the plaster and deal with it, was usually her motto. *But oh*, she thought, a knot in her stomach tightening. *How will I bear it if he doesn't feel anything for me?*

Things settled down a little during the following week, and Lily turned her mind from her heartache by working hard on any task Wolfie gave her. He was delighted and said he'd give her another raise as business was booming and he was doing a lot of work on conveyancing and other types of contracts.

'It's so much easier to get through the files of each case with your brilliant new system,' he said when Lily came into his office to get a signature on a document. His pale blue eyes were warm as he looked at her. 'But now you can slow down and take some time off if you want. You must be tired after all the work you've done.'

'No,' Lily protested. 'I love the work. And now that there is perfect order here I feel very much at home.'

He looked thoughtfully at her for a moment. 'Are you feeling all right? You look a little pale. No problem with your grandmother or anything?'

'No, she's in great form. She looks as if she's got a new lease of life. She's planning a great project that will be announced as soon as she has everything in place. And,' Lily added, smiling, 'I think she has a boyfriend. But please don't tell anyone. Or laugh.'

Wolfie held up his hand. 'I swear. I wouldn't laugh. There is no age limit to love. And if it happens to people late in life, it's even more wonderful than when they are young.'

'That's very true,' Lily said, still smiling as she remembered the glow in her grandmother's cheeks, the new look of happiness and hope in her eyes. 'I hope it works out for them.'

'And for you,' Wolfie cut in. Then he turned back to his

computer screen, looking as if he was sorry he had said it. 'Never mind. Your private life is none of my business.' He waved his hand at Lily. 'Carry on with whatever work you want to do. Or take the rest of the day off.'

'Off?' Lily asked. She checked her watch. 'Well it's nearly lunchtime. I might take a long lunch and go for a walk along the harbour as it's a nice day.'

Wolfie nodded. 'Good idea. I might see you down there when I've finished dealing with this document.'

'Okay. See you later.' Lily walked out, took her jacket off the stand in the reception area, picked up her bag and went out into the fresh air and sunshine. A quick sandwich in the nearby café and a stroll along the harbour would clear the cobwebs out of her head and cheer her up.

The walk certainly lifted Lily's spirits. The blue water of Dingle Bay, where fishing boats were coming in to dock at the quays, the warm breeze with the tang of salt and seaweed and the call of the seagulls gliding above her, gave Lily a boost of pure joy. After a while, she sat on a bollard and turned her face up to the sun, closing her eyes. It was a heavenly moment that made her forget her worries for a while.

'Hey, Lily!' a voice called.

Lily gave a start and opened her eyes, squinting against the sunlight at the figure coming towards her. She nearly fell off the bollard when she saw it was Dominic.

'Hi,' she started, getting to her feet. 'What are you doing here?'

'Walking, like you,' he replied, smiling at her.

'Lovely day.'

He looked up at the sky. 'Ah sure it's a grand day.' Then his gaze drifted back to her. 'How are things with your sisters and your grandmother? Still trying to work out a solution to the ownership of the property?'

'Oh, eh, I suppose you haven't heard,' Lily started, relieved to be distracted from all the feelings that had risen inside her at the sight of him. 'It's all okay now. Arnaud arrived at the end of the party and suggested they go into a partnership. But she refused and then something amazing happened. I found the deeds and an old letter that proved Granny is the legal owner of Magnolia Manor. The house was given back to our family years ago, only nobody knew. So we're fine and now Granny wants to go ahead with her grand plan...' She looked up at him through her eyelashes. 'Which you know about, of course.'

'Grand plan?' he asked, looking confused.

'Yes, the serviced apartments for older people,' Lily told him. 'Didn't you work with Granny on it?'

'Not as far as can remember.'

'But you did a full survey of the structure,' Lily argued. 'Granny told me. Why didn't *you* tell me?'

'Oh that. Well, I...' He looked decidedly awkward, but was interrupted by his phone pinging. He took it out and glanced at the text. 'I have to go. I'm needed at a house nearby that I'm working on and there's been some kind of power cut.' He stopped and looked at her for a moment. 'How about that breakfast I invited you to? We can do that on Sunday morning, if you're free. We do need to talk, I feel. About what you just mentioned and a lot of other things...'

'I know.' Lily met his eyes, her heart beating. He seemed so anxious to see her and sort things out, which gave her a dart of hope. Either way, it would be good to have the opportunity to ask all the questions that had been troubling her for so long. 'Okay,' she said. 'Sunday morning it is.'

His face broke into a happy smile as he moved away. 'Great. I'll make breakfast and then we can walk on the beach. See you then.' He walked away, breaking into a run further away.

Lily watched him running with an easy stride, feeling the familiar butterflies whirling around as she thought of their date on Sunday.

This is it, cards on the table, all questions answered and the air cleared, she thought. *I might come away from it sad and heartbroken, but at least I'll be able to move on and not have to second guess how he feels. If he doesn't share my feelings, I might at least find out if he's been dishonest. That is more important than anything...*

26

After a restless night, Lily woke up early. She looked out the window at the clouds scudding across the sky and the branches of the trees shaking wildly. Windy and overcast but no rain. Great. The bike ride to Ventry would be hard but not impossible. She could take the car but felt that the fresh air and exercise would calm her. She dressed quickly and went downstairs to make herself a cup of tea while she waited for the skies to brighten and the visibility to improve. The butterflies in her stomach whirled around as she thought about what she would say to Dominic. Two things had to be cleared up: that letter from the Bernard firm she had seen on the top landing, and also the woman in the photo. But it was the possible involvement with the Bernards that gnawed at her the most. Whether he was single or in a relationship had to do with her emotions, and that simply had to take a back seat for a while. Her family had to come first. His explanation about the letter might clear the air and put her mind at rest – if there was an acceptable reason for that correspondence. Lily said a quick prayer that this was the case and then finished her tea, put on her jacket and went outside to find her bike, closing the door softly behind her so she wouldn't wake Rose and have to answer a lot of questions. She had come in very late after a night out with friends so she was probably fast asleep.

As Lily set off, her legs burning from pedalling up the first slope, she felt a strange sense of exhilaration looking out over the ocean and the waves crashing in against the rocks below the road. The air smelled of salt and seaweed and the seagulls gliding on the wind above her emitted plaintive cries. There was nothing more uplifting than the ocean and the sea air and the cries of seagulls to Lily, and she realised how lucky she was to live here and how right she had been to come back.

It didn't take long to reach Ventry beach and Lily stopped for a moment to admire the view from the top of the hill. The horseshoe-shaped beach with its white sand and blue-green water was stunning even on a cloudy day in early spring. Lily remembered coming here for picnics and swimming during her summer holidays. They had enjoyed ham and cheese sand-wiches made by Nora, washed down with orange squash and then ice cream from the stand near the shop after their long swim in the crystal-clear water. Wonderful memories of lazy summer days, and now she could do all that again.

Lily got back on the bike and freewheeled down the slope to the path that led to Dominic's house, where she got off and led the bike down the lane lined with rhododendron and camellia bushes already in bloom. The gate was open when she arrived at it, as was the front door as she came into the little front garden. She could hear the waves crashing onto the shore below and thought it must be lovely to live so close to the sea. Listening to the sound of the waves would be a wonderful way to go to sleep.

Dominic stood just inside the door and shot her a wide grin. 'Hi there. Hope you're not too tired after the bike ride in that wind.'

'The fresh air was a huge boost.' Lily tried her best to smile cheerfully despite her beating heart. She stepped inside after leaving her bike on the grass, took off her jacket and hung it on the row of pegs by the door. 'The exercise woke me up too.'

'Yes, that usually helps. I've made pancakes for breakfast, the American kind.' He gestured at the table in front of the large picture window. 'Sit down and dig in. I'll make coffee. Or do you prefer tea?'

'No, coffee would be great,' Lily said as she sat down at the table where there was a stack of pancakes on a plate, a jar of honey, a bowl of blueberries and raspberries, another bowl with muesli with a tub of yogurt and a jug of orange juice. 'Lovely breakfast,' she said to Dominic as he busied himself with the coffee machine.

'I made a bit more than usual. I don't often have the time to cook, but as it's Sunday and you were coming...' He stopped and laughed. 'Okay, I was trying to impress you with my cooking skills.'

'You succeeded big time.'

'Great.' Dominic brought two steaming mugs to the table and sat down. 'Dig in. I'm sure you're hungry.'

'I'm starving.' Lily momentarily forgot her concerns as she helped herself to pancakes and then put some of the muesli and berries in the bowl by her plate.

Dominic poured juice into her glass and then they ate in silence while Lily looked at him, trying to think of a way to ask about the letter.

'What?' he suddenly asked as he put down his knife and fork. 'You look as if you're bursting with questions. So spit it out or you'll choke.'

Lily squirmed. 'Well I...'

'Yes?' His eyes were teasing as he looked at her.

She took a deep breath and put her mug on the table. 'Okay. First of all, I have to ask you about a letter I saw on the landing the last time I was here. Please don't think I was snooping. It was there on that little table and I just happened to see the name on the envelope. A name that has been like a red flag for us all for quite a long time.'

Dominic looked at her for a moment without replying. 'I know which letter you mean,' he said slowly. 'And I also think I know what went through your mind when you saw it. I wish you hadn't though.'

'But I did see it,' Lily said in a near whisper. 'What was it about, Dominic? I need to know.'

Dominic leaned forward and met Lily's worried gaze. 'Okay. I'll tell you. It was about a scheme that kind of didn't work.'

'You were scheming?' Lily asked, her stomach contracting. 'Against us? The Fleurys?'

'Not *against* you,' he corrected. '*For* you. I was trying to help you all, you see. I thought if I contacted them and pretended I wanted to work with them I could get them to give up their demand for ownership. So I offered to do a survey, which they accepted and then I sent them a bogus report saying the house would be impossible to rebuild because of dry rot and rising damp and all kinds of mould and rotten beams in the roof. In fact I laid it on so thick, they saw through it. That letter you saw was from the son, Henri Bernard, telling me they wouldn't pay me for any of the "work" I had pretended to do. That's all.' Dominic sat back and drew breath. 'He was pretty ticked off, I have to tell you.'

'Oh,' Lily said, staring blankly at Dominic while she tried to take it all in. Then she started to laugh, not so much because she found it funny, but because of the relief and all the pent-up emotions she had felt ever since she saw the letter. 'I'm sorry,' she said when she had calmed down. 'But it's kind of ridiculous. Here I was, trying to understand why you were plotting against us, and all the time you were actually trying to help. Not in a very professional way, I have to say.'

'I know,' he said with a self-derogatory smile. 'I wouldn't be a good double agent. Or any kind of agent, actually.'

'You'd be caught in ten minutes,' Lily said, laughing again. 'But I'm really touched that you tried to help. And I'm sorry that I thought the worst of you.' Their eyes met for a moment. 'With everything I've been through, it's hard for me to trust men.'

'That's okay, Lily,' Dominic said softly. 'I'm glad that's cleared up.' He took a swig of coffee. 'So what was the other thing you wanted to ask me?'

'Oh, well...' Lily blushed. 'I wanted to know who that woman is. The one in the photo upstairs.'

Dominic looked blankly at her. 'The woman in the... What photo? On the landing?' Then it seemed to dawn on him what she meant and he started to laugh. 'Oh *that* woman.'

'Yeah. That woman,' Lily said, her voice cold. 'I saw the photo at the same time as I spotted the letter. Not that it's any of my business, but, well, after the night of the party, and that moment full of emotion between us that nearly ended with a kiss... I was wondering... I mean,' she babbled on, 'the photo was there on the little table and I spotted it when I...' She stopped, near to tears with embarrassment.

Dominic nodded, a little smile playing on his lips. 'I see. So you thought she was some kind of girlfriend or something?'

'Well, yes. Is she? Please tell me the truth.'

Dominic looked at Lily for a moment, his eyes dancing. 'If you must know I'm madly in love with her. Who wouldn't be?'

'I see,' Lily said miserably. 'Okay. I understand.'

He laughed and shook his head. 'Hey, hold on. I was stringing you along.'

Lily frowned. 'You were? Well, it's not funny.'

'I know,' he soothed. 'I'm sorry.' He paused before he spoke again, still looking highly amused. 'Okay. Here's the truth. Are you ready?'

'Yes,' she whispered, bracing herself for what would come.

'I don't know who she is.'

Lily stared at him. 'What? You don't know?'

'Nope. No idea.'

'But... but...' Lily tried to understand what he had just said. 'How can you not know?' she asked, feeling so confused she didn't know how to react. 'You have a photo of a complete stranger up there on the landing?'

'Calm down, Lily. It's okay.' He took her hand across the table and squeezed it hard. 'Listen for a minute. That photo, which actually isn't there any more, came with the frame I bought in a gift shop in Dingle. You know how those frames sometimes have pictures of people in them? I was so busy with my scheming against the Bernards, I just put the frame there and forgot about the photo.'

'Oh.' Lily suddenly felt both very stupid and relieved. She'd been agonising about that woman for over a week and it turned out to be some random model. She let out a nervous laugh. 'Now you must think I'm really silly.'

He smiled fondly at her. 'Of course not. I understand how you could have made the mistake. I don't know why I just put the frame there without removing the picture. I needed it for a photo of my parents on their fiftieth wedding anniversary last month and now they're in there smiling at me. You can go up and take a look if you like.'

'I will later,' Lily promised, her cheeks still burning with embarrassment. 'I'm so sorry I suspected that you were plotting against us. And that you were cheating on some girlfriend with me. I feel really stupid now.'

'You're not stupid, Lily,' he said gently. 'You just have a warm and tender heart and that's one of the things that I like about you.'

Lily felt herself blush again. 'Thank you. Can we forget about this now?'

'I don't think I can,' he said, letting go of her hand, his eyes tender as he looked at her. 'Because if you were worried I had a girlfriend, that means that you care about me as much as I do about you.'

Lily suddenly felt overwhelmed by everything: his eyes on her, her feelings bubbling up to the surface, the unreasoning fear of falling in love only to be left heartbroken again. The trauma of the divorce was still so real. She was terrified of it happening again. The hard shell of reserve she had built up was slowly breaking and she didn't know if she could survive without it.

'You do?' she whispered.

'Yes.'

A shaft of sunlight blinded her momentarily and she had to look away out to sea, where blue-green waves rolled in towards the shore. She shielded her eyes with her hand and looked back at him. 'It's very bright in here.'

'Yes, the early morning sun can be blinding as it's low this time of year.' He looked at her side-on, clearly unsure of the change of subject. He inhaled. 'Lily, I—'

'Could we go outside? I'd love to see the beach in this lovely light,' she said all of a sudden. The warmth of the sun was stifling. She needed fresh air and a little distance from Dominic.

'Yes, let's go to the beach. I think it would be easier to talk out there. And Larry needs a walk.'

'Where is he?' Lily asked, looking around the room.

'Trotting around in the garden, I think. Come on, let's go and find him.'

Dominic rose and went behind Lily to pull out her chair. His warm breath on her neck as she got up made her nearly dizzy. She stepped away and walked to the door, throwing it open and taking deep breaths of the cool air. Then she put on her jacket that Dominic handed her and walked ahead of him to the gate. Larry suddenly appeared out of nowhere and wagged his tail furiously as she patted him on the head.

'Coming for a walk?' she asked him, to which he barked and bounded off through the gate and down the lane that led to the beach. Lily started running after him but had to stop halfway down the beach to catch her breath, which was where Dominic caught up with her.

He took her by the arm, looking into her eyes with a strange expression. 'Are you running away from me?'

Lily tried to slow her breathing. 'No. From myself,' she finally said. 'I felt so awkward in there when I asked about that photo. And then you were so sweet about it and said such nice things...' She stopped as tears welled up. 'It scares me,' she said. 'I have this weird fear that it's going to happen again.'

'What's going to happen again?' He paused. 'Do you mean you think I'd behave like your ex-husband?' he asked incredulously. 'From what I know he doesn't sound very nice.'

Lily nodded. 'Something like that.'

Dominic took a deep breath. 'Okay. I should be insulted but I get it. Even though you never told me much about him and what he did.' He paused. 'And I never told you what happened to me.'

'No you didn't,' Lily said, wondering what he had been through. The reason he left London to come to Kerry and change his life.

'But I will in a minute,' he said, letting go of her arm. 'I think we've both tried to forget, but it never goes away, does it? I mean, being dumped by someone you thought loved you and then, when you meet someone else, you have a kind of déjà vu feeling. Here we go again, you think, seeing the same scenario in your head and running as fast as you can away from it.'

'But you're not running,' Lily said.

Dominic smiled. 'Not from you, and that's a first for a long time.' He suddenly sat down on the sand, waving at her to join him. 'Let's sit here for a bit and talk now the sun is coming out.'

'Okay.' Lily sat beside him and wrapped her arms around her knees. 'Can I go first?'

'Of course. I'm listening.'

Lily stared out to sea as she started to tell Dominic about Simon and what he had done to her, how he had begun to drift away when he realised that the Fleury family were not as wealthy as he had first thought, and that the manor house was a wreck in need of major renovations. How he had then started to flirt with other women and been sour and rude to Lily.

'He thought he had married into a family with money who lived in a big posh house. He had seen Magnolia Manor in old photos and heard about the wonderful gardens. But the reality was far from what he imagined. I knew then he never really loved me the way I loved him.'

'What a gobshite,' Dominic said with feeling when Lily had finished.

'I know. I was carried away by his looks and all the lovely things he said that he didn't mean. He made me feel so good about myself. For a while.'

'And then he dumped you.'

'Yes.' Lily shifted sand through her fingers. Then she looked at Dominic over her shoulder. 'So that's why I'm afraid to fall for anyone again. It has nothing to do with you, though.'

'I know that. But hey, listen, you gave your love to someone who didn't deserve it. Are you going to let him ruin your life forever? If you don't allow anyone else in, you'll never know the difference between real love and that fake stuff he fed you.'

'Are you talking to yourself?' Lily asked.

He sat up, leaning his arms on his knees. 'I suppose I am. As I told you, I've been through something similar. A few years ago, I was in love with a girl who left me for someone else. I had asked her to marry me and had bought her a diamond ring and everything. Cost me a month's salary and an arm and a leg,' he added with a wry smile. 'She said yes, but only a week later told me she had met someone else and packed her stuff and left. She kept the ring too.'

'How awful. Did this happen in London?' Lily asked.

'Yes. Five years ago. I've been on dates since I came here but never met anyone I felt I could trust or even go on a second date with. Until now.'

'And...?' she asked, holding her breath as she waited for him to elaborate.

'And now I'm here with you.' Dominic put his arm around Lily and pulled her closer. 'I feel safe with you. As if I've met a kindred spirit. We seem to love the same things, dogs, nature, this place that is so unique and lots of other things too.'

'Like order and tidiness,' Lily said with a laugh, leaning her head on his shoulder. It was lovely to sit here with him, feeling so close and protected with no pressure to be anything but herself.

They turned their heads towards each other and, as their lips touched, Lily melted into his arms, kissing him back, breathing in his warm, clean smell. Then they pulled back and looked at each other and smiled.

'I'll never forget this moment,' he murmured, his eyes full of tenderness.

'Neither will I,' Lily said, knowing this was real and true, even if it felt too soon. 'But I'm not—'

He put his finger to her mouth. 'Shh. I know. We're just test driving this to see where we go. I don't need anything else. I know how I feel, and I get an idea of how you do just by looking at you.' He smiled.

Lily nodded. 'Thank you. That makes me feel less panicky. I have so much on my mind right now, I need a little peace and time to think and settle into what's going on with us.'

'Exactly. We've only known each other a few months and

we have a whole lifetime to get to know each other.' Dominic scrambled to his feet and held out his hand. 'Come on, let's continue our walk and enjoy this lovely morning.'

Larry suddenly bounded towards them, tongue lolling in a huge doggy smile. Dominic picked up a stick and threw it into the water; Larry raced after it, barking. They both laughed and ran along the beach, the wind blowing their hair and making them breathless.

Lily felt full of joy and hope. She knew she was falling in love and that was wonderful. She didn't have to worry any more or feel it would all end in tears. It wouldn't. Not this time, not with Dominic. But there was one question still niggling her.

'Just one more thing,' she said after a while.

He stopped walking and looked at her. 'What?'

'The structural survey. Not the fake one you tried to fool the Bernards with but the one you did for Granny. Did she tell you why she wanted it done?'

'No, she didn't. I thought it had something to do with a new roof or renovations of some kind. Then she said she'd tell me what it was about when the time was right.'

'Why did she want to keep it secret?' Lily asked. 'If it was just a survey to make sure the structure of the house was okay.'

'I think she didn't want anyone to know what she was planning until she had all her ducks in a row.'

Lily sighed. 'Typical. Always keeping everything secret until the very end. And here I was, thinking you knew but didn't tell me.'

Dominic laughed. 'Well, I could hardly tell you something I didn't know. If I had known, I would have told you. Even if Sylvia had sworn me to secrecy. I know that sounds dishonest, but I had a feeling it had something to do with whatever was going on with the house and all that mess. I would have done anything to calm your fears.'

Lily smiled at him. 'I love that. Thank you. Anyway,' she

said and resumed walking, 'I'll tell you what it was all about while we walk.'

Dominic fell into step with her. 'Okay. So tell me.'

'Okay, so this is what she wants to do...' Lily proceeded to describe Sylvia's plans for the house and gardens, Arnaud Bernard's involvement in it and how Sylvia had spent the best part of a year networking locally with all kinds of people in order to get the project started.

'That's why she was calling into the building where my office is. She was meeting an architect on the first floor who will design the whole thing.'

'Amazing,' Dominic said when she had finished. 'But as far as I can see, this will take time. The planning application alone could be tricky. Kerry County Council might not like it at all and if the building is listed, that will put another obstacle in her way.'

'It's not listed. And did I tell you that we found the deeds? They were in an envelope stuck behind that painting Brian's granny had in her room in the nursing home. Caroline, my great-granny, gave it to her many years ago.'

'Incredible,' Dominic remarked. 'So Brian's granny was the keeper of the secret all along.'

'Exactly. The deeds were in the best hiding place ever. So at least the ownership has been sorted and the building not being listed removes another obstacle.'

Dominic nodded. 'That's good. And my structural report will also help move things along. So it might be possible after all, even if the planning application takes a bit of time.' He looked at Lily. 'How do you feel about it? I know you had other plans for the place that you might have preferred.'

'I did.' Lily stopped again, the strong wind making her breathless. 'But when I thought about it, I realised what a good idea it is to provide flats for older people who are not ready for a nursing home but still need company and support and a little extra comfort. Rose agrees with me and I'm sure her firm will be handling the property once it's up and running. I think I'll eventually be able to realise part of my dream, too. There is going to be a garden centre and a café that I could run. But that will be in a year or two, or even more. In the meantime, I will try to talk Granny into moving everything to Wolfie just to have legal help nearby.' Lily drew breath and started walking again.

Dominic took her hand. 'That's great to hear. So now we can concentrate on us and just being together. I'm beginning to enjoy this date. Let's make it last all day. Lunch, then watch a movie, then dinner and then... who knows? How about it?'

Lily laughed and squeezed his hand back. 'The perfect date.' Her heart skipped a beat as she looked up at him, wondering if it was really true that they were here together or if it was a dream. But her legs ached from cycling, and walking in the heavy sand, and that felt real.

She had been so unsure of herself for so long that she had thought nobody could love her, least of all a man like Dominic. But he had proved her wrong on so many levels. He wanted them to be together and liked her for who she was.

27

Sylvia sat at the desk in her study filling in forms and writing emails and letters on her computer. A lot of work had to be done before the enormous project was up and running. An engineer connected to the County Council had to inspect the house and then planning permission could take months. Then they had to fill in a separate application for the proposed garden centre and café. But the biggest headache was the funds to pay for it all. Arnaud was putting in a lot of money, but he couldn't pay for all of it. She had to find sponsors or maybe set up a limited company and take out a loan. Then the question of ownership of the flats had come up. But they had agreed to discuss this later when they went for their walk in the gardens.

'If the flats are owned by their occupants and then pass away, their families will inherit and then they will start renting out the flats to all kinds of people,' Arnaud explained while they walked. 'Holiday lets for example. That is not the purpose of this scheme.'

'No,' Sylvia agreed. 'Then we lose the whole idea that is so close to my heart.'

'And mine,' he said, smiling fondly at her. 'It's a wonderful idea. I never thought I'd find something like this to invest in. But I did, thanks to you.'

'And we found each other,' Sylvia said, breathless from trying to keep up with his long strides. 'I think we'll have a wonderful business partnership once this thing is off the ground. It's so nice to be on the same page. We have so much in common,' she continued. 'Old age, losing our spouses and all kinds of other things.'

'Old age doesn't seem to bother you much,' he remarked with a fond smile, slowing his pace. 'You're as sprightly as a fifty-year-old.'

'I'm lucky to have excellent health,' Sylvia replied, smiling. 'But it is a bit of a struggle to keep up with everything sometimes.' She had managed to find out that he was seventy-eight, so four years younger than her. She hadn't revealed her age, but let him assume she was much younger. Not that it mattered at all, they were getting on so well in everything now that the problem of the ownership was solved. 'It's nice to have such a sympathetic business partner,' she said.

He stopped and looked at her. 'I hope we'll be more than business partners. I find you so charming and amusing. And I love your Irish accent and all those Irish sayings.'

'Your French accent is more to my taste,' Sylvia said, feeling a warm flush of affection for this handsome, kindly man. 'It's very alluring, you know,' she said, fluttering her eyelashes to make him laugh.

'Oh like Maurice Chevalier?' he asked with a wink as he launched into a well-known song in an exaggerated French accent, adding Sylvia's name to the last line.

Sylvia giggled. 'It should be Louise, but that's so funny. I think Maurice laid on the accent big time. He probably didn't speak like that at all normally.'

'I'd say not.' Arnaud took Sylvia's hand, tucked it under his arm and resumed walking at a gentler pace. 'Isn't it marvellous to talk about old stars that nobody of the younger generation knows anything about? That's why I like being with you. We remember the same things, the same times and all the same movies, music and books.'

'We remember being young,' Sylvia filled in. 'But with you, I don't feel old or young. I just feel like myself.'

Arnaud nodded. 'Yes, me too.' He stopped walking again and looked at her. 'We have so little time left, you and I, so we should not waste it. We've only just met, but I know I'd like to be with you as much as I can. Here, in this beautiful garden, but also in the South of France, where it's warm even in the winter. Would you come and see me there?'

'I would love to,' Sylvia replied, looking into his velvet eyes. 'We will travel back and forth for as long as we are able.'

'Winter in France and summer in Ireland?' He nodded. 'Yes, that sounds perfect. And we will work together and see this new project through. We could have a little flat on the ground floor and be independent from the rest of the house.'

'I have already had plans drawn up for my flat, and there is plenty of room to make it bigger so you can have your own quarters,' Sylvia said after a moment's reflection. 'That way we can have our own space as well as being together. What do you think?'

He picked up her hand and kissed it. 'Perfect, *ma chère* Sylvia.'

She slapped him playfully on the arm. 'You old charmer. Don't you know that kind of thing is totally irresistible.'

'But of course,' he said, smiling. 'But I also know there is no way to get around you if you do not agree to something. I am going to let you sit in the driver's seat at all times.'

'Can we have that in writing?' she asked, looking at his

gleaming white hair, tender brown eyes and square shoulders. He had charmed his way into her heart and, for the first time since her husband died, she felt something akin to love. No matter what happened or how long they would both be alive, she knew she would always remember this moment.

28

When Lily called in to say hello to her grandmother one evening later that week, she found Sylvia working at the desk, shifting papers and muttering to herself. She looked unusually dishevelled and stressed, a pencil stuck in her hair and the collar of her silk shirt was wrinkled under the unbuttoned cashmere cardigan.

'Granny,' Lily exclaimed. 'Are you still working? It's after nine o'clock. I thought we'd watch the news on TV together.'

Sylvia blinked and looked at Lily. 'Is it that time already? I was just going to take a quick look at the plans. Arnaud was such a great help but now that he's left I feel a little lost, I'm afraid.' Sylvia sighed and got up from her chair. 'Silly of me to become so dependent on him, but he felt like an angel from heaven the way he so quickly agreed to help finance the project and become my business partner and—'

'Then it became something more than that between you?' Lily asked softly.

Sylvia nodded, her cheeks pink. 'Yes,' she murmured and sat on the sofa, stretching out her hand to the glowing embers of the fire. 'The logs have nearly burned down and I didn't notice.'

Lily sank to her knees, put some kindling and two more logs on, then sat back on her heels as the flames started to flicker. 'There. That should take in a few minutes. I let the dogs out too. They were whining at the door.'

'I forgot about them and everything else,' Sylvia said, looking slightly shocked. 'I must get more organised and maybe get someone to help me with all this stuff.'

'I could do it,' Lily offered. 'I have less work now that the files are organised in the office. So it'll be fun to sort your stuff out. You know how I like that sort of thing.'

Sylvia smiled fondly at Lily. 'Yes, that's that orderly streak in you. You have that from your grandfather. Liam was a wonderful organiser. And so is Arnaud.' She sighed. 'Oh dear, I miss him already.'

'When is he coming back?' Lily asked.

'In a few weeks.' Sylvia looked wistful. 'I hope he will stay a bit longer this time. I was thinking I'd organise one of the bedrooms for him, the one with the adjoining bathroom to mine. If you don't think that's a bit... well, you know. Not quite fitting or something.'

'I think that's a wonderful idea, Granny.' Lily got up and joined Sylvia on the sofa, putting her arms around her grandmother. 'Whatever makes you happy is fine with me and all of us, you know.'

Sylvia looked doubtful. 'People might talk.'

Lily laughed. 'So let them. Who cares? Those who love you will just be delighted that you have found a man to be happy with.'

'That's a lovely thought.' Sylvia pulled away and studied Lily for a moment. 'And what about you? Have you found a man to be happy with? I hope that is why you have lost that mournful look you had when you arrived.'

Lily smiled. 'Yes, Granny, that's why. Dominic and I are

dating and we have so much fun together. That's all for the moment. Nothing more.'

'And nothing less,' Sylvia filled in. 'I'm so happy for you. I think you're perfect for each other.'

'Well we agree about most things, that's for sure. But perfect?' Lily considered this for a moment. 'Nothing is perfect, but this time I feel safe. Does that sound weird? That's how I feel with him anyway.'

'That is what I would call as perfect as it can be,' Sylvia declared.

Later, as she FaceTimed with Dominic before going to sleep, Lily told him about her evening with Sylvia. 'She is totally besotted with Arnaud, which is sweet. I'm happy for her.'

'I hope we'll be together and still in love when we're that age,' Dominic said, his voice sleepy.

'If we're both alive, I have a feeling we will,' Lily replied, smiling at the screen. 'You look half asleep.'

'I am. We had those two gigs Saturday and Sunday night and I was working on that new house all day, sorting their electricity and doing all kinds of odd jobs. But we're nearly finished so I'll be all yours very soon.'

'I promised to help Granny organise all the material for the Magnolia project,' Lily said. 'So I'll be a little busy for a while.'

'I can help you with that,' Dominic offered. 'I do love putting everything in its place.'

'Oh that would be great,' Lily told him. 'We can do it together, then we'll be finished a lot faster.'

'Sounds good.' Dominic stifled a yawn. 'Look, I'm falling asleep here, I just want to say one thing before we sign off. A question.'

'Yes?'

'I was wondering... And please tell me if it's too soon... if we could perhaps live together?'

Lily was both surprised and apprehensive. 'You mean you want me to move in with you?'

'Yeah,' he said, looking a little awkward. 'But only if you want to.'

'Oh sweetheart, of course I do,' Lily replied, near tears. 'It would be so great to be together all the time. But I'm not sure how Rose would feel being here all alone when she comes for her visits.'

'You did it for a while. It didn't seem to worry you. Rose is an adult too.'

'I know, but I needed to be alone then.' Lily sighed. 'Rose is different. She needs company and support.'

'You can stay with her at the gatehouse when she's here. Would be good for you both to have some time together.'

Lily nodded. 'That's a good idea. But it's not only about Rose, it's Granny too. She needs me to be nearby.'

'Do you have to be so dutiful all the time?' Dominic asked, a touch of annoyance creeping into his voice. 'Give yourself a break from being the big sister and the eldest granddaughter. Rose is an adult; she has to face life's ups and downs on her own and deal with it her own way. And your granny coped perfectly well all those years when you were in Dublin. She also has Nora nearby, remember. You need to think of yourself more. Have some me time, do fun stuff just for you.'

'I suppose you're right,' Lily said, touched by his concern for her.

'No supposing. I am right,' Dominic stated. 'Lily, please think about it. I know I said we'd take it slow and not rush into anything but here I am, loving you and missing you like crazy. Not because I'm lonely, but because I want to be with you all the time and wake up to see your lovely face every morning. I love you for caring for your family the way you do, and for many other things too, but I want us to be together, not apart like this, saying goodnight over the phone.'

Lily felt a rush of warmth all through her body at his words. She felt the same and suddenly knew what he said was right. She couldn't live Rose's life, or her grandmother's. She knew she loved Dominic with her heart and soul in a way she had never loved anyone else. She wanted to be with him too.

'I could move into the gatehouse, of course,' he suggested with a slow smile. 'But I doubt Rose would love to find me there when she's home.'

'It would get a little cramped,' Lily said, laughing softly. 'But maybe she'd like having a handyman around. So many things need to be fixed in this house.'

'She'd never stop nagging me. So let's scrap that idea.' Dominic yawned. 'Sorry, sweetie. Must go to sleep. Let me know what you decide.'

'No, I'll tell you right now!' Lily exclaimed. 'The answer is yes. I'll move into your house as soon as I can. I've always wanted to live in that house anyway.'

'Is it me or the house?' Dominic asked, laughing.

'Both, but mostly you.'

'Then I go to sleep a happy man. Goodnight, my sweet, beautiful Lily.'

'Goodnight, my darling,' Lily whispered, knowing he was already asleep. But she was now wide awake and thinking about how she would break the news to Rose. Dominic's words drifted into her mind and she knew he was right. Rose had to learn to fend for herself. Maybe that was the only way for her sister to finally grow up.

Lily smiled into the darkness, imagining herself living with Dominic in her dream house, going to sleep beside him to the sound of the waves. It seemed like a fairy-tale, but it was real. No matter what the future brought, they would face it. Together.

EPILOGUE

It took over a year for the building project to get off the ground. But by then everything had fallen into place: the planning permission granted, the agreement between Arnaud and Sylvia signed, all the investors' money in the bank and then builders and contractors hired and ready to start. Two architects had been on the job to make sure the façade of the building and most of the inside remained intact, and they had done a wonderful job with the plans. None of the character of the house would be destroyed and the restoration would be done with the utmost care. The main staircase was being restored to its former glory, the intricately carved banisters beautifully displayed with a new red carpet ordered to give it a finishing touch. The whole of the two top floors, including the old servants' quarters, would be completely changed, however – the many rooms turned into ten studio flats – which would be a huge undertaking.

All that was only at the planning stage, the builders having just got started, knocking down walls, ripping up floors for the new plumbing and getting on with all sorts of other construction work. The noise was deafening and there were clouds of dust everywhere. Despite all that, everyone was delighted it was all ready to go, especially Sylvia, who seemed to find all the noise and mess hugely satisfying.

Sylvia and Arnaud had announced their engagement last autumn to everyone's surprise and delight. But their relationship was a little unusual to say the least. They would lead separate lives part of the year and be together in spring and summer. Arnaud had asked Sylvia to come and live with him in the South of France in the winter, but she had refused. 'I'm a Kerry woman,' she declared, 'and we don't give up on our home for a little bit of rain.' So Arnaud had given in and they came to an agreement that suited them, even if it caused many raised eyebrows in the area. He would live mostly in the South of France in the winter months and come to Kerry for the spring and summer. In any case, Sylvia said, she had to stay around and keep an eye on things, as you never knew what people might get up to if she turned her back on the big project that was about to get started.

The old couple were going to live in the gatehouse while the house was being rebuilt and would move into their quarters in the new apartment complex as soon as it was finished, which could be another year or more away. Arnaud had spent the winter in the South of France but had come to Ireland for a last family Christmas at the old manor before it changed. And what a fun Christmas it had been, with the three sisters, their grandmother and her fiancé, Nora, Martin, Dominic and even Wolfie and his father, who had been such a help with legal matters all through the past year.

At first, the Fleury women were wary of Arnaud and his son. After all, they had threatened the manor and upset Sylvia so much. But, as they were going to work together, they had to bury the hatchet, Sylvia had declared. 'All is well now and we have to move on.'

'Yes, but Arnaud's son has to be punished for what he did to you,' Rose had protested as they were in the kitchen putting the last touches to the Christmas dinner. 'Is he really going to be let off the hook just like that and we have to pretend nothing happened?'

'Yes,' Sylvia had said with a stern look at Rose. 'We are going to behave with style and be polite. And I'll not have any bad manners at Christmas time. Especially from you, Rose. Is that clear?'

'Yes, Granny,' Rose had mumbled.

'Good. Now take the smoked salmon and the bread into the dining room and put it on the sideboard,' Sylvia had ordered.

Lily smiled at the memory as she drove to her new home one evening in late June. She knew they should be angry with Arnaud for what he had done, but she hadn't been able to conjure up such feelings when she talked to him. With his white hair, beguiling smile and twinkly dark eyes, he was charming and kind and had a great sense of humour. He seemed to make Sylvia happy and that was the best part. To give his son his due, he had apologised to them all for the letter he had written without his father's knowledge. Sylvia had said he was forgiven and that they were looking forward to working with him on the project, given that he had huge experience in that field – his firm had worked on many similar buildings in France and Germany.

Granny looks so happy now, Lily thought as she drove down the hill and parked just above Dominic's house. *How wonderful to have found love again so late in life, even with a man we feared would destroy us. But it seems so right now, like the perfect end to a very long story.*

Lily felt as if ten years had passed since that day when they discovered the deeds and heard about Sylvia's plans for the manor, rather than just over a year. Her life had also changed in ways she couldn't have imagined in her wildest dreams, which added to the feeling that a lot of time had passed. She was now living with Dominic in the house above Ventry beach and they were planning to get married in the near future, as soon as it could be arranged and everyone could be there.

Lily got out of the car and, as always, stood there to look out over Ventry beach. It was a warm evening and the mellow sunshine gave the sand a golden glow. The blue-green waves lapped the shore and the sound was like a gentle whisper in the air. She thought back to that afternoon and her visit to the doctor, who had confirmed her suspicions. The nausea and fatigue she had been suffering from the past few weeks was not caused by some nasty virus, but by what felt like a miracle. Lily touched her stomach and tried to take it in. She – they – were going to have a baby sometime in early January. And now, here she was in this heavenly spot, about to share the lovely secret with the man who had become the most important person in her life.

Lily took a deep breath and hitched her bag higher on her shoulder. She could see smoke rising from the front of the house and knew Dominic had lit the barbeque. She started to run down the hill and along the lane, ducking under the bushes, then continued through the gate that was open and around the corner to the patio in front of the house. 'Hi, sweetheart,' she panted, trying to catch her breath.

Dominic looked up from the food he was preparing. 'Hey, Lily. What's up? You look fit to burst.'

'I have something to tell you.' She gently took the knife from his hand and put it on the table. 'Leave the food for a moment.'

'Okay.' He looked at her with a mixture of confusion and worry. 'What's going on? Is there something wrong?'

'No. Not wrong. But our lives will change forever after this.'

'This – what?'

'This little person,' she said, taking his hand and putting it on her stomach. 'We're going to have a baby.'

'What?' His eyes lit up. 'We are? Oh Lily, that's... I don't know what to say. It's fantastic, that's what it is.' His eyes gleamed with tears as he put his arms around her. 'Now we have to get married soon. Even if it means it'll only be me, you and a priest or a mayor or someone from the registry office or whatever.'

'We don't have to,' she argued. 'This is not the eighteenth century, you know. People have babies without getting married these days.'

'We are not people and I'm old fashioned and I want to be married to you,' he said in a tone that did not allow arguments.

'I know.' She stood on tiptoe and kissed him. 'We'll make plans tonight and then get going on the wedding. I know exactly where I want to be married.'

'So do I,' he said, returning her kiss. 'Now go and change and then sit down while I serve you food and spoil you rotten until that little person is born.'

'That sounds like a plan,' Lily said. 'And we'll talk about the wedding. I want it to be really romantic.'

'It will be,' he promised.

Later that summer, Lily would remember those words as they were married under the magnolia tree in front of the manor. The work that was underway was not yet visible from the outside and the sun, from a clear blue sky, shone on the guests gathered on the front lawn, watching Lily and Dominic say their vows. Lily wore a white embroidered kaftan, Caroline's pearls and small white roses in her hair. Dominic looked handsome in a beige linen suit, his eyes so full of love as he looked at Lily that it made everyone there cry.

'I'm so happy for them,' Sylvia said to Nora, dabbing her

eyes with a lace handkerchief as they lined up to congratulate the happy couple. 'They will make wonderful parents.'

'I can't wait to babysit,' Rose declared.

'Me neither,' Vi chimed in. 'We'll be taking turns to look after that little boy or girl.'

'We can help out too,' Arnaud said, putting his arm around Sylvia. 'In some small way, I mean.'

'We'll just watch the young people and give them advice,' Sylvia cut in. 'Which they will ignore, of course. My dear Arnaud, we are too old to babysit. In any case, I might just take a little break in France with you next winter. Just to see if I like it.'

'That would be wonderful,' Arnaud replied with a broad smile.

'Only for a visit,' Sylvia warned. 'I need to see this house rebuilt too.'

'Always the house,' Arnaud remarked with a shrug. 'That is your first love, I know. I just have to accept it.'

'Yes you do,' Sylvia said with feeling. 'The Fleury girls will always be part of this house whatever shape or form it has. Rebuilding it and making it come alive again is the best thing we can do. Magnolia Manor will rise from the ashes and give us comfort and shelter and companionship for a long time to come.'

'Amen to that,' Dominic said in Lily's ear as they stood under the tree. 'You're a Magnolia girl and always will be. And I love you and this house and all that you bring to my life.'

'And you to mine,' Lily whispered back, knowing that part of her would always be in the old house even if she didn't live there any more. She felt blessed that her new husband not only understood how she felt but loved that part of her too.

Today was a new beginning. Both for them and Magnolia Manor.

A LETTER FROM SUSANNE

I want to say a huge thank you for choosing to read *The Keeper of the Irish Secret*. I was so excited to start a new series with a whole new cast of characters. The setting, this time, is the Dingle Peninsula, an area with a stunning landscape where we have a little house. It's truly a magical place and I hope I brought you there in your imagination, even if you're reading it far away from Ireland. The Fleury family will be featured in all the books in this series and I am hoping to take you with me on their adventures.

If you did enjoy it, and want to keep up to date with all my latest releases, just sign up at the following link. Your email address will never be shared and you can unsubscribe at any time.

www.bookouture.com/susanne-oleary

I hope you loved *The Keeper of the Irish Secret* and if you did I would be very grateful if you could write a review. I'd love to hear what you think, and it makes such a difference helping new readers to discover one of my books for the first time.

I love hearing from my readers – you can get in touch through social media or my website.

Thanks,

Susanne

KEEP IN TOUCH WITH SUSANNE

www.susanne-oleary.co.uk

f facebook.com/authoroleary
X x.com/susl
g goodreads.com/susanneol

ACKNOWLEDGEMENTS

As always, I want to thank my brilliant editor, Jennifer Hunt, and all at Bookouture for their never-ending hard work and support. Also my friends and family, and above all, you readers out there who constantly cheer me on and send me nice messages. Many, many thanks to you all. Your support is what keeps me writing!

PUBLISHING TEAM

Turning a manuscript into a book requires the efforts of many people. The publishing team at Bookouture would like to acknowledge everyone who contributed to this publication.

Commercial
Lauren Morrissette
Jil Thielen
Imogen Allport

Cover design
Debbie Clement

Data and analysis
Mark Alder
Mohamed Bussuri

Editorial
Jennifer Hunt
Sinead O'Connor

Copyeditor
Faith Marsland

Proofreader
Becca Allen

Marketing
Alex Crow
Melanie Price
Occy Carr
Cíara Rosney

Operations and distribution
Marina Valles
Stephanie Straub

Production
Hannah Snetsinger
Mandy Kullar
Jen Shannon

Publicity
Kim Nash
Noelle Holten
Myrto Kalavrezou
Jess Readett
Sarah Hardy

Rights and contracts
Peta Nightingale
Richard King
Saidah Graham